THE PALACE
OF
FANTASIES

Delver Maddingley

First published in Great Britain in 1993 by
Nexus
338 Ladbroke Grove
London W10 5AH

A catalogue record for this book is available from British
Library.

ISBN 0 352 32842 8

Typeset by Type Out, London, SW16
Printed and bound in Great Britain by Cox & Wyman Ltd,
Reading, Berks.

To students of nineteenth-century literature

CONTENTS

ONE

RESERVED COLLECTIONS

Except for the heavy panelled door and the green velvet drapes pulled across the window to exclude the late February sunshine of Southern California, the walls are entirely lined with books. Row upon row of leather-bound volumes stand ranged upon mahogany shelves. The gold tooling on their spines gleams in the light cast by a desk lamp on the table. Soft green calfskin covers the top of this table; it is quite bare apart from the stand supporting a closed folio volume of opulent appearance.

A girl enters the room, closes the door behind her and locks it with a brass key which has been entrusted to her as a privileged research student. She places her handbag and a small pile of books and papers on the table, draws out a heavy leather-upholstered chair and sits for a moment staring at the closed volume on the stand. Her blouse is white and slightly transparent, so that the back of her bra shows through the material, its clasp overlaid by a thick chestnut plait tied with a black ribbon. In contrast with the crisp, laundered whiteness of the blouse, her shoulders and arms gleam soft and ivory-hued in the lamplight. She reaches forward to open the book.

It is an album, its stiff pages displaying a collection of old photographs, most of them sepia-tinted. The girl catches her breath at the sight of these. As she turns the pages she looks away from time to time, shaking her head and nervously wringing her hands. But always she returns fascinated to the pictures, and as her scrutiny proceeds a blush suffuses her cheeks and neck.

These photographs were painstakingly assembled and

1

mounted in the album by a wealthy connoisseur in the nineteen-thirties. After his death they had remained as an embarrassment to his family until, a few years ago, more pressing embarrass-ments of a financial nature obliged them to sell the album at an undisclosed price to the University of Banesville. Here, the Department of Reserved Books, Prints, Manuscripts and Photographic Materials, usually known simply as Reserved Collections, furnishes a temperature- and humidity-controlled repository for these treasures. The pictures, some of them dating back to the earliest years of photography, are available for inspection by accredited scholars and a few lesser enthusiasts pursuing their studies under the supervision of the departmental librarian. One of these enthusiasts is the girl now turning the pages, a graduate student called Gloria Sweetbutts.

As she slowly turns the pages of the album Gloria's left hand wanders to her lap. She pushes her chair back from the table. Her fingertips scrabble at the powder-blue muslin of her long wraparound skirt. Impatiently she uncrosses her knees and pulls aside the garment to reveal a leg clad in a black silk stocking terminating halfway up the thigh. A red suspender secures the stocking top, and the red, black and blue items with their different textures offer an attractive contrast to the soft cream-coloured flesh, the fluffy bush of brown hair of which only the lower part is uncovered, and the wet pink slit bisecting it, into which a dainty finger now slides. Every now and then she leans forward to turn another page with her free hand.

The pictures are indeed such as to bring a blush to the cheeks of this modest young lady from New Hampshire. By now, of course, she has grown fairly immune to the hefty-hipped, small-breasted Venuses leaning tipsily against sundials and birdbaths, the apparently hairless impudicities between their huge thighs tastefully concealed by a hand, a scrap of drapery or a frond of ivy. The smiles fixed on their darkly painted lips call forth no sympathetic response from the depths of her own being. In these lifeless poses the photographers have aspired vainly to the status of true artists. But interspersed among these are other photographs, intended to move the beholder not just to an aesthetic thrill but to an instant physical response.

In conceiving these more interesting works, their creators had as their primary object (after that of making money) the erection of the male organ. Yet Gloria is finding them just as effective in raising her clitoris to a condition of lustful turgidity. She presses down gently on the little bud with the tip of her thumb while wiggling two fingers of the same hand in her vagina.

The pictures that are turning her on depict unrestrained lewdness. No attempt has been made to disguise the sexuality of these debauched models, some of them mountainous heaps of flesh and others mere slips of undeveloped girlhood. The hair which academic artists would have painted away sprouts unashamedly from sweaty armpits and gaping pussies. Arseholes wink rudely from parted buttocks. Breasts are wrenched upwards, their nipples forced into their owners' slobbering mouths.

As well as representations of poses such as these, inviting the spectator to enter the picture and violate the willing model, there are others which show couples and groups performing lecherous acts or in a state of visible readiness for such acts. In one of these a huge shaven-headed black guy, his muscle-bound torso gleaming with sweat, services a slender white woman. Both are nude but Gloria observes that the man's ankles are shackled and attached to a heavy chain while the woman sports a glittering tiara, a jewelled collar, silver bangles on her arms and many ropes of pearls. Her lips and nipples are dark with lipstick, a gem winks from her navel and her pubic hair has been trimmed into the shape of a heart. This woman's elbows rest on pump luxurious cushions, but her thighs are supported by her black lover's hips as he forces the first six inches of his ebony rod into her quim. Unlike the other pictures, this one bears a caption in fancy script, the spelling suggesting that it is either a home-produced article or designed in some sleazy Parisian atelier for the American market. It reads: 'A Nubian slave enjoys the favors of the Queen of Sheba'. Under stress or sexual excitation it is easy to misread familiar words. Gloria pauses for a moment, wondering how the black dude can appreciate the *taste* of this honey-flavoured chick without going down on her.

Ms Sweetbutts moans, lies back on the table with her legs dangling down over the edge and frigs herself vigorously with one hand while proceeding to fondle an exposed breast with

3

the other one. She is too far gone to need further visual stimulation. She draws her heels up until they find a purchase on the edge of the table, letting her knees fall wide apart. With three fingers thrust deep into her hot cunt she lifts her bottom from the green leather, revealing a patch of dampness that has trickled down from her self-abused organ of lewdness. She utters a throaty yell as waves of lust swell up and burst within her. And when the third wave bursts, flooding her whole being, it is as if a star has exploded in her head, momentarily blinding her as her body bucks in orgasmic shock.

But that dazzling burst of light was no mere illusion triggered in Gloria's head as her loins released the tide of passion. It was an electronic flash deliberately set off by the Captain as he held her shameful display in sharp focus, making sure that her features were easily recognisable as well as the full extent of her abandon. He had been watching throughout her performance, his trusty Leica to hand. By opening the door of what used to be some kind of fuse box on the wall of his office he was able to peer through a hatch and between some carefully displaced books on one of the mahogany shelves of the adjoining room. For most of the time he had been patiently looking over her shoulder from his hidden viewpoint as she turned the pages of the album. Although it was hardly an accident that his camera was poised at the ready, as he carried it with him everywhere, it had indeed been a stroke of good fortune that on the approach of her crisis she had mounted the table and adopted a position facing his lens.

With the camera still hanging round his neck the Captain took a key ring from his pocket and made to unlock the door of the room in which Gloria had just disgraced herself. The door opened silently and he entered to find her still stretched out on the table in immodest disarray, exhausted.

'Oh! Dr Haggler!' she cried, blushing scarlet in her confusion as she lay open-thighed and blushing on the library table. She swung her feet down to the floor and tried to conceal her cunt and exposed tit. 'I'm so ashamed,' she confessed. 'Guess I don't know what came over me, Dr Haggler.'

The Captain, who for professional purposes had adopted the

4

name of Haggler from one of the law reports he was in the habit of reading back home in the United Kingdom, put a fatherly arm round her shoulder. 'Don't fret yourself, my dear,' he advised in silky tones. 'You've merely succumbed to an occupational hazard quite common in this branch of research. After all, you were only responding in the way the photographers intended.'

'But isn't that the − the intentional fallacy, or whatever? In any case, I was just trying to cool off. I guess it's real warm today.'

Like all visitors from the Old World, the Captain knew that Americans felt hot when he was shivering in their icy conditioned air, just as they complained of cold when the central heating brought the sweat to his brow. But Gloria's explanation would hardly wash, and she knew it. 'The ambient environment in here is thermostatically monitored,' he improvised gravely. 'Why you should have to remove your underwear on account of the heat is beyond me. You needn't feel shy about the natural reaction of a healthy body − and a very lovely one at that, if I may say so.'

Gloria flared up indignantly. 'I never removed my goddam panties,' she blurted unguardedly. 'It was so hot I didn't put any on this morning.'

'That may well be the case, although it hardly explains the exposure of your left nipple, does it? But I'm telling you, you needn't worry. Nobody has to know you were abusing yourself over those obscene pictures. Not if you're sensible.'

'I wasn't doing anything of the kind, Dr Haggler − I'd never get off on materials that exploit and degrade women,' whined the humiliated girl. She sat down on the edge of the table, buttoning up her blouse with rapid but fumbling movements, too upset to realise that her skirt was still open to the hip and so hitched up and twisted that her pussy remained exposed to the ambient environment and her supervisor's sidelong gaze.

The Captain patted the camera hanging round his neck. 'All right,' he said. 'Maybe you weren't, or maybe you didn't mean to. But didn't you mention the doctrine of the so-called intentional fallacy just now? When people look at the picture I've taken of you, what counts won't be what you thought you were doing but what they'll presume you were up to. And that can be summed up in two words: no good.'

'You mean you took a picture of me? And you're going to show it to people?'

'Depends. Just calm down, my dear. I wouldn't really want to harm your career. You're a nice kid.'

'So you'll give it to me and we'll forget all about it? Say, Dr Haggler, I guess you're kinda nice yourself.' Gloria twisted round on the table, threw her arms around the Captain's neck and kissed his cheek.

'I'll give you a copy,' he assured her, 'but I need the negative for my own private collection. It's something I'll always treasure. I promise you it'll never be seen by anyone who could injure you — not unless you let me down or disappoint me. You wouldn't want to do that, would you now?'

'I guess not.'

'Well, come on, baby. Let's be friends. Want a job?'

'What kinda job? I hardly started this thesis.'

'I need a part-time PA. Nothing to it — just to be on hand when I need you and come with me when I travel. Won't interfere with your research. A couple of hundred dollars a week, and free hospitality on the road. You're hired, Ms Sweetbutts. We're in business!'

Still clinging to his neck, Gloria looked up at him with relief and wonderment. 'Say, Doc,' she cooed, 'I didn't know how I was going to get through the semester. Thought I'd have to sell something — but I sure don't have much to sell.'

'You have your talent, my dear young lady. I intend to make full use of it and you may be certain that your co-operation won't be in any way detrimental to the success of your thesis.'

'Yeah? I truly am grateful, Dr Haggler. I thought maybe I was a bit of a nuisance round the department, like getting between you and your magnificent collections?'

The Captain's hand moved down from her shoulder to the naked top of her thigh. 'Listen, sweetheart,' he said. 'I don't let anyone get between me and the objects of my desire. In any case, I'd much rather have you hanging round the bookstacks than some crazy bitch wanting to deface or destroy anything that makes women look good.'

By this time the admiring Gloria was reduced to putty in his hands. He patted her pubis before helping her down off the table and leading her across to a comfortable couch. This he had caused to be installed for the use of readers who preferred to take their pleasures lying down. Because he had often thought with sympathy of the embarrassment suffered by users of the British Library, who were allowed to peruse books of an erotic nature only under supervision, one of his first actions on taking over at Banesville had been to set up this small, thickly carpeted reading room as a place where devotees could pursue their interests undisturbed. Security was taken care of by the little hatch through which he had just been monitoring Gloria's activities.

Gloria seemed to appreciate the facilities. 'You got things real nice here,' she commented.

'We like to put our clients at their ease,' he replied. 'This room's my own favourite hideaway when I have the department to myself. I think of myself as a sort of sultan or pasha surrounded by all these images of females lined up for my enjoyment and all these books offering me a life of the most refined sensuality. I lie here and think of the place as my Palace of Fantasies.'

'Say, that's neat — the Palace of Fantasies. Can I ask you a question, Doc?'

'Go ahead.'

'You said something about your own private collection?'

'That's right.'

'So when do I get to see it?'

The Captain hesitated. 'It's got no historical importance, you know — just personal memories. I keep it in my apartment. Wait a minute, though — I may have a couple of specimens with me here.'

He got up and hurried into his office. Gloria heard the opening and shutting of drawers. Her supervisor returned with a brown envelope. He removed his jacket and tie and sat down beside her again. 'Which picture in the album impressed you most?' he asked.

'That's pretty hard to say,' she replied. She had been most powerfully affected by those in which sperm was shown spouting

7

from tumid cocks or leaking from invaded cunts, but was reluctant to admit this. 'I guess the ones based on historical characters like the Queen of Sheba.'

'I thought you might say that, Gloria. I always suspected it was the intellectual element that attracted you to this branch of the humanities. Well, I've got something here with a touch of the intellectual in its conception.'

From the envelope he withdrew a plastic folding frame. It contained two colour snapshots facing one another. The left one depicted a girl and the right one a youth. Both these these young people stood in sunshine beside a derelict wooden building but apparently facing in opposite directions. They pointed cameras at the spectator, leading to the inference that they were in fact taking pictures of each other. Gloria examined these pictures with interest. The youth, clad in a black leather motorcyling tunic and boots, was displaying himself shamelessly. Between boots and tunic a pair of short stubby thighs, paper-white but scribbled all over with ink-black hairs, supported a dense black thicket. Below this thicket hung a bare bulging scrotum, while out of the thicket sprouted a monstrous prick, upright and red. The girl, who must have been about eighteen and was really pretty, stood with her head tilted very slightly to her right and a thick yellow plait falling forward over her right shoulder. She wore nothing but a cool, slightly loose white top. It was just a rectangle of white cotton which wrapped round the chest and buttoned down the front, supported by shoulder straps. The right strap had fallen to droop loosely down her upper arm. Only the top two buttons were fastened, and below them the front hung open, so that the whole of her gleaming belly was bare. Her weight was supported on her lean left leg, while the right one was flexed slightly outwards and backwards. Because of her natural slimness and this elegant posture a hint of living muscle was evident on her thighs, especially the right one, braced back as it was. These contours were echoed by the suggestion of abdominal muscles tensed under the gleaming skin of her belly, so that the small hipbones and central tract from the opening of her garment down over the navel towards the cunt were highlighted by the afternoon sun. Paler than the creamy-pale of the surrounding skin, the negative image of

8

absent knickers or bikini bottom could be detected below the level of her hips. Not much of this white image was to be seen, though, for it had clearly been a diminutive garment, and the main part of that triangular region was tufted with a light, gingery-blonde bush, close examination of which showed that it terminated in a little peak hanging down between the thighs. The tuft masked the inward curve of the buttocks, but just visible was the beginning of this curve at the top of the right thigh, darkly shaded by overhanging fuzz.

'That's my friend Melanie,' the Captain explained. 'I hope you get to meet her some day.'

'And who's the guy with the hard-on?'

'Oh, he's just some creep who went with her. Derrick, he was called. Look, I've got one more in here.'

He took out another photo, evidently taken with a flash. Stark naked, a girl who could not have been more than sixteen years old lay on a crumpled purple sheet. Against it, her body looked purest white. These two dominant tones delightfully set off the few contrasting details: dreamy blue eyes; two golden plaits (one on the sheet, the other draped forward over her shoulder) tied with scarlet ribbons; a black velvet choker decorated with a red rosebud; the lighter pink rosebuds of her parted lips and the nipples crowning her plump little breastlets; the shining gold tuft about the smooth-shaven V. She lay with her right arm thrown back above her head to expose a childish armpit. Her left palm rested on her lower belly, the fingers spread out so that the index and middle ones, forming an inverted V, masked the edges of the tuft, their tips just resting in the creases between mound and thighs. Thanks to the way she sprawled with legs wide apart her labia were displayed, moist and slightly open, adding a final touch of shiny pink to the delicious scene. A naked youth of about the same age, his neck similarly adorned with choker and rosebud, knelt between her thighs, his rod fully extended. From its glowing head hung a viscous white thread which formed a vertical connection, some two inches long, between the glans and the girl's sodden pussy. Her tummy, fingers and tuft were awash with his hot white jelly, already beginning to run down the channels of her groin.

'Supposed to be a couple of newly-weds,' the Captain

explained. 'That girl Melanie organised a sort of mock wedding. The picture shows the result of the bridegroom's first attempt — he aimed too high and had a bit of an accident.'

It seemed to Gloria that she had been transported to another world, a realm of delicious sensual indulgence, as she reclined here in the Palace of Fantasies with this middle-aged but tolerably well preserved man of the world. Afraid that the seepage from her cunt must be leaking on to the couch, she lifted her buttocks and twisted round to rest her weight on her right hip, facing the Captain. He took this as a hint, and whipped out his stiff-standing prick. In no time at all he had lifted her left leg and thrown his head and shoulders between her thighs so that he could raise the back of her blouse. He unclasped her bra and reached round to the front to squeeze her breasts. Even as the covered nipples sprang out like pebbles, his organ forced its way rudely between the oozing leaves of flesh and slid up her cunt. Then began the long, luxurious pumping. His left hand traced a caressing path down her belly to the yearning clitoris. Gloria Sweetbutts closed her eyes and tried to think of New England. But she had already yelped three times in violent release when her supervisor crushed her body back against his own and trembled as he flushed out her cunt with repeated gushes of thick, creamy semen.

One day the following week the Captain was relaxing in his Palace of Fantasies when Gloria Sweetbutts entered from the office.

'We got a visitor, Doc,' she announced, chewing. 'A Professor Burdle from UCLA?'

He ran his hand up one of Gloria's legs, lingered a moment on the warm flesh above the stocking top and wormed a finger into her knickers. 'Tell him I'm in conference right now,' he ordered.

'He's a she — a lady in hotpants?'

'Oh, very well, then. Show him in. Her, I mean.' He scratched PA's cunthair, pinched her clitoris, withdrew his hand, put the book he had been studying out of sight, checked that his flies were properly zipped up and advanced to meet the visitor.

Professor Burdle was a tall and impressive lady of about thirty-one with a strong jaw, swept-up black hair very slightly streaked with gold, and unbelievably long legs. These were encased in sheer black tights over which, as Gloria had said, she sported a pair of snug black shorts. A blue T-shirt was stretched across a pair of firm breasts, their nipples protruding so shamelessly that the Captain half expected to see traces of colostrum staining the material.

She extended a suntanned hand. 'Dr Haggler? Dee Dee Burdle.'

The Captain welcomed her. 'And what do the initials stand for, if I may make so bold?' he inquired.

'They stand for Dee Dee — D-E-E, D-E-E.'

He motioned her to the low couch. She sank down and sat with her knees primly together, the golden hands clasped over them, while he drew up one of the heavy chairs and sat peering down at her. 'And what can I do for you, my dear madam?' he purred.

'Well now, I guess you're from England. I just love you Brits? Maybe I'm the one who can do something for you. You placed an advertisement in last fall's issue of *Bibliopoly Quarterly*?'

In fact, he had placed differently worded versions of this ad in a number of publications, ranging from that obscure quarterly to *Hustler* and *Hot Beavers*. It was a request, on behalf of the Department, for information concerning the whereabouts of any pornographic literature likely to have antique or rarity value. In the last few months it had elicited a flood of musty-smelling old pin-up magazines, the busty models often leprous with the greyish or greenish white ejaculations of yesteryear that had spattered over them. This garbage had been trashed without compunction as being beneath the notice of serious scholarship, So far, no offers of a genuine nature had been received. It seemed unlikely, however, that this elegant woman had travelled from Los Angeles to off-load her husband's sleaze.

'My department is interested in augmenting its collections,' he explained. 'I have funds at my disposal, and full discretion in the matter of acquisitions.'

The visitor unclasped her hands and raised the left one to rest on the nape of her neck. The firm left breast rose with the movement and a smooth armpit was exposed, slightly filmed with a fragrant exudation that caused the Captain's nostrils to flare. 'In that case,' she continued, 'you may care to take a look at this?' From her slim briefcase she withdrew a folder and handed it to the Captain. 'It was brought over from England by my family in the eighteen-thirties,' she said. 'Its provenence is hard to authenticate, but I can show that the family had connections with John Murray, the publisher? These are some stanzas by your Lord Byron — Murray refused to print them.'

Scarcely able to contain his excitement, the custodian of Reserved Collections opened the folder. Within it lay a single sheet of pale blue paper. A crease showed it had once been folded in half, but now it was displayed flat. Copied quite neatly in faded brown ink were three stanzas. The Captain scanned them expectantly.

Don Juan knew he could not rule out treachery;
Our flesh is heir to many mortal shocks.
Before he girded up his loins to fetch her, he
Weigh'd up the odds a Grecian gift of pox
Would be the wages of such wanton lechery —
Should he avoid the fate of rasher cocks
And, penetrating her with probing fingers,
Subject her to the joys of cunnilingus?

He brought her to his chamber, offer'd money
Discreetly, for this practice, tho' obscene, is
A precondition for the kind of fun he
Intended. Then he took a teat between his
First finger and his thumb, and lick'd her cunny
While she, responding lewdly, touched his penis
With lips and tongue, and fondled to perfection
His dangling cods, until he reach'd erection.

But now, before he melted in liquidity,
Forgetting all his former fears, he shunted
His throbbing engine with extreme rapidity
From out her honey'd mouth, and loudly grunted;
Then shifting till his mistress's lap hid it, he

12

Pressed home his suit. The weapon quite encunted
Within the scabbard of his fair conductor
To love's Elysian fields, he soundly fuck'd her.

Certainly the *ottava rima* with its impudent flouting of decorum
and its jaunty Hudibrastic rhymes had the familiar ring of
Byron's comic epic. But one had to be absolutely sure. Professor
Burdle interrupted his cogitations to reassure him. 'Oh yes,'
she said, 'there's no doubt it's the poet's hand. I'm sure you're
familiar with it, Dr Haggler?'

As she leaned forward on the couch to peer at the paper in
his hand, her breasts hung down and the top of her T-shirt gaped
just enough to reveal a glimpse of the hardened nipples. 'And
hold it in front of the lamp,' she said, standing just behind him
and reaching her right hand round his waist to assist him. 'What
you have there, as you can see, is a sheet of contemporary laid
paper, originally folded to measure eighteen by twenty-one point
seven centimetres, with horizontal chain lines two point five
centimetres apart, countermarked *Joseph Coles 1818.*'

The Captain was enchanted by the raunchy natural perfume
of the body now pressed against his back. But he was also
impressed and somewhat intimidated by what he was being
shown and told. A find like this would surely enhance his
standing in the academic community. The manuscript must be
acquired at any cost. Well, not, strictly speaking, *any* cost. He
needed a bit of time to ascertain what such a manuscript might
be worth.

'My dear Professor Sweetbutts,' he began, confusing his
visitor's name with that of his new PA and reaching a hand
behind him to fondle one of her buttocks through the shorts.

'Burdle.'

'My dear Burdle. This is clearly a most valuable piece of −
of − merchandise. I think we may have a deal. What sort of
price were you thinking of?'

'Well now. Don't you think it's rather up to you to make me
an offer? The kind of offer I can't possibly refuse?' She broke
away from him and flopped down on the couch, her legs apart.

'Tell you what − I'll see if I can come up with a firm bid
later today. I know what it's worth to us, of course, but it will

13

be necessary to clear a sum like that with the library committee. Can I meet you tonight?'

'Sure. You'll find me in the Ramblers Motel at Trautwein and Buena Vista, Room 203, any time after eight?'

She rose, hitching her hotpants up into her crotch. As this cool lady bestowed a valedictory smile on him the Captain was pretty sure he saw the tip of her tongue projecting between wet lips. But allowance had to be made for the fact that she was standing in the gloom beyond the dazzle of the desk lamp. He showed her out into the bright, functional office, and sat down to consider the position. A couple of phone calls quickly established that three thousand pounds sterling had recently been paid at Sotheby's in London for a late copy of one of Wordsworth's late sonnets arguing the humanitarian and religious desirability of the death penalty.

That evening he zipped himself into his leathers, donned his goggles, mounted the gleaming Harley-Davidson and easy-ridered through the deserted boulevards of downtown Banesville. Helmets were not legally required in California, and although he felt some reservations about foregoing that protection, it certainly led to quicker kissing. Soon he was taking a right at the intersection of Trautwein Avenue and Buena Vista Drive and swinging in under the tall illuminated sign proclaiming 'RAMBLERS MOTEL — $40 SINGLE — POOL — ADULT MOVIES'. An outside staircase just beyond the deserted but floodlit pool led to a walkway running the length of the two-storey building. He found Room 203 and tapped on the door. After some moments Dee Dee Burdle admitted him to the softly lit motel room. She wore a white bathrobe and a towel was wrapped round her head. 'Hi,' she said, 'I just love leather.'

Her visitor grinned. 'Feel it,' he suggested, taking her hand and placing the palm over his stomach. She didn't slide it downwards as he had half expected, but moved both hands to his hips and pulled him up against her. Her mound pressed into his hardening penis.

'Steady, big boy,' she breathed. 'Don't I just know you bikers? Get a nice girl and all you can think of is park and make out. You caught me in the shower, Dr Haggler. Look, I'm still

14

all wet.'

Pushing him back from her she undid the loose bow at the waist of her bathrobe, letting it hang open. The robe now covered her nipples, but not the listening expanse between them. A soft white hillock rose on each side of the suntanned breastbone. Inevitably the Captain's eyes wandered down over the flat belly with a drop of water spilling from the navel, to the sodden bunch of black hairs between her thighs. But Dee Dee wrapped the robe round her once more and made for the shower, rolling her hips with an exaggerated motion and indicating an array of bottles.

'Fix me a highball, will you?' she said. 'Icebox over there. Oh, and help yourself to whatever. You do drink, don't you, Dr Haggler.' This last question was delivered as a statement of unimpeachable fact.

The Captain tossed a handful of ice into a tall glass and did his best to mix her a beverage that would be palatable, highly potent but non-emetic; for himself he poured a stiff Jack Daniels. After unzipping the front of his jacket to expose a hairy chest dewed with beads of perspiration, he carried the drinks into the bathroom.

Dee Dee Burdle stood naked in front of the mirror, her feet apart and her knees bent outwards. In the reflection he could see that she was dabbing the damp pubic hair with a towel. Looking at her directly from behind, he couldn't help noticing her pink arsehole and the black-fringed purse of her sex puffed out there between her thighs, just waiting for a feel. He set the drinks down beside the washbasin and rested the fingertips of his right hand on her right hip. 'You can take your drink right out of here and wait for me in the bedroom, you bad man,' she snapped, twisting away from him and wrapping the towel round her waist.

Chastened by this setback, he withdrew to sit on the edge of one of the two large beds. When the tall professor finally emerged, however, the Captain felt rewarded for his restraint and concluded that her behaviour had merely been intended to signal her wish to be in control of the situation. She was still naked from the waist up, apart from a string of large red beads hanging down between her breasts. Her lips and nipples were made up in exactly the same vivid tint of lipstick and the colour was echoed in a broad red band around her head. But what gave this appetising picture real distinction, or so it seemed to the Captain's practised eye, was the imaginative improvisation with which she had dressed her lower parts. What was probably the girdle of her bathrobe, a length of towelling about two inches wide, was tied round her hips and knotted at the side. Tucked into this girdle at the front and back hung a pair of eight-inch-square face flannels, probably provided by the motel.

'Washcloths, courtesy of Ramblers Motel?' she said in confirmation of his unspoken guess. As she uttered these words she half turned away from him and flipped up the cloth at the back. Then she propped up the pillows on the other bed, stretched out on it voluptuously and took a long sip from her glass.

Her guest raised his own glass and drank before addressing her. 'Professor Burdle,' he began, 'I've come here on behalf of the University of Banesville to make you an offer.'

'Well?'

'A thousand bucks,' he said.

'I guess you don't know diddly about the market for holograph documents, Dr Haggler,' was her withering response.

The Captain took another sip and pulled himself together. He must not let himself be outmanoeuvred. 'My dear madam,' he proceeded, 'you need to appreciate that it would be professionally unethical of me not to seek the best deal for my principals, in this case the president, provost and librarian of the university. I am acting as their agent — I am in honour bound to do so. But at the same time I am sensible of the strongest motives for obliging such a lovely lady as yourself. Such an attractive personality! Tell me, though — if you have no faith in my valuation, why don't you put it up for auction?'

'Simple. First of all, it's kind of important to me that a family heirloom like this should end up in a truly prestigious collection not too far from home. Second of all, I could use the cash right now. And third of all, I don't see why I should be screwed for commission.' She clasped her hands behind her neck, exposing her smooth-shaven armpits, and smiled enigmatically at the Captain.

'Three thousand.'

16

'Five.'

'Four.'

'We got ourselves a deal.' She raised her left knee and patted the right-hand side of the bed in a gesture of invitation. Her leather-clad guest sprang into action to clinch the deal. Kneeling beside her he straightened her leg once more, rested his cheek on her belly and pressed a palm against the face flannel. Through it her mound felt firm and plump.

'I guess *you* can screw me for commission, Dr Haggler,' she murmured. 'I'm through haggling.'

He raised the flap, opened his mouth wide and fitted it lengthwise over the whole extent of the neatly trimmed black hair. Then he stretched his lips round the edges of his teeth and squeezed the fleshy fruit with a hard but harmless bite. Professor Burdle lay passive. It was easy now to thrust a hand between her legs and open them to an angle of sixty degrees. He unclamped his mouth from the twitching pubis and after licking the fingers of one hand used the tip of his tongue to lay open the engorged sex lips, releasing a tangy, seductive odour. As his tongue thrust deep inside her he slid the hand up under her bum and worked the first joint of his thumb into her anus. The hot cunt contracted so violently that his tongue was forced out. He slashed it up the silky length of her slit and let it play teasingly with the hardening bud at the top of its run.

At this point she seized him by the ears and dragged him painfully up until he was extended full length on top of her. The nectar he had sipped from her genitals was transferred to her mouth. She writhed beneath him, relishing to the full the sensation of supple leather in contact with her bare skin.

When he pulled back to look at her she opened her grey eyes very wide and asked him a question. 'Do you have a name, Dr Haggler? What do your girlfriends call you?'

'They call me the Captain, mostly. That's what I encourage.'

'The Captain. Say, were you in your Special Services or something, Captain?'

His answer was oblique. 'Sometimes, when he's called upon to do it, a man's got to do what only a man can do.'

'I'm impressed, I truly am. You and I are gonna make sweet music, Captain.'

But instead of rubbing their instruments together in erogenous harmony, she rolled him off her stomach and rose from the bed. 'Adult movie time,' she laughed, fiddling with the TV set supported on a swivelling wall bracket. 'If we're making our own music we can manage without the sound.' He stiffened in anticipation as she stood there sideways on to him, her scarlet-tipped breasts hanging firmly with no hint of sagging and the slightly concave cheek of her right buttock catching the light between her front and rear face flannels.

Dee Dee Burdle returned to her new lover and dragged down the zip of his flies. The long, hard prick flew out of its leather hiding place and quivered like a steel spring. She stooped to lick the tip. 'That's real good,' she sighed, 'but first let's lie back and see if we can pick up some ideas from this two-bit movie.'

The action on the flickering screen, however, fell far short of inspiration. The film or video they were watching would never have merited a place in the Banesville Reserved Collections. It was all mechanical bonking, sucking and frigging, with extended sequences showing close-ups of the pained faces of men and women bouncing up and down and rare glimpses of cock and cunt. But after a few minutes of this dreary stuff, when he was just about to turn his full attention to his companion, the Captain's eye was struck by the beauty of an auburn-haired girl who had just entered the room in which this unimaginative orgy was taking place. He waited as she pulled her yellow sweater over her head. Why yes, that face looked familiar — but surely it couldn't be his old flame, Gina Wootton? What would she be doing in an American porno movie? Made up as she was, it was hard to be sure if it was her. Those breasts were about the right size, and she had Gina's freckles, but so had many girls with auburn hair, and the same could be said of the chestnut-coloured triangle of fur briefly revealed when she pulled down her jeans and panties. Thereafter, her face was mostly buried out of sight between the thighs of her fellow actors and actresses. Well, if it was Gina she was clearly enjoying a fulfilling new life of her own. The Captain had other fish to fry.

Turning his back on the TV, he lifted Dee Dee's arm and

used the head of his cock, swollen and glib with the clear fluid already welling from its tip, to paint the smooth, soft armpit. She brought the arm down and enclosed his hardness in warm flesh. Then she raised and opened her knees, and turned up the flannel so that it lay on her belly. Still fucking her armpit, the Captain leaned sideways to peer at the treasure she had brought to light. The complicated lips of her cunt were pink and puffy, and had parted to reveal their inner surfaces shining wetly. He rested his middle finger lengthwise between them; they closed over it like a clam. The first joint of the finger sank into the fleshy wetness, then the second and the third. With his thumb he attacked her clit, dragging the nail carefully across its sensitivity. As a final titillation the tip of his little finger tickled her arsehole. With a great shudder Dee Dee Burdle's athletic thighs clamped together over his hand. Her bum lifted from the bed and she moaned out her pleasure as the Captain's hot come flooded into her armpit and trickled down to the sheet beneath.

When their spasms subsided, she lay back and let him lick the armpit dry. The task was not a distasteful one. After each flat-tongued stroke he brought his lips to hers and thrust the coated tongue deep into her mouth. In no time at all he felt the vigour pumping back into his loins.

He glanced at the TV. A new film now seemed to be showing — rough, raw and red-blooded. The whole screen was filled with a succession of gaping pussies, spending pricks and girls' faces dripping with sperm. He leaned back and smiled at the professor.

'How would you like another thousand?' he asked.

'A thousand fucks?'

'A thousand bucks. We haven't started fucking yet. I'll write you a cheque on the departmental account for six grand.'

She seemed puzzled, so he spelt out what he had in mind. 'You'll get six from me,' he said, 'and I'll get a thousand from you. That's how I get my commission — OK?'

She raised her eyebrows. 'Fine by me, Captain.'

That settled, he turned her over, got her to stick her bum up, raised the flannel and started fucking her in earnest. He had just conceived the outline of a brilliant scheme.

19

TWO

A BRILLIANT IDEA

A fortnight later, on the other side of the Atlantic, March rain was falling on the roof of a little cottage just outside Upchester. An attractive girl of nineteen sat upstairs in a dormer window, preparing to write another entry in the spasmodic journal she had begun more than a year ago as a student at nearby Cunlip College.

This fair-haired diarist was none other than Melanie Winspur, the indecently exposed photographer depicted in the double portrait the Captain had shown to Gloria. For the Captain, too, had Cunlip connections. And so had Miss MacDonald, in whose cottage Melanie was now residing. In fact, Miss MacDonald was the only one of this trio to maintain her connection with the college. Although she was as deeply implicated as any of them in the scandal which had brought about the principal's resignation and made it necessary for the Captain to leave the country, the subsequent investigations had failed to uncover her role. She was still employed as mistress in charge of English and Physical Development. Under the new regime, of course, she had to conduct herself with great caution, but she still contrived to extract considerable satisfaction from the job.

Miss MacDonald had not yet driven home from the college, where she was supervising a hockey match. Melanie had the place to herself and had gone up to her room, where she took out the yellow notebook. Smiling at the developments she had to record, she began to write.

Mac had letter from the Captain yesterday morning. Out there in California he's had what he calls a brilliant idea. We're not sure, but it *might* work, so we'll give it a whirl.

When letter came Mac wouldn't let me see it at first. She chuckled over it at breakfast and took it to work with her. Didn't get home till half eleven — said she'd already eaten and was too tired to talk. I could smell girl on her and guessed she'd been with that pushy little Anne Amory who pretends to be so demure, or even Helen Lascelles, if she hasn't been expelled from Cunlip yet. Had a godawful row and I insisted on sleeping in own bed.

After sleepless night took cup of tea to Mac. She smiled at me but I kept mouth shut and went back to bed. A bit later heard her calling. Felt hot and sticky, so changed into cool blue playsuit — the pale blue cotton one I often wear in the summer. I mean the one that has a little, bust-hugging top with shoulder straps and a trimming of white lace above bare belly. Just love the high-cut knickers, loose and frilly round hips but snug at crotch, with lace at waist. Well, I went to her room, crept into the big bed and snuggled up to her.

Mac was wearing her yellow cotton robe that opens down front and has just two bows, one at throat and one at bust. Her dark hair was undone and spread over pillow. She hugged me, kissed me and put hand on cheek of bottom, working fingers round under knickers into groove at back. We had chat about last night's (Friday's) bad feelings.

MAC: What got into you last night, dear?

ME: You'd been with one of the girls again, hadn't you?

MAC: Look, Melanie, if you don't like it here you can always go and live with your parents. You know we agreed to give each other as much freedom as we needed, within limits.

ME: Yes, but I don't seem to need quite as much freedom as you. Doesn't seem fair, somehow. Don't you get enough of it with me?

MAC (*wriggling finger in opening of bum*): Darling, I can never get enough of you. Know why you don't fancy any of the outside talent? Partly because you never get out to see any, and partly because when you're not doing it with me you're doing it to yourself. Now that's not healthy for a girl of your age, not when there's an alternative.

ME: It was you who told me to stay indoors in case the police are still looking for me. You know what? I don't believe they ever connected me with that *Fanny Hill* business.

MAC: But they must have got their hands on all the videos. I'm just surprised they never got round to interviewing *me*. Let's have a kiss, and I'll tell you about a little surprise I've arranged for you.

We went into a tight clinch. Mac shifted her hand down so thumb prodded my arsehole and fingers reached round cleft. Felt first finger slip into pussy while tip of next one gently patted clit. As we kissed I undid her two bows and got both hands on her boobs. Pushed a knee up between her legs — she worked her way down till her cuntlips, all wet and open, were sucking on my thigh. I brought one of my hands down to frig her, and we both came as easy as falling off a log. Then we relaxed on our backs, each with a hand resting lightly on the other's furry mound, and went on with interrupted conversation. ͨ

ME: You said something about a surprise.

MAC: We're having visitors tomorrow. A little tea party.

ME: Who? Do I know them?

MAC: Oh yes. You remember Carla Merryweather and Anne Amory?

As if I'd have forgotten them! Even if they hadn't been involved in that fantastic dorm feast of mine last June, anyone at Cunlip with eyes and ears would have known those prim-looking little misses and their sluttish reputations. Mac just trying to cover fact that she's been going with Anne all this term. Well, Anne's a desirable baggage all right — that's why I picked her as my special partner that night. Felt quite jealous when Captain stuck his prick in her, and glad it wasn't hers but Nikki's cunt he came in after having it up all eight of us. Anyway, I tried not to let her see I was miffed. A tea party with those young ladies might be something worth waiting for, after all.

Then she told me about Captain's letter. He's in charge of this famous collection of smut, and has tons of money to buy up even more. What he wanted to do is rather naughty, but I'm not turning my back on chance of making a few thou, which is what he has in mind, and I think that goes for Mac too, though she made out she still wanted to think about it. He'd remembered how I wrote that porno version of *Romeo and Juliet* and what Max had done with the episode we acted from *Fanny Hill*, and that was why he'd chosen us.

He wanted us to put our heads together (our *heads*?) and write some pieces in the style of famous authors like Dickens and Jane Austen (spelling?). Idea is that these pieces are supposed to be rejected bits from their books, never printed because they were too dirty. When we've written a few, he'll come over and if he thinks they're any good he'll find a way of fabricating manuscripts in authors' handwriting so his library can buy them and we'll all be in clover. Maybe it's a crazy scheme — Mac rather seems to think so — but the actual writing could be fun.

On the next day, Melanie was far too busy to find time for writing and it was not until the weekend was over that she sat down with her diary once more to enter her account of the tea party which had kept her so occupied.

Mon, March 18

Yesterday (Sunday) afternoon Mac drove over to college and came back with the two girls. Carla had grown a bit taller since I last saw her but no change in Anne, even though there can be quite a difference between sixteen and seventeen, which is what they must both be now.

23

Having their Sunday glad rags on instead of Cunlip uniform made them look younger because of contrast between what they think of as grown-up clothes and their young faces.

Must try to describe what they look like. Carla still has long black hair. She had it done in two thick plaits with red bows and that gave quite a little-girl effect in spite of red lipstick. She took off cardigan. Wore a close-fitting black top of thin material, probably to show off little buds that have developed since last year. It was sleeveless. We could see she had quite a lot of black hair under her arms now. Top was tucked into tight red knee-length skirt with black belt and brass buckle. Buttons left undone on slit up right side of skirt, all the way up to top of thigh, where you could see tops of black stockings. Must admit those stockings looked good on her. Think her legs have improved a bit if that's possible — even curvier than before. Red shoes to match skirt, and personal stereo over head to complete picture, but took it off when Mac made sarky remark — just like a teacher!

Anne wore her pretty straw hat with wide brim and flowers in band but took it off when she sat down. Her yellow hair done up in pony tail at back and combed down in fringe over eyes. Those lovely violet-coloured eyes!! Unlike Carla, no make-up on. Demure white blouse with long sleeves, high neck with cameo brooch at throat and lots of frills down front. Long wraparound skirt of mauve Indian muslin — sandals on bare feet. As ravishingly pretty as ever — no wonder Mac's got the hots for her.

Girls kissed me on cheeks when they came in and Anne pushed her body against mine rather obviously. I was dressed more casually in faded jeans and baggy sweater. Oh, and Mac in usual claret-coloured tracksuit. We sat down a bit stiffly in front room and Mac went to kitchen to make tea. Didn't really know what to talk about. Quite an age difference between their seventeen and my nineteen. Embarrassing. Wished we all had Walkmans (Walkmen?) and would have turned on radio except that Mac thinks it's rude when you have visitors. (So do

Mummy and Daddy but they're older.)

Things got much easier when Mac came back with tea
and cakes. She did take-offs of Cunlip staff and got the
girls to let slip all sorts of gossip about what's going on
these days. After a time, talk came round to A level texts.
Anne and Carla both doing *Middlemarch* with Mac. I'd
read it myself, but years ago when I was too young.
Thought I was going to be bored by this chat, but then
it got interesting.

MAC: What do you really think about Dorothea's
marriage to the Reverend Edward Casaubon? Can you
imagine what their wedding night must have been like,
and the parts of the honeymoon George Eliot feels she
can't describe for respectable Victorian readers? You
remember Mr Casaubon, don't you, Melanie?

ME: Was he that awful dried-up old clergyman with
bad breath and a white mole on his face? And wasn't there
a hair growing out of the mole? I remember he was
supposed to be like a mummy, buried in the dust of dead
civilisations. Is that right?

MAC: Yes. Actually he had *two* white moles with hair
on them. And I'm not sure about the bad breath, but you
might say that was implied.

CARLA: Is that what you call halitosis, Miss Mac-
Donald?

MAC: That's right dear. Anyway (*talking to me again*),
poor innocent Dorothea Brooke, who doesn't want to
know she's got the sort of bodily needs healthy young
women are bound to have — Dorothea thinks she's in love
with him because he looks like the philosopher Locke and
she's taken in by his scholarship, even though it's a bit
of a sham, and sees him as a father figure she can care
for and revere.

CARLA: He's really more of a mummy than a father,
isn't he, like Melanie said!

ANNE: He reminds Dorothea of the poet Milton,
doesn't he, Miss MacDonald?

CARLA: And wasn't Milton blind, and used to beat
his daughters?

MAC: My word, you are catching on, you two. How far had we got? Oh yes. I was reminding Melanie that the self-sacrificing Dorothea decides to devote her life to him, but for quite the wrong reasons. You must remember, Anne and Carla, that she thinks 'the really delightful marriage must be that where your husband was a sort of father, and could teach you even Hebrew, if you wished it'. Casaubon's incapable of love, of course. He marries her because he's getting old and needs someone to look after him. Someone bright enough to help him with the boring and pointless book he's trying to write, his *Key to All Mythologies*, but not clever enough to realise the book's never going to get written.

ANNE: He underestimates Dorothea, doesn't he, Miss MacDonald?

MAC: Most men underestimate women, dear. Anyway, Melanie, Casaubon and Dorothea get married and go off to Rome for their honeymoon. She doesn't really know what to expect — in those days young women really didn't know. But she soon suspects something's wrong when he spends all his time shut up in libraries, leaving her to wander aimlessly through art galleries full of upsetting erotic paintings and sculptures.

ME: Sounds like an opening for our little scheme? Just what the Captain wants.

MAC: Doesn't it just. But what do you girls think — was the wedding consummated?

CARLA: What exactly does *consummate* mean?

MAC: Well . . .

ANNE: It means having intercourse, doesn't it, miss, like you keep explaining in Physical Development? You're supposed to do it on the wedding night. In the olden days the bride used to be a virgin and her husband had to take her virginity. That's why they wore white wedding dresses — so you could see the blood to prove it was her first time. I don't think that disgusting old Casaubon was capable of getting it up.

CARLA: No, but he probably made her do all sorts of other revolting things. Oh yes — I'm sure that when he

26

got back from his libraries he used to mess her about with his bony old fingers. I bet she had to kiss his moles or something like that. And all the time I bet she was secretly seeing that young guy who was falling in love with her — know the one I mean?

ANNE: Will Ladislaw, Mr Casaubon's cousin.

CARLA: No, I didn't mean him, silly. I meant his friend, that German painter.

MAC: Naumann.

CARLA: That's right, Naumann. Will's all soppy and romantic but you can tell Naumann's really got the hots for her. — I don't want to be rude, Miss MacDonald, but this tea tastes a bit funny.

MAC: Well, I did put a wee drop of something in it, to warm us all up.

CARLA: What?

MAC: Rum.

CARLA: Can I have some more?

Actually, it was quite warm already in cottage — on this dull day Mac had central heating on full blast and had lit fire in front room. Now she drew curtains. Really cosy with sound of wind in chimney and rain pattering against windows. Bottle came out and tea was more thoroughly doctored. Could see slightly blurred look in girls' eyes.

Mac said everyone had to do a turn — give a little performance. Said she didn't mind what, as long as it was some sort of a dance. Put on CD with ballet music — *Swan Lake*, I think. Carla volunteered but insisted we switched off lamps so she could dance in firelight.

Carla's a natural, of course. Took full advantage of slit up side of skirt to show off right leg, stretching it out and stroking up length of it all the way to bare flesh above top of stocking. She pulled her top out at waist and slowly rolled it up till it just covered her little titties — then we got benefit of all that white skin shining in flickering light between black top and red skirt. Wriggled her hips about and made faces at us, sticking tongue out.

After a bit she undid belt and stepped out of skirt.

27

Except for her small bust and schoolgirl plaits she looked really sophisticated now in the red suspender belt and slinky black stockings. Her snatch and bottom were just about covered by little black knickers with 'Merry Xmas' at front in red. Not quite right for time of year but nobody complained. Winking, she rolled her top up the last bit over her small, hard nipples. I started to feel wet and sticky between legs. Now Carla was really ready to prance about and do some fabulous high kicking. When a break in music came up she turned to face fire, bent forward and eased knickers down over bum. Reached a hand up between thighs and played with herself there for a moment, then kicked knickers right off and turned to face us. With hands on hips, she made rude writhing movements and shoved darkly furred patch towards us. Everyone clapped. Carla bowed and sat down.

Next it was Anne's turn. Anne's not such a natural mover but she was quite clever tripping across room on tiptoes and leaning forward with an arm stretched out in front and a leg behind, and twirling round so her long skirt lifted up to show her bare legs. And now and then she'd just lift one side of it to show us the whole length of lovely pale thigh.

She fiddled with brooch at throat and unfastened buttons, then opened front of blouse so we could see she was wearing pretty white lace bra. With boobs her size she doesn't really need one, but we all know how girls that age are and it did look pretty on her. Blouse came right off and she danced about reaching up with arms to lift bust. Shaven armpits, or maybe the hair was so fair you couldn't see it in dim light.

After a bit of twirling and bouncing so her pony tail bobbed up and down, Anne lay down on her back. Put her hands under bottom and rolled knees right back to chin, then stuck legs straight up into air with her bum held up from floor. Mauve skirt fell down her legs till everything was uncovered — slim legs, round white bum, and just a hint of blonde fur where her thighs were pressed together. She started bicycling with her legs, which made

28

her bare bottom quiver and the leg muscles ripple in the reddish firelight. When she'd finished she brought her legs up straight again, with the feet together in their little white socks. But only for a moment. As if she was doing some sort of Yoga exercise, she slowly opened her legs outwards, keeping them straight, until they made a wide V. The three of us gathered round to gawp at her goodies.

Now we could see just how much (or little) hair she had on her. It was a tiny triangle of yellow fur, too fair and fine to hide the pretty slit of her snatch. Really short yellow hairs fringed the slit, just making those fat outer lips shine like golden velvet. Felt a strong urge to get down there and run my tongue over lips, then plunge it into the slit and use it to prise the pussy open. But as we watched, the inner lips started to fall open of their own accord and we got clear view of all this pink oily wetness. The smell was heavenly.

Anne couldn't hold position any longer. Brought legs together again, then started making scissor movements. One leg was lowered to floor while other one was pulled back to her face − then the other way, so that all the time her legs were passing at the halfway point and those moist inner lips must have been sliding against each other, though I could only guess this from expression on her face. Suddenly she jumped up, snatched off skirt and bowed.

'Please, Miss MacDonald,' Carla piped up, 'don't let her sit down. I want to dance with her.'

Well, I'd seen Anne doing a kind of dance with my dorm-mate Emily to attract the boys last summer down behind the old pavilion − the Captain was with me while we spied on them. So I clapped my hands and asked Mac to let them do it. At first Anne seemed a bit shy, which was surprising after how she'd just been entertaining us, but soon got into swing of things. There were the two of them with their contrasting colouring, Anne wearing just her lacy white bra and white socks turned down to her ankles, and sexy Carla in red suspender belt, red bows on her plaits, black stockings and black top rolled up right under armpits. They got together in ballroom-dancing

29

clinch, but instead of waltzing round the little room they stood and did it on the spot, just like Anne and Em did it that time at Cunlip.

As they swayed about in time to the music, they did their best to give Mac and me glimpses of the various points of contact. Their lips kissed, Carla's nipples brushed lightly against the tips of Anne's bra when Anne's breasts weren't squashed against Carla's chest, Carla's stockinged thighs clashed rhythmically with Anne's bare ones and they ground the mounds of their cunts into each other. They seemed to be getting pretty randy and so were me and Mac from watching the show. In the end they just stood hugging one another, hands on bums and fingers trying to worm their way into arseholes.

'That's enough of that, you scamps!' said Mac and made them sit on separate (spelling?) chairs. 'It's Melanie's turn now.'

I didn't see much point in hanging around — no need to work myself up slowly or anything like that. Just peeled off my sweater and jeans and let them all see dainty green G-string I was wearing instead of knickers. Little tufts of pubic hair sticking out through lacy floral design, and pouch so small quite a lot of ginger hair not covered, both at base of tummy and round edges of thighs.

Instead of dancing I just stood there and played with my tits till the nipples went dark red and stuck out long and hard. Went on working them — began to get lovely yearning feeling low down in tummy with all those eyes watching me. Suddenly feeling got much stronger, and I could tell the love juice was welling out of me. Put hand on G-string. It was all wet. Looked down and saw it was nearly covered with spreading damp patch. Carla laughed, so I went up to her and shoved crotch into her face. Then I stood in front of them frigging myself through G-string. As it got wetter and wetter I pushed it bit by bit into my twat until the lips closed over it in front the way bum closes over back part. They loved that!

Now I had to slip finger under waistband and work it down to tickle clit. But after a few minutes of this Mac got up and came over to me. 'We'd like a decent view,' she said, and yanked G-string down to give them a really indecent view. As the sopping lace was dragged out of cunt, it brought the lips out with it, all pink and puffy. I stood with legs apart and G-string halfway down thighs, playing with myself. Knowing they wanted their 'decent' view, I lifted the hood back so clit stuck out like pink pea.

Then I announced that I wanted them to stick their fingers in me, one after the other. I let the G-string drop down to my ankles, stepped out of it and picked it up with one hand while I went on holding my sex lips and hood stretched back with the other one. Went over to Carla and held damp garment over her nose. Felt her finger searching for my opening — rather long nail a bit painful but OK once she got inside. Taken by surprise when pad of her thumb landed on clit. She pinched thumb and finger together and I could hardly bear it.

Quivering and on point of exploding I pulled back from her and went over to little Anne, who was sitting all agog on edge of chair. I was still holding myself wide open and stood with hips thrust forward. Anne looked up at me, blushing, then the sly puss grabbed my bottom and crushed my twat against her face. Felt her nose rubbing on clit and tongue licking up and down between lips till it hooked up into entrance of cunt. Waves of lust coursed through my lower belly, as they say in the dirty books. But I didn't want to come till all three of them had taken a turn, so I reached under Anne's chin and tipped her backwards.

Mac stood up as I approached her. Unlike the girls, she didn't look all that sexy in her tracksuit, so what did I do? I got hold of waistband and eased trousers down over her bum and hips. And then I got my first major shock of the evening.

The MacDonald wasn't wearing any knickers. Instead, she had a kind of harness of tapes holding an enormous rubber cock with smooth but realistic balls. We hadn't noticed it before, I suppose, because tip had been tucked up under waistband, but now it dropped down to horizontal position, sticking out eight or nine inches from her pussy and nearly two inches thick. I recognised it as the one she keeps in her lab for demonstration purposes in physdev classes. I 'borrowed' it once to use as ritual object at that mock wedding I laid on for Captain. Some punch it packs!

Well, I was shivering with surprise as Mac looked me in the eyes. She pulled me to her and I felt softness of her damson tracksuit top against my bare breasts. She kissed me. Her hand reached between my legs and I felt her fingers scooping out the sticky juices. Then she drew back and smeared them all over artificial cock till it was dripping with the goo.

'Right, girls,' she said, 'I'm sure you're all dying for a man up you by now. We don't get so many real men coming to this cottage but that doesn't mean it's a fuck-free zone. Down on your knees, side by side — heads on floor and bottoms up!'

Something in her voice told us she was serious. I knelt down first in front of the fire, with Anne on my left and Carla on my right. Noticed difference between Anne's bare leg against my left one and Carla's stocking against right one. I turned my head first one way and then the other and saw they were excited.

Carla was first to get it. Her eyes almost popped out of her head. Her tongue lolled out and she dribbled on the carpet. I saw Mac's hand reach round Carla's right side and under her to stroke the tight little nipples. Could feel her other hand force its way between my right thigh and Carla's left one, and guessed she was having her clit massaged. The old in-and-out got under way, fast and furious, till Carla squealed and collapsed flat on floor with Mac on top of her. Look on her face one of exhausted bliss.

As Mac climbed off her I braced myself to take the dildo. But no — she was ramming it into poor Anne and it seemed to be such a tight fit she might as well have been buggering her. In fact I strongly suspected she was, but had no way of being sure. Anne herself was much too far gone to say anything. Mac leaned forward over her and undid her bra, which dropped to floor. The lovely little tits with their pink nipples dangled loose, swaying in time with the MacDonald's thrusts. Just like Carla, Anne had her clit worked while this was going on. She too collapsed with Mac on top of her and got wet kisses all over her blushing cheek.

I heard a sucking, plopping sound as rubber prick was pulled out, unstoppering whichever hole it had been plugging. A powerful hand reached round my side and tugged my left boob. At the same time another hand thrust its way between my thighs and was clamped over my mound. A thumb pushed up into my fanny.

Without warning I was rolled over on to my right side, partly on top of Carla, who was still sprawling there panting. Mac's thumb was yanked out, and getting a purchase high up on my right thigh she got me on my back and forced my legs wide open. Then she was on me, between my thighs, and the end of the great bludgeon was nudging against my quim.

'Wake up, girls,' she yelled. 'I want you to run your hands up the insides of her thighs and then pull her cuntlips open for me.'

I felt their fingers sliding up towards their target. I felt them stretching me and I felt the rubber cockhead forcing its way up the entrance to my quim. And then I had my second major shock of the evening.

The door opened, and into the room walked Derrick, all shiny in wet black leather, his black hair sticking up in spikes and his face pale under the black stubble. (Whenever I see him in his biking gear I think of Captain, but Derrick's never given me a thrill like that famous nude ride on the Upchester bypass.) Without asking Mac, because she wouldn't have liked it, I'd let Derrick borrow my key to have a copy cut so he could creep in nights to visit me when Mac didn't need me in bed. Well, not seeing any lights through the curtains the silly prick hadn't realised car outside meant Mac *must* be at home, and he'd just walked in 'to have a look round', as he told me afterwards.

Confronted with lurid firelit scene in front room, Derrick thought he'd really done it now, and was about to make dash for front door. Actually, though, he couldn't have arrived at a better time. No more need for rubber cock-substitutes!

Mac pulled out of me and we all stood up, with gleaming truncheon still waving about at base of Mac's belly. Anne and Carla very embarrassed and tried to keep pussies hidden with hands. 'You all know Derrick, don't you?' I asked rather lamely. Of course they did — he got his job at Cunlip back after Captain had to go, so they must see him pottering around grounds and peeping out of bushes every day.

The MacDonald gave him a kiss and laughingly unstrapped dildo. 'We can dispense with this old friend now,' she chuckled. 'Get those leather trousers off, Derrick, but keep the jacket on.'

Well, he could hardly refuse. When they were off he looked really diabolical in that reddish glow from the fire. His short stubby legs were all shaggy with black curls and his huge purple-headed dong, which leapt out of his pants as if it was spring-loaded, stuck up even bigger than the dildo and much more inviting. Always thought it funny there's no hair on his pillocks, just light pink wrinkled skin hanging down — or just now stretched tight and shiny — under woolly mass of pubic fur. Prefer Captain's hairy scrote, I think.

He was impatient, old Derrick. Saw a drop of clear liquid welling up out of slot in tip of prick. Mac wanted to bring him to boil slowly, though, and made him sit down with rest of us while she went to kitchen to make fresh tea. Girls giggled awkwardly, keeping legs crossed and arms folded across chests. But I leaned back casually with one leg over arm of chair to give him eyeful. His prick looked as if it was getting even harder, right up against leather of jacket. He must have been hot with that jacket in front of the fire — beads of sweat rolled down his forehead. He didn't say anything. No small talk, our

Derrick — *that's* not what he's famous for.

Mac came back with tea and we sat drinking it politely and nibbling slices of Battenburg while she complimented him on his manliness.

MAC: Got a nice one there, Derrick. I was just telling these youngsters it's not every day they're lucky enough to take tea with a real man.

DERRICK: Well, I . . .

MAC: You're Melanie's boyfriend, aren't you?

DERRICK: Well . . .

MAC: And you've seen these two rascals at Cunlip, I'm sure. This is Carla and that's Anne.

DERRICK: Oh, I'm . . .

MAC: Ever had a chance to fuck them, Derrick?

Derrick choked on a crumb and doubled up, spluttering, while Mac thumped his back. Both the girls blushed, though Carla also laughed.

CARLA: He's never got that close to us.

MAC (*to Derrick*): But I bet you've seen them all bare like this, haven't you?

DERRICK: Only when . . .

MAC: And seen them doing it to each other when they thought no one was watching? Fancy the idea of doing it now while he watches, Anne? (*Anne blushed deeper pink and looked down at her lap.*) Is it true you and Carla sometimes do it in public, dear?

ANNE: We — we try to keep ourselves to ourselves, miss.

MAC: But not always very successfully, eh? Now listen, everyone. What we've got here, as you can see, is ripe cockflesh. We needed it and now we've got it. And we're going to use it.

ANNE: Please, miss, I think it's time for us to be getting back to college. Would you mind driving us back, like you said?

MAC: Don't worry, darling — I had a word with the principal and told her you might be staying overnight. You can relax now.

Anne didn't seem to relax at all but hugged herself and

shivered in spite of a roaring fire. Carla's reactions were a bit more positive, I could tell, but she played coy for a while. Then she went over to her friend and knelt down beside her, whispering in her ear. Anne shook her head petulantly. Carla whispered something else and a little smile flickered at corners of Anne's mouth. 'Oh, all right then,' she said.

Mac explained in a cosy, chatty way that she had something rather elaborate in mind which we'd have to do on big bed upstairs. But she was afraid Derrick wouldn't last long enough without spilling. She thought his flesh was so ripe it would be best to have some preliminary fun and drain off first emission in front of fire.

CARLA: You mean like a dry run?

MAC: I don't mean anything like a dry run. I mean he's going to take each of us in turn but very quickly and without any pumping once he's inside. Melanie and I must time it − half a minute in each of us. He can frig us and we'll see how many of us he can bring to a climax before he comes himself. I'm the hostess, so he can begin with me. Oh, and for a change, Carla, you can take your stockings and suspender belt off − no, not yet, but so Derrick can see while he's in me. Anne, dear, I'd like you to keep those cute socks on.

Anne pulled the white socks up over her calves. Ran out of room and returned with her pretty straw hat. Mac was delighted with her taste and said she could wear it.

Cushions were laid out on floor and Mac pushed Derrick down on his back, legs together and prick stretching up bare belly and dribbling that clear sticky stuff over leather of jacket. Mac stood astride him, her brown-fringed pussy on full display. Then she swooped down, flexing athletic legs like shiny steel springs. Told me to do the honours, so I bent D's cock to upright angle and then slightly down. He winced. Mac had two fingers of each hand hooked into cunt, holding it open so I could steer the big knob into her as she lifted her bum slightly. When it was in place she plumped down on him and his whole length was sleeved in the one plunge.

She leaned forward and kissed him lightly on mouth, then sat up straight with hands linked behind neck. Naturally, this had effect of lifting her firm boobs and making D notice them. He reached up and gave them a working over till nipples were brown and tight. 'Ten seconds,' I said, looking at my watch. He dropped his hands to her crotch and dug around feeling for her clit, a bit distracted by Carla's antics as she peeled off stockings and suspender belt.

By this time Mac must have been burning on very short fuse. No sooner had his fingers touched sensitive part than she yelped out loud, her head went back and her hips shot up into air. D's prick was released, thickly coated with the MacDonald's spendings, and twanged back against his belly. It looked bigger and angrier than ever.

I helped Mac to armchair, gave her a shake and reminded her she had to keep an eye on watch, as I reckoned it ought to be my turn next, seeing as I'm the one Derrick goes out with. I straddled him and bent the rigid tube back so I could guide it into me. Massaged own tits while D squeezed my bottom then got to work on love bud. He didn't touch it directly but squeezed fleshy lips over it with one hand while tickling my gingery curls with other. Very hard to resist natural temptation to bounce up and down but remembered rules of game and just let cunt muscles keep tightening around D's cock. Felt like I was in Paradise — in fact it truly did begin to feel like eternity of bliss because the MacDonald got carried away and forgot about timing us till nearly two minutes were up.

Randier than ever when I climbed off. Carla took next turn. She'd kept her black top on, rolled up under armpits. Maybe it was because she thought D might not like her flattish chest — I think it's ace myself — that she got on him other way round, facing his feet. He went in really easy, and reached in front of her to give her the works. But that wasn't quite what Carla wanted. She took his hands round behind her and stuck one of his fingers into bum-hole. D got the idea and shoved it right up while stroking buttocks with free hand. Carla did her own frigging round the front and collapsed as she came, bent double over his thighs.

I was dying for it to be my turn again and afraid I might climax before it came round. But I sportingly helped Anne to pull Carla off. We stretched her out on carpet beside Derrick, so Anne, who seemed to need a lot of encouragement, could look at her girlfriend while she was being spiked herself. Prick couldn't find its way in — kept pushing in wrong direction and hurting her, so I made her kneel up, licked my fingers and worked them all round her slot. Then I put one hand firmly on her buttocks and grabbed D's tool in other one. Brought her down on him as I held him at just the right angle. She moaned as she sank down. Didn't seem too interested in what he was doing to her clit. Couldn't take her eyes off lovely sight of Carla flat on her back beside him, her hands under her head to show off the musky black tufts under her arms. Carla's curvy legs were pressed together and darkly furred mound was like a high round hill where thighs joined the flat tummy. Anne reached across and laid palm of hand on that inviting pussy.

But her time was up. She needed no help getting D's thing out of her and snuggling down beside Carla. Mac out of game because she'd already come, so now it was me again at last. This time I was so excited the prick felt like red-hot poker going up me. I shuddered and melted before it was halfway in.

That was three down and one to go (Anne), not counting poor old Derrick himself. Would he be able to outlast her, I wondered. In a dream, I raised myself really high to let his cockhead out, then lifted my leg over him and flopped down at side. Timid Anne got up reluctantly to take my place. She didn't look too happy as she took stiff wet cock fastidiously between finger and thumb, pointed it back and brought her pretty blonde-fuzzed cunt down on it.

Her fears of being stretched even more were ill-founded, though. It only took the touch of her little golden hairs as she approached him, slightly off-centre, to bring the spunk surging up in fierce jets. Heavy white dollops of it splashed all over the undersides and pink nipples of her breasts, her rounded tummy, where they flowed sluggishly towards the hollow of her navel, the inner thighs and especially over the golden mound. When the actual squirting had stopped, the stuff still kept welling up out of the slit and running in thick layers down the column, over Anne's hand which was still holding it and down to irrigate his bush and bollocks. It smelt like the sea. Everyone was well satisfied, including Anne, who doesn't seem to have much time for Derrick.

Now that edge had been taken off D's appetite and we were all shining with sweat, Mac led way up the steep stairs to her bedroom. Whole of room taken up by big bed, so we all flopped on it, glad it wasn't quite so hot up here. Mac explained that what she wanted us to do was quite simple once we got into position. Point was that we could make it last a really long time. But first we had to get Derrick stiff again. Mac pushed Anne down on her back and knelt at head, holding her shoulders down. Carla sat between her knees to keep them apart. Then Derrick and me had to lick his spunk off her.

Although it was starting to dry into crisp flakes round edges, most of it was still warm and moist because deposited so thickly. I began up at boobs and D, who had stripped off completely, down on insides of thighs. I nuzzled my way down fairly quickly while D was lingering round entrance to love trap. Soon we were nose to nose, our tongues pinching one of her inner lips between them. Our tongues met and prised the lips open. Without having to discuss it we knew what to do − the double tongue slid upwards, splitting the sealed petals apart, till it came to the pip. Then we took up independent activity again, independent but co-ordinated. Our tonguetips titillated the tiny clit from two directions and at same time tickled each other. Out of corner of eye I saw Mac bend forward and give Anne upside-down kiss. Glancing other way, I noticed Carla was rolling D's semi-limp cock between hands and mumbling its head with her lips.

39

Anne, who had managed to hold herself back when we were downstairs, suddenly tensed her tummy muscles and stiffened out. 'That was lovely,' she murmured, as Mac lifted mouth from her lips. And the excitement of being down between her legs while she got off like that had done trick for Derrick, too. I sat up and watched as Carla slid her distended mouth along length of resurrected prick and then released it in all its purple-headed glory.

So now we were ready to take up our new positions as directed by Mac. Thought it was really nice of her to ask if I minded D fucking her again for this one. I said of course not, that was the least I could do for her. She curled up on her right side and raised her left knee. D, also on his right side, nudged up against her and she helped him bed cock in her cunt. Then I moved into place just behind him. I lay on same side as both of them and raised left knee just like the MacDonald. D had to angle his body away from her and rest right cheek on inside of my right thigh. His right arm reached under this thigh and his left one over my left hip. Between his two hands he could now squeeze Anne's bum and her pussy as she too lay on her right side behind me. To complete the formation, her head was wedged between Carla's thighs while I felt around on bed above my head till I found Carla's tits. The tits may be tiny, but her nipples get huge when you rub and pinch them. Her left hand just reached as far as Mac's left boob, which it fondled vigorously.

I lifted my left thigh a bit higher to let Derrick slide head right up into crotch where he could lick me all over sexy parts and give me good tonguing in arse as well as twat. And now we all got to work in earnest, but in a leisurely way, trying to make pleasure last as long as possible. I think it must have lasted more than half an hour. Some of us females may have had mini-orgasms along the way, but D only spunked into Mac when we'd all worked each other up to a sensational multiple eruption that nearly shook bed to destruction.

Today I'm still quivering when I think about it. It wiped me out. I'm stiff and aching in every muscle. Must try

40

to be a bit less physical for a few days — find some nice sedate occupation.

I know. I'll have a look at *Middlemarch*.

On writing these words, Melanie closed the diary and went straight to her companion's bookshelves, where she soon found the fat paperback. The Captain's bright idea was destined to be realised.

THREE

LOVE AMONG THE RUINS

Melanie, who was a gifted mimic, studied the relevant chapters carefully. As soon as she had persuaded herself that she felt at home with George Eliot's mental processes and the Eliotic idiolect, she dashed off a draft chapter. In doing so, she kept before her the image of this Victorian woman of formidable intellectual powers, passionate nature and equine appearance who had had the temerity to defy the prudish social code of her day and live for so many years with a married man. George Eliot, surely, was no prude. But remembering something Miss MacDonald had told her, Melanie had to ask herself an awkward question which might, she thought, have some oblique bearing on the case of Casaubon and Dorothea. When in old age the writer eventually married a younger admirer and took him to Venice for their honeymoon, why had she hurled herself from the balcony of their apartment into the waters of the Grand Canal? This was a riddle Melanie was unable to solve, but as she struggled with her material she gradually came to feel more at home with such contradictions.

Miss MacDonald read the chapter critically, and asked her to rework several paragraphs. When she was satisfied that her young friend had done her best and that this best was approaching the requisite standard, she brought her own talents and experience to bear and subjected the chapter to a further stage of transformation. This involved the insertion of historical, cultural and topographical details of the kind despised by modern youth, for whom they hold little enchantment. Melanie, who found such stuff boring in the real *Middlemarch,* could not help admiring the effect as she lay in bed beside her beautiful patroness and cast her eye over the finished work.

An author much given to wide-ranging generalisations has declared few revolutions to be of more profound influence upon the inward constitution of the human heart than those in which the rosy confidence of dawning affection is subverted by the encroaching harsh light of common experience. We all of us exist in a medium compounded of hopes and fears, and at those crises of our lives when our fears gather into oppressive thunderclouds threatening to overwhelm the tender rills of youthful hope, it can seem that the very ground of humanity is undermined beneath our feet.

Such indeed was the case of Dorothea when, as Mr. Casaubon's bride of a few hours, she set forth with him on their wedding journey. They travelled in some style, as Sir James Chettam had good-naturedly placed his brougham at the disposal of the happy couple, in exchange for the use of Mr. Casaubon's ancient chariot during their absence. After the excitement of the wedding Dorothea was not sorry to throw herself back on the cushioned seat beside her husband while Sir James's man John, who was to drive them, mounted the box and the apprehensive Tantripp climbed up next to him.

Now, for the first time, Dorothea felt doubtful of her new position. All her reading had taught her that a bridal pair's first moments alone together were likely to be marked by tenderness and passion, which, in relation to Mr. Casaubon, had in her imaginings taken the form of her rendering a detailed account of her aspirations to improve the lot of his poorest parishioners, and on the side of her husband a warm exposition of his plan for the studies that were, he assured her, a secondary object of this visit to Rome. And yet her anticipation of these leisured and uninterrupted delights had been somewhat shadowed by a foreboding of other procedures sanctioned, nay, sanctified, by the matrimonial state, procedures at which her sister Celia had hinted obscurely after being

43

taken in hand one morning by Mrs. Cadwallader. As she took her place in the coach, the new Mrs. Casaubon left a seemly distance between herself and her bridegroom. If this was to be the occasion of the first embrace, she was determined not offend his refined sensibilities by appearing forward, or deficient in the decent wifely reticence she deemed becoming in women of her class.

She had been prepared, then, for a warm discussion of matters dear to both their hearts; and, if not exactly prepared for something so far outside her experience, she would at least have been unsurprised by a physical earnest of Mr. Casaubon's esteem. What she had not, however, expected was the great sigh, the yawn and the interminable succession of snores (punctuated only by occasional but alarming groans) that now ensued as their conveyance passed through Middlemarch and rattled southwards on the London turnpike.

When at last they pulled up in the courtyard of the inn where they had planned to seal the bond of their new condition, the evening was far advanced. The landlord regretted that his best room was already taken by a young, newly married couple. "Anyone else I would shift out of that great bed to make room for a man of the cloth such as your honoured self," he assured Mr. Casaubon. "But you and I, sir," — and he winked as he leaned forward to speak in confidence — "you and I would not be after depriving such a riggish pair of the delights of their first night together, saving your reverence, now would we? Why," — and he leaned further forward — "the blushing bride was all a-twitch for it, sir. But let me see, now. I have very decent lodgings for you in the front of the house, with a fire already laid. And for your daughter, sir, there's a cleanish coffin-bed in a closet next the bridal chamber. Your servants will find fresh straw for themselves in the stables."

Hearing these words, Dorothea felt a sense of guilty relief that the bright wedding ring of which she was so conscious remained concealed within her glove, and her warm sentiments towards her husband were rekindled by his passive reception of the innkeeper's misunderstanding. The matter was not mentioned while they partook of a light supper; indeed, Mr. Casaubon seemed quite unresponsive to the various topics she attempted to start, pleading fatigue and the effects of a long-standing digestive disorder. She planted a chaste kiss upon his noble brow and retired with a rushlight to the narrow, windowless closet.

No sooner had she undressed to her shift, extinguished her light and stretched her travel-stiffened limbs as far as the dimensions of her little bed permitted, than she became aware of disturbing sounds in the adjoining room. What puzzled her was the way these sounds, which her ears quickly registered as human voices, one male and one female, seemed to convey both hilarity and horror. Lying in the musty darkness, little by little she made out the presence of a door, outlined by thin lines of light: a door separating her strait accommodation from the bridal chamber beyond. And now she could see that even more light was spilling through the keyhole. She rose, wrapped a shawl around her shoulders and knelt before that source of radiance.

The sight that met her dazzled eyes appalled her. Infernally illuminated by a blazing fire which supplemented with its reddish flickering the harsher light cast by a glittering chandelier, a bed stood some two yards from her point of vantage, positioned sideways to her. On the bed, immediately in front of Dorothea, a lovely, youthful and blushing girl was seated, the bride for whom she, the new Mrs. Edward Casaubon, had been required to make way. This girl was attired in nothing but a white cap and a shift of transparent lawn, open at the front to display a plump bosom crowned with two coral tips. "Oh, sir!" Dorothea heard her cry. "You have quite worn down my defences. But will you not spare a poor girl you have already driven to the brink of madness?"

"Indeed no, madam," came the deep-throated reply from the husband, who was stationed outside Dorothea's field of vision. "The time is come when I must press my suit to the utmost. I would remind you of the vows you have sworn this very day. Make ready!''

At this the girl, who seemed to have been half playing the part of coyness and half leading her consort on with dissembled forwardness, gave a laugh and impudently stuck out her tongue. She then threw herself back so that she was lying flat on the bed with her bare feet hanging down to the floor. In this posture, she lifted her hips and drew up her shift to her waist. Dorothea trembled with shock and the anticipation of irrepressible pleasure. The bride's smooth white legs sagged wide apart, so that her secret centre of attraction was presented directly to the keyhole.

It is often conjectured by the youth of our enlightened and better regulated times that young ladies raised in the first two reigns of this century were accustomed to a certain slovenly laxness in matters of personal propriety. But Dorothea's ardently devout disposition, nurtured as it had been in the Puritanical soil of Lausanne, had flowered into such exemplary chastity that now, at the age of twenty and on the threshold of married life, she had never gazed or felt the desire to gaze upon the most intimate parts even of her own body. Her sister Celia, to be sure, was of a more flesh-bound temper and, knowing no scruples as a child, had frequently flung herself, naked, into the arms of her darling Dodo, begging her to kiss her from head to foot. Dorothea, however, had gently repelled these ingenuous advances; although Celia's charms had been exhibited to her freely and without shame, she had never allowed her eyes to rest on them or on those of any other female, herself not excepted.

Thus it was that the still unravished bride of Mr. Casaubon found herself, against her better judgment, peering through a keyhole upon such beauties as she had scarcely dreamed of. Set like a ruby amid the alabaster of this girl's thighs and quivering lower belly, a shining boss of flesh winked out at the head of a pink, double-crested cleft. The enticing ravine was fringed with yellow

46

curls, and a profusion of such curls adorned the plump mound above. As Dorothea peeped, it appeared to her astonished gaze that the moist lips fell apart as if spontaneously.

But whatever treasures they now disbursed were hidden from her illicit scrutiny. A dark form of considerable bulk interposed itself between the bed and the keyhole; it resolved itself into the figure of a burly man, attired only in his shirt and standing between the girl's dangling, outspread legs. He stooped forward, and Dorothea interpreted the cessation of the young bride's giggles and whimpers as a sign that he was claiming a nuptial kiss. Such delight, however, overwhelming though it might seem to Dorothea's fevered imagination, did not assuage his heaving lust for long. Rearing himself up to his full stature, the eager bridegroom lifted his shirt over his head and cast it aside. Dorothea marvelled at the rippling muscles of his shoulders and back, and the brawn of his hirsute thighs. Whatever manly qualities Mr. Casaubon might harbour beneath his clerical garb, she did not suppose they could rival the picture of virility she now beheld.

Suddenly, this veritable Mars hurled himself forward upon his waiting Venus, whose legs flew up and clasped themselves around his waist. In this new posture, his white posteriors were prominently displayed, and Dorothea, who was surprised to feel something warm and moist running thickly down the inside of one of her own thighs, became shyly aware of the bulging sac depending between his. As she had never looked upon the naked appurtenances of another person of her own sex, the reader will hardly wonder that she was a complete stranger to the male form. To her, the sculptor's fig leaf represented the daring *ne plus ultra* of æsthetic contemplation. And yet, as her eyes took in the electrifying scene before her, she was not totally puzzled by this dark-skinned sac, for Monk, her great St. Bernard, sported something smaller but not dissimilar between his hind legs.

The sturdy groom was battering against the belly of his

bride; the bed shook and unheeded cries of protest begged him, ineffectually, to desist. Dorothea gasped as the posteriors clenched, the shaggy legs stiffened and the muscle-roped body crushed itself down with all its force. The girl's bare feet kicked wildly in the air. She emitted a drawn-out, chilling scream which gradually modulated into a cooing, purring murmur of contentment. The man, relaxed and limp, slid down to the floor.

Dorothea caught her breath and found herself inexplicably clutching her own immodest parts. Open to her view beyond the keyhole was that secret place on which she had feasted her eyes before the intrusive male figure had plundered it. But how different in aspect from the trim organ in its still virgin condition! The crisp golden curls were wet and flattened. Splashes of bright blood besmirched the alabaster thighs and had soaked into the bedsheet. Now, even as she watched, a foaming white substance, flecked with crimson, oozed thickly from the swollen, ravaged lips. Instinctively, Dorothea knew she had now been vouchsafed the knowledge of what it meant to become a woman. Nevertheless, her carnal education remained incomplete: nothing in the scene enacted before her had yielded a hint as to what it meant to be a man. The groom had not once turned his back upon the bride, and thus the means by which these rosy, pearly effusions had been summoned forth remained a mystery.

The following night the Casaubons reached London. This time they were able to share a comfortable room with a capacious bed at the Bull in Aldgate. On retiring, Dorothea, mindful of what she had learned from the scene she had witnessed, threw herself on the bed with her legs dangling over the edge and her shift rolled up to her waist. Her husband, who had been busying himself with some papers beside the fire, approached her in his tasselled nightcap and long shirt. Instead of placing himself between her thighs, however, he merely reproached her for her immodesty and warned her that she was putting herself in the way of taking cold. "Dorothea, my dear," he continued, "you must not think me unmindful of my

48

conjugal duties. But the unwonted rigours of prolonged travel and the lively anticipation of joys yet to come when we reach the Eternal City combine to persuade me that we shall do well to defer our union until our arrival. In the meantime, you may be assured of my warmest regard for the wifely treasures you have laid up so long for our mutual enjoyment within the strict but delightful bonds of wedlock. The relishing of such treasures is said to be the acme of our merely mortal comfort." Having spoken, he climbed into bed with her slowly and stiffly, politely kissed her cheek and turned to lie with his back towards her, as if he had seen nothing to arouse his baser passions. Nevertheless, had Dorothea been possessed of the power to peer into his soul, she would have beheld a cockpit of tumultuous if sluggish stirrings centred on the vision of her proffered flesh.

They were proceeding towards Dover the next morning when she closed her eyes and affected to fall into a profound sleep. As she lay back on the gently swaying seat with her legs deliberately parted, she was aware of Mr. Casaubon stealing closer, raising her skirts and petticoats, easing open the cambric of her drawers and resting a trembling, bony hand upon her most sensitive place. He heaved a shuddering sigh, withdrew his hand and rearranged her clothing.

That night, which was spent in Dover, she lay awake many hours, listening apprehensively to the storm which raged outside and seemed to echo the dark tumult within her own heart. At length she drifted into uneasy slumber, tormented by dreams of tempest-tossed nausea and shipwreck. On awakening, she was conscious of her husband stumbling about the room and splashing water as he stood at the washstand. Dorothea said nothing, pretending to be still asleep, but she was disturbed to find that her shift had worked its way right up to her armpits. Even more disturbing was the small patch of a cold, oleaginous fluid she felt running slowly down her side from her navel. Since setting out on her wedding journey, she seemed to be discovering that the female body was

49

liable in the married state to exude strange, unguessed-at substances from the most unlikely orifices, but the true nature of the processes she observed was still a profound mystery to her.

The greater part of humanity inclines to dignify the past of its half-remembered, half-imagined childhood with the picturesque attributes bestowed by a romantic haze. But those of us capable of contemplating the condition of things some forty years ago with an eye unblurred by nostalgic sentiment must acknowledge that the truth was often harsher, and that, however delusive our age's panacea of Progress might be in general, it has brought us undeniable benefits in some particulars. One such inestimable benefit is the convenience of being propelled not merely from coast to coast, but overland from the Gallic shore even to the mighty barrier of the Alpine peaks by the agency of steam. It took the travellers whose early married life we are chronicling six tedious weeks over rough roads to reach Rome, weeks enlivened only by the occasional stirring sight or happening.

Mr. Casaubon's curiosity was narrowly confined to whatever vestiges of classical antiquity might be espied or conjectured along the way, but Dorothea insisted that they should turn aside from their itinerary to offer up a sigh upon the field of Waterloo. As they alighted from their vehicle, she startled her husband by taking his arm, gazing into his eyes and murmuring, with a tremulous sigh: "Stop! — for thy tread is on an Empire's dust!" To Mr. Casaubon, the effusions of Lord Byron were a closed book (and perhaps one better left unopened); his wife might have become a babbling lunatic for all he could tell, but to humour her he paused and looked down. At his feet he saw something in the lush grass and stooped to pick it up. It was a human skull that had lain there ever since the awful events enacted in this solemn arena seventeen years previously. The sight of the desiccated cleric blinking into those empty sockets was strangely moving to his young bride. Dorothea could not but be struck by a certain resemblance between the quick and the dead — the grinning death's head wanted but a covering of sallow skin stretched over it, the sparse adornment of some hanks of grizzled hair and the dull lustre of a pair of sable orbs, to appear a veritable simulacrum of her consort. This moment was a memorable one, but thereafter their progress blurred into a succession of jolting highways and ill-prepared, unfamiliar meals consumed in the malodorous inns that furnished their way-stations. By day she did her best to accommodate herself to her husband's dry and infrequent discourse, and during the hours of darkness to his nocturnal eructations, crepitations and other still more disagreeable habits.

Nor could she hope for relief in the company of her faithful maid, Tantripp, who, as well as being studious not to disturb the privacy of the honeymooners, seemed totally absorbed in the company of her fellow-servant John. One evening when they had broken their journey somewhere on the upper reaches of the Rhine, Dorothea missed her reticule. She descended to the courtyard of the inn to search for it inside the brougham.

Inexplicably, the blinds were drawn down and the spring leathers creaked loudly as the vehicle rocked from side to side. On opening the door, she was astonished to find these two persons on the seat, locked in a tight embrace, and even more astonished to see that their lower limbs and rumps were naked to her view. She withdrew, blushing. Her ardent and theoretic nature was strangely disturbed, and it was many weeks before she was once more able to look Tantripp in the eye. Thereafter the maid grew daily more impertinent, while John made little attempt to conceal his state of constant inebriation.

At last the snowy pinnacles of the Alps towered above them, and Dorothea gave herself up willingly to the transports of the sublime. Her spirits were raised, her breast animated and her cheeks suffused once more with the rosy hue that had abandoned them since her departure from her native shores. Even her husband's costive irritability affected her somewhat less; she was relieved

51

to find he had no desire to lengthen their journey through Switzerland by striking westward to visit her old school in Puritanical Lausanne. And this sense of elation remained with her during their descent into the plain of Lombardy, their progress across the Apennines down to the sparkling Ligurian sea and finally along the coast by way of Leghorn until the seven hills of Rome arose before their eyes.

Through the offices of Sir James Chettam, a spacious but gloomy apartment had been reserved for them on the Piazza di San Pietro in Vincoli, on the Esquiline Hill. (As they laboured up the steps of the Via San Francesco di Paola to gain this piazza, Mr. Casaubon explained in dry tones that the learned Varro derived this hill's denomination from the noun *excultus,* in allusion to several ornamental groves laid out upon the slopes by Servius Tullius, most popular of the ancient kings of Rome, before his overthrow by the violator of the chaste matron Lucretia, Tarquin the Proud. Furthermore, he disclosed, the impious daughter of Tullius had driven her car over the dead body of her sire on the very spot at which they now stood, from which act this steep ascent had anciently been known as the Via Scelerata, the accursed street.) The concierge conducted them through the lofty rooms of the apartment and threw open the double doors that gave access to the bedchamber. Dorothea gasped. The entire expanse of the walls, except where they were interrupted by the doorway and the tall, shuttered windows, was hung with paintings and tapestries depicting scenes of the most voluptuous debauchery. Now, not once but fifty times at a glance, a large part of her ignorance was dispelled, for each of these libidinous pictures displayed anything from one to a dozen *membra virilia,* most of them primed to their full extension and many of them engaged in the generative act. The concierge grinned at Mr. Casaubon and addressed him with flashing teeth and eloquent hands: "*Ecco il tempio d'amore matrimoniale, signore* — the temple of the matrimonial venery." He indicated the lubricious decorations, and continued: "*Per infiammare il gusto sensuale.''* Mr. Casaubon's jaw dropped. *"A fine di stimolare l'appetito voluttuoso ed eccitare i sensi lussoriosi* — for make a stand a the pego, your holiness.''

Mr. Casaubon blanched to a more sepulchral shade of grey, pressed a coin into the outstretched palm of the concierge and, bidding the fellow *arrivederci,* hurried him out of the apartment.

Poor Dorothea soon discovered that, even in the presence of these gross stimulants, her husband's self-command was that of a saint. Had he forgotten, she asked herself as she lay beside him on the third night, his promise to begin discharging his conjugal obligations once their destination were reached? So far, the joys to which he had looked forward in Rome had been confined to long hours in which he had toiled over dusty manuscripts in the Vatican library while she had savoured the city's various sights of ruined glory and incomprehensible art. The sole relief from all this suffocating strangeness came when she visited the Protestant cemetery to pay her respects to the poetic genius of Shelley and Keats, but the respite had been brief. That night, pondering the blasted magnificence of which she had been an unenthusiastic spectator and closing her eyes to the images of immodesty that winked at her from the shadows around the bed, she fell into a slumber troubled by a dream of alarming vividness.

In this dream, she found herself standing at the back of the orchestra in a great concert hall intolerably overheated by the flames of a thousand candles. She hid behind a towering double bass, a little girl once again in petticoats reaching no further than her knees. The orchestra had just begun to perform an heroic concerto, known as the ''Balkan'', which had supposedly taken the capitals of Europe by storm. On this occasion the work was being directed by the composer himself, a Serb known for his vertiginous genius and unpronounceable name. Mighty chords thundered out in celebration of the pure, patriotic aspirations of his oppressed nation. Dorothea's thighs shook with emotion. As they shook, she realised that they were completely bare. Her clothes had fallen from her childish form, and nothing but the bulky bass stood between her and the spellbound audience. The music grew louder, slower and more discordant. She could see that the notes in front of her were marked *Molto rallentando*; each crashing burst of sound seemed to be prolonged interminably, although her confused wits were able to grasp from the nodding of the metronome suspended above the platform that the muddy semiquavers were in fact being churned out at the rate of seventeen to the minute, decelerating slowly.

Distracted by this calculation, she had failed to notice that she was now seated at the front of the orchestra, right on the edge of the platform. Her instrument had shrunk to the size of a violoncello, which she clasped between her girlish thighs, while she herself had grown. Her form and development were still those of a child, but she had now acquired the stature of a healthy maiden of fifteen or sixteen.

As the opening orchestral *tutti* approached a climax of expectation, it dawned upon her that she, who had never played a stringed instrument in her life, was to be the soloist. Adept upon the pianoforte, she could see that the music before her was of diabolical difficulty. What poor sounds could she hope to coax from the unfamiliar object betweeen her legs? Panic now gripped her, even as she raised the bow and prepared to draw the horsehair across the vibrant strings. Vibrancy, however, was the last quality that could be expected from them: all four strings hung slack and useless. Dorothea struggled vainly to tighten the keys at the neck of the 'cello, but knew that even if she managed to do so she would be quite unable to tune the awkward instrument. She felt sick.

The deafening music heaved itself into a rising cadence, as if ready to pounce, and stopped, its dying agony continuing to reverberate around the domed auditorium. Dorothea closed her eyes. When she opened them she was standing, and the 'cello had contracted to the size of a useless violin which she clutched before her private parts.

The audience held its breath, then gasped as, before its eyes, the youthful soloist was transformed into a well-grown beauty boasting the full twenty years Dorothea had lived in the world. She glanced down and saw her bosoms budding into rose-tipped globes, veined with blue. Her hips and thighs filled out, and the plump triangle hidden behind the violin became darkly shadowed. A pretty thicket of chestnut curls now sprouted around the central cleft and spread up the lower reaches of her belly.

But the lusty Serb was growing impatient. He glared at her, his whiskers bristling, while the audience began to cough with embarrassment. Then he spoke. "You must stroke the belly," he explained. "And you must rub your hand up and down the stem. That is how we all do it." Ignoring his advice, Dorothea raised the violin to her chin; the crowd roared its appreciation as her parts of shame were wantonly displayed. In her anguish, she uttered a prayer to the virgin goddess Diana, a prayer which was immediately answered. The bow she held in her right hand became an arrow, which she hurled at the fulminating composer. It pierced him to the heart and he crumpled at her feet.

The urgent need now was to cover her most intimate part again. She lowered the violin and let it hang there, but it had dwindled once more and was now no larger than a kit, or dancing-master's miniature fiddle. Dorothea felt nothing but self-loathing for the impudent exhibition she had made of herself and anger at the fraud to which she had been subjected. "How could anyone think that I would be satisfied with — with *this*?" she shouted. "It ought to be getting bigger all the time, but instead it can only shrink." Throwing herself down on the chair she had used while still a 'cellist, she parted her thighs and pressed the tiny kit against the hot opening that at all costs had to be concealed. To her horror, the diminutive instrument disappeared inside her, leaving the nether mouth fully exposed. The inflamed mob was mounting the platform, eager to conjure harmonies from her vibrant young body . . .

55

She awoke, bathed in almost hectic perspiration. Her hand clutched something cold, wet and sticky. To her consternation, she discovered this to be the shrivelled excrescence which graced her husband's loins in the place where the gods, heroes, fauns and satyrs disporting themselves on the chamber walls were distinguished by more impressive tokens of their prowess.

The following evening, Mr. Casaubon informed Dorothea that he proposed to consummate his connection with her that very night. "But first, my dear," he said, "I must leave you for an hour or so. During this constrained absence you may for once forget your character as a Christian lady and utilise the licentious ornaments of our apartment to bend your mind to more pagan delights. Submit yourself to the soft enticements of Aphrodite, in order that you may be ready to receive me on my return.'

Dorothea's heart shrank as if her husband had laid an icy hand upon her breast. But when she heard the door close behind him, she was ashamed to acknowledge to herself that a seductive warmth was beginning to course through her veins. She stood at the window and peered down to watch him as he hurried towards the shadowy ruins of the baths of Titus, whence he turned his footsteps in the direction of the Colosseum. Looking westwards, she was aroused by the sight of a blood-red sun declining above the twin eminences of the Capitoline, steeping them in a sanguine radiance. Five years later a touring English poet was to ejaculate in disgust at the contrast between legend and reality: —

> Is this, ye Gods, the Capitolian Hill?
> Yon petty Steep in truth the fearful Rock,
> Tarpeian named of yore?

To Dorothea, however, impressed by the consonance between the lurid aspect of the hill seen at this hour and her husband's account of felons being hurled from the Tarpeian rock into the foaming waters of the Tiber, this scene was filled with awful foreboding. She closed the shutters, lighted the candles and dutifully gave herself up, as directed by her spouse, to the contemplation of those inflammatory productions from which she had hitherto held her gaze averted.

As she passed from painting to painting, her knees began to tremble and she found it needful to support herself against the wall. The sights that confronted her in rapid and seemingly endless succession were such as she had never before beheld, although she had reason to suspect that her uncle possessed some engravings of a similar kind which he kept locked in a cabinet in his library.

A large canvas depicted the rape of the Sabine women in more flagrant detail than is to be seen in the pictorial representations of that event which grace the public galleries of the great cities of Europe. As is usual in such representations, Romulus and his warriors were shown carrying off the naked and half-naked virgins in their brawny arms. But another part of their bodies was also exhibited in a state of brawny preparedness, and in some cases this member had already forced its entrance into the receptacle of the indignant victim. In the background, Dorothea observed a girl who had been overlooked by the ravishers. She had raised her flimsy garment and was displaying her secret but neglected charms in the hope of yet attracting one of the virile Romans for her own enjoyment.

Two smaller pictures formed a pair. One showed a voluptuous, drowsy-eyed Leda receiving the attentions of a great white swan. The artist's imagination had so far departed from traditional iconography as to show the bird with its head and most of its neck engulfed between the girl's rounded thighs. The patch of reddish fur at the base of her belly contrasted beguilingly with the whiteness of the downy neck, and the ingenious artist had used a subtle palette to hint at a flush of passion upon the curve of her stomach. In the companion piece, a plump Pasiphaë was being covered by a high-mettled bull with smoking nostrils; the brute battered from behind at the portals of her modesty, in full and oustretched readiness to sire the monstrous Minotaur upon her.

Even without benefit of all the mythological instruction her husband had pressed upon her since the earliest days of their acquaintance, Dorothea would have recognised the blushing youth in the next painting which caught her eye as Ganymede, cupbearer to Jove. Yet nothing in Mr. Casaubon's exposition of the tale had prepared her for the indignity the impressively proportioned father of the gods was now offering to inflict upon his callipygian minion. She fled in horror, seeking a less perverted scene.

Scarcely older than the abused Ganymede, a bashful Adonis strove to resist the caresses of Venus, who had discarded on the grassy hillock forming their bed the scant, gauzy drapery that had ill concealed her beauty. Those parts of her body dedicated most particularly to the rites of love were portrayed in a condition of high emotion: the rosebuds of her breasts were concentrated into long, hard teats of ruby and her wantonly smiling lips were puffed, moist and slightly parted, as were those other lips, neglected by the pencils of respectable artists, at any rate in those of their works exhibited in public buildings. Venus bent over the reluctant boy, using one of her hands to cup the swelling purse between his thighs, while with the other she grasped the wilting member for which she reached with the tip of her tongue.

Mrs. Casaubon tore herself away from this moving spectacle and, her head swimming and her bosom bursting, moved along the row of pictures, until one of a somewhat different *genre* caught her eye. The execution was cruder than that of the productions she had so far scrutinised, but its subject was clear to make out. In a setting of gothic arches dominated by a great black crucifix, half a dozen monks, their habits knotted up around their waists, were seen debauching four young nuns, whose lower limbs were similarly denuded. Two of these cowled brothers might thus have been thought superfluous to the requirements of the self-sacrificing sisters, but they had devised a means of making themselves serviceable. One had placed his staff entirely within the mouth of a nun whose more appropriate opening was already occupied as she sprawled on the altar. The other had ripped open the front of this same girl's garment. Standing between his two confrères as they lavished pleasure upon her at both ends simultaneously, he waved his bulbous rod above her, showering her breasts and belly with spurts of a margaric liquor that ran down and coated her sides. It was pleasurably shocking to our innocent Dorothea's Protestant sensibility that such a pungent satire upon Popish practices should be displayed, albeit in private, barely more than two miles from the Vatican itself.

Dorothea summoned Tantripp. As soon as the maid had helped her out of her simple day dress of Corinth blue trimmed with *cendre de rose* and unlaced her stays, she was dismissed; the feverish fingers of her mistress completed the disrobing and Dorothea stretched herself in full nudity upon the damask counterpane.

At the foot of the bed, on the wall immediately before her, hung a painting of middle size which she conjectured to be the prize of this collection. It could have been from the brush of Boucher himself, so lifelike was the luxurious imagery calculated to challenge the celibacy of any occupant of this bed. The picture showed a deeply upholstered sofa piled with plump cushions and rich, crumpled drapery, and a discarded rose lying emblematically on the floor beside it. A beautiful, naked girl was extended face-down upon the sofa; she too had the poignant air of having been lately used and discarded, although Dorothea found it hard to understand how any lover could have torn himself away from such enticing charms. The texture of this ripe girl's bareness was heightened by juxtaposition with the tumbled velvets, satins and silks upon which she was so negligently displayed. Her right elbow, furthest from the spectator, was raised to rest on the curved arm of the sofa, and the hand supported her chin as she seemed to gaze in a betrayed stupor after her departed companion. Her fair hair was braided and bound up on her head. With her left elbow on the seat-cushion and the fingers of her left hand just touching those of the right, her trunk was slightly raised so that the profile of a pendulous breast could be discerned. The girl's thighs were spread apart, the left one hanging somewhat over the edge although the foot remained up on the seat, while her right leg sloped up a large cushion which leaned against the back of the sofa, its lower corner stuffed beneath her loins. With his model lying in this position, the artist had most expertly delineated the tender curves of her posteriors. Sated with the grossness of the images she had contemplated before coming to bed, Dorothea nevertheless felt herself beginning to melt once against at this more artful titillation. With the eye of her newly awakened faculty of lubricity she supplied the rear view the painter had implied but delicately left unrepresented: the open groove running down darkly between those soft buttocks, the little puckered orifice winking shyly forth and the curly-fringed pink slit of moistness spilling the overflowing tribute so recently offered up by her master, which dripped and soaked into that opulent cushion.

Dorothea lay on her back, her skin filmed with a dew exuded under the double stimulus of the hot atmosphere and the heady thoughts aroused by this masterpiece. One of her hands had attached itself to a hardening nipple; the other had strayed to the moist treasures between her legs, which she found herself to be plundering without conscious volition. A powerful sensation had begun to suffuse her entire corporeal being, but just as it threatened to accumulate into overwhelming, explosive intensity, the door opened and her husband strode into the room.

He greeted her with a look of approval rather than affection, and glanced at the picture on which her eyes were still fixed. Taking his hint from the artist, he commanded Dorothea to turn over on to her front. He seized her by the hips and pulled her down the bed until her legs were hanging down to the floor. Then he removed

60

a plump pillow from under the covers and stuffed it beneath her belly so that her rump was thrust up into the air. Now it was the work of a moment for Mr. Casaubon to strip to his shirt. Dorothea turned her head sideways and saw that this garment was lifted up like a tent by the long rod of flesh it concealed, albeit she could easily supply its general appearance from the pictorial representations she had been studying during his absence.

In a flash he was upon her, showing no mercy. She recollected the painting of Jove ravishing Ganymede as her most private and shameful place was invaded first by a wet tongue which lubricated it and the surrounding area most liberally, and then by something hard, hot, gross and throbbing. The terrible weapon was pressed against her forbidden opening with all its might and, as it was pressed, the opening tightened in pained resistance. She felt Mr. Casaubon, who now seemed even more of a stranger than on the day of their marriage, roughly tearing apart the cheeks of her behind in his efforts to effect an entrance. Poor Dorothea cried out in pain. As she did so, and perhaps precipitated by the sense of manly power this reaction conveyed to her husband, a modest quantity of luke-warm, thin fluid was sprayed over her buttocks and into the ravine dividing them.

Mr. Casaubon collapsed on his bride's back, utterly exhausted and drained. She lifted herself to roll him off her; the sight and odour of the wet, slug-like appendage, redolent of the fish market and the merest ghost of its active self, made such a distasteful impression upon her that she rolled him over once more so that it was his turn to lie face down. The sight that now confronted her caused her to gasp in alarm. From the midpoint of this frail man's back, the point at which his shirt had become caught up, down over his skinny posteriors and right down to the backs of his knees, he was covered with a bloody network of weals and welts. Her heart softened towards him, for she supposed him to have been set upon by cowardly villains during his recent perambulation. When she pressed him for an account of the affair, however, he mumbled some incoherent and wholly unconvincing remark about calling at a cloister in the shadow of the Colosseum with a view to investigating, experimentally, the spiritual benefits claimed by its inmates for the practice of flagellation. Despite the narrow scheme of her education, Dorothea had, in the vaguest terms, heard of such excesses. But when, the next night, she stole from the apartment to seek out the cloister of religious devotees, the only intact building she found in that quarter proved to be under siege from devotees of quite another persuasion, led on by the objects of their adoration, who were luring them willingly into that *maison close* by the most impudent exhibition of their privities.

Nothing more was said of the episode, and indeed little intercourse of any description passed between husband and wife for the next few days. Then, one fine afternoon, Dorothea was surprised to receive a call from Mr. Casaubon's young cousin Will Ladislaw, of whose presence in Rome they had been quite unaware. Holding her fascinated with his laughing eyes, Will explained that he had been residing there for some months in a studio he shared with a German painter of his acquaintance, familiarising himself with the antiquities and magnificent works of art in which the city abounds. Dorothea blushed, glancing involuntarily towards the door of the bed-chamber. It was closed, and the remarkable collection of paintings behind it remained hidden.

Ladislaw was invited to dine with the couple the following day, and in his turn accompanied them to meet his friend Naumann, a wild young man who succeeded by means of flattery in persuading Mr. Casaubon to sit for him while he executed a sketch of his head as St. Thomas Aquinas, to be used in the large canvas on which he was presently at work. But the German's true purpose in making the sketch was to lend countenance to his proposal that he should attempt a full-length portrait of Mrs. Casaubon, a project that would entail her attendance at the studio every day for the next week at least. Her husband, whose researches in the Vatican left her for so many hours neglected, could hardly object to this proposal.

In the event, two portraits were taken and a charcoal sketch. In the first, Dorothea wore a striking gown of Modena red taffeta, close fitting and extremely *decolletée*, with modish imbecile sleeves and a narrow gold *ferronière*, a gift from Will, adorning her brow. This portrait, destined to be presented to her husband, showed her standing beside a bust of Socrates, fanning herself with a silk hand-screen. But the second painting was altogether more *gewagt*, as Herr Naumann put it. He knew he would be able to dispose of it for a very respectable price, and hoped that one day it might establish his reputation, if not that of his model, by gracing the walls of a great public gallery. On her own insistence, Dorothea posed for it in total nudity upon a sofa, in precisely the attitude of the young courtesan whose picture had so impressed her as she reclined on her bed that evening in the Piazza di San Pietro in Vincoli. The genial German's third production, however, small though its dimensions were, outdid the other two in the emotional effect it was calculated to arouse in the beholder; its nature was such as to ensure its retention in the private collections of the artist himself. With quick, nervous lines and great subtlety of shading he reproduced the spectacle of Dorothea and Will, both as naked as they had been born, engaged in consummating the very act which, to her chagrin and frustration, Mr. Casaubon had failed to execute. Dorothea had left Middlemarch as a virgin bride, but was to return, despite the inadequacies of her husband, to take her place in society as a fully qualified married woman.

Melanie sighed with pleasure and surprise as she laid aside the bundle of papers and turned to embrace her co-author. 'We'll never get away with it,' she said. 'It's just too filthy.'

'Too filthy?' laughed her companion. 'It's because it was so filthy that poor George Eliot got cold feet and didn't try to publish it. But what do you think of it apart from the filth?'

'Isn't it a bit top-heavy? Maybe we've rather rushed the

business with Will and Naumann.'

'It just sort of turned out that way,' said Miss MacDonald, 'but I'm quite pleased with the effect because critics will see that as another reason why it was chucked out. Georgie girl decided she wanted to make much more out of what those two got up to, and that's how it is in the real *Middlemarch*. Any other comments?'

'Apart from that, I'd say it's fairly convincing because it's so bloody boring. I just love the boring bits — maybe that's because you did most of them. Yes, it'll do. But that's enough for tonight — let's celebrate finishing it at long last.'

The two women threw back the bedcovers, discarded their nightdresses and buried their faces in each other's cunts. Their literary labour and the work to which it had given birth were nor forgotten as they devoted the next few hours to joys that Dorothea had never dreamed of. As for her original creator, it is certainly possible that George Eliot had dreamed of or even experienced such ecstasies. In old age, plagued by rotten teeth, she was courted by a number of female admirers. But, as Miss MacDonald had to admit to Melanie, the pen that had produced *Middlemarch* had nothing to communicate on the subject of any indiscretions of that kind — unless, like the chapter now scattered on the floor beside the bed, such confessions were still awaiting discovery.

FOUR

GETTING IT TOGETHER

The Captain gulped a large Glenlivet as he sat jumpily in the lounge bar of the Kensington Moorlands Hotel. He pretended to devote his attention to the pages of *Country Life* while keeping a keen eye on the street entrance. Pleading acute jet lag, he had packed Gloria off alone in a taxi. Admittedly, he was sorry to forgo the New Vibrations Modern Dance Group's nude production, *The Twenty-Fifth Day of Sodom,* for which they had tickets, but if Gloria returned with a good report of it he would try to take her to another performance.

The magazine slipped from his hands as the glass door swung open and a good-looking woman entered the bar. But no — this was not the young lady for whom he was waiting so nervously, even though it was already twenty minutes later than the time they had surreptitiously agreed that afternoon at the Royal Academy.

Gloria had insisted on taking him to a controversial exhibition of erotic photography in pursuance of her research. While she passed through the galleries with a show of affronted disdain, the Captain had trailed behind to relish at his leisure a rather conventional but nonetheless striking set of black-and-white prints which would have merited a place in his Palace of Fantasies back in Banesville. He had stiffened in his trousers as he stared at them and he stiffened again now at the recollection.

In the pictures, a bearded man in a white shirt and black socks held up by suspenders was debauching his much younger bride in a hotel bedroom of the twenties. Improbably, she still wore her headdress and veil, lace gloves and white silk stockings, but her other garments had been tossed aside. In the first view she knelt to take her groom's straining cock into her mouth. The second one showed a rapturous grin on her pretty face. A trail of semen ran from the corner of her mouth. The man had his lips clamped on one nipple, while the other breast was thrust towards the camera. The next picture gave a close-up of the supposedly virginal pudendum, the labia held open by the bride's gloved fingers. Her groom's cheek rested on her belly; his tongue reached into her blonde curls, questing towards the clitoris. In the final shot the couple were shown joined in consummated matrimony: the girl knelt on all fours on the bed, her tits hanging down and her bum in the air while her consort entered her dog-fashion. Most of his manhood had disappeared up the cunt pouting out from between the conjunction of buttocks and thightops — only the wet root emerging from the tangle of black hair remained in sight. Clamped between his lips wagged a phallic cigar.

So engrossed was the Captain in this scene that he had not noticed the tugging at his sleeve. But the silky voice of the girl who had approached him brought him back to the real world. 'Haven't we met somewhere before?' she asked.

The Captain stepped back and ran his eye over her. At first he was distracted by the elegant chalk-striped costume, a smart couturier's parody of masculine business attire. But the auburn hair, despite its modish styling, soon prompted his memory. 'Why,' he had cried in genuine delight, 'if it isn't Gina Wootton! Give us a kiss, then, for old times' sake.'

Although he had fucked her only twice during his sojourn at Cunlip College, Gina had been the dearest object of the Captain's desire ever since he had witnessed her willing violation in the showers, the instrument of her ravishment being a salami. The salami had projected from another girl's cunt and the two had linked themselves on the floor, cheered on by their classmates while the Captain peered down through a skylight. When he and Gina had at last come together in happy copulation, he had formed the impression that she was not altogether immune to his charms; for all he now knew, if fate had not separated them they might well have become lovers. For Gina was beautiful and had what, for want of a better word, he could

66

only call *class*. She was a sexy snob, to tell the truth. And she had still looked like a sexy snob as she stood there patronising the exhibition, transformed though she was from a freckled schoolgirl to a well-groomed woman about town. As she smiled up at him with her seductive green eyes, he had caught a distant glimpse of Gloria Sweetbutts moving back in his direction, and hastily scribbled a message on Gina's exhibition catalogue: 'See you 7.30 Kensington Moorlands Hotel'. It was now seven minutes to eight.

Anticipating disappointment, he set his empty tumbler down on the table beside him and gazed out through the glass door at the street. There were few cars about and fewer pedestrians, and the April sun had long since gone down behind the buildings opposite. At that moment a cool pair of hands were laid over his eyes. The Captain sprang to his feet, breaking away from his fragrant-smelling assailant. Before him stood a radiant Gina Wootton, who laughed at his discomfiture as she kissed his cheek.

She was now wearing a modest but extremely smart black lightweight coat with lime-green accessories, including a cute little pill-box hat, a lime-green band to bind back the bunch of coppery curls, gloves, shoes and a small furled umbrella. Her lipstick was chosen to form a piquant contrast with the green.

'Have a drink?' offered the Captain.

'Better not,' she said. 'This is just the sort of place I might run into Mummy.'

The Captain had already had a bottle of Bollinger sent up to his room and had bustled about packing Gloria's belongings away before coming down to the bar. He gave Gina the room number and asked her to follow him up there after a few minutes' delay for the sake of discretion. This gave him time, on reaching the seventh floor, to draw the curtains against the last rays of the setting sun, switch on some seductive lighting and change into a silk dressing-gown before a light tap was heard on the door and he admitted his elegant caller.

When Gina handed him her coat, he gasped at the simple but beautifully tailored lime-green costume with its high-standing mandarin collar. Downstairs she had been a vision of black offset by green; now the proportions were reversed and the

67

touches of black were provided by a jet brooch on her flattish bosom and the sheer silk tights (stockings?) that clung to the slim curves between knee-high hemline and dainty shoes. When she threw her arms around his neck and kissed him with surprising fervour, his hands on her back could feel no telltale indication of a bra. As to knickers, his investigation of the smooth curves of her bottom was inconclusive. His cock rose and thrust out through the opening down the front of his silk gown. As its head tried to bore into Gina's belly, she pulled away from him.

'Hold on!' she laughed. 'You won't be my friend if you spill anything on these clothes.'

While she began to work briskly on her buttons, the Captain took the champagne from its silver bucket and fumbled with the wire and cork. He turned with two foaming glasses and presented one to his old flame.

Jacket and skirt had been discarded and laid, neatly folded, on a chair. Gina stooped with her back to him, smoothing the skirt. At first he received the impression that from her waist down her body was clad in black tights — a slight disappointment, perhaps, when he had hoped for stockings and suspenders, but he had to admit that their texture and colour contrasted beautifully with the girl's shining white back; almost as beautifully as the hanging bunch of auburn hair clasped in its green band. The little hat still perched on her head. When she straightened up and turned to face him, however, it was evident that it was not tights that encased her nether limbs after all, but the lower part of a semitransparent black garment that sheathed her trim figure from neck to toes, probably the kind of thing they called a body stocking. She pivoted slowly round for him to admire her and he took in the design of this sexy item. Above her waist, the front part was stretched tight over her breasts. The nipples thrust hard and orange-tinted through its taut, close mesh, and their covering, rising as high as the throat, was secured with a bow tied behind her neck. This left her slim but rounded arms, her freckled shoulders, her sides and her back bare. The fragile material stretched around her hips and came together in a plunging V at the very base of her spine, inviting the insertion of a finger between the swelling cheeks of her bottom. For the present the Captain declined this tacit invitation, registering with interest that the transparency of the garment allowed him to make out that she wore beneath it a tiny pair of green bikini-style briefs, barely more than a G-string.

He winked at Gina and they raised their glasses, setting them down after a couple of long, cool draughts. She winked back at the Captain, removed her hat carefully, kicked off a shoe and flexed her knee as she bent down to take off the other one. It dropped to the floor and she stroked the inside of her raised thigh, smiling up at him provocatively. Allowing the front of his dressing gown to fall open as he approached her, he took her in his arms, strained her to him and screwed into her mouth with his tongue. Her back felt warm and smooth to his fingers and as she raised her arms to cross them behind his neck he was aware of a suggestive fragrance emanating from the shaven underarms. His lips disengaged from hers and his nose burrowed into the urgent moistness of her right armpit. 'Do you get to see any of your old Cunlip friends?' he mumbled.

'Oh yes,' she answered, giggling in her ticklishness. 'I'm in touch with quite a few of them. We have fun at weekends, though I don't know what's happened to Melanie. And I used to see a fair bit of the Muttock, though not since the new year.'

Mary Muttock had been the unconventional principal of Cunlip College while the Captain had served as odd-job man there, and her forced premature retirement had coincided with his own, being occasioned by one and the same scandal. 'Perhaps you could arrange for us all to get together soon,' he suggested. 'Didn't you know? Melanie's living with the Macdonald now. I've promised to go and see her — we've been writing to each other. You still seeing that ill-favoured boyfriend of yours — what was his name — Joker Jennings?'

'Not in public. Leastways, not when I can help it. But now and then, yes. You know — when I feel like something a bit rougher than I brush up against every day in personnel management.'

'That's what you're doing now?'

'That and a bit of modelling and filming.'

If it had been physically possible the Captain, stirred by his memory of a certain adult movie watched with Dee Dee Burdle, would have touched and fondled every part of this young woman's body simultaneously. As this was beyond his power, he endeavoured to carry out the programme serially, eager to complete his exploration before being overtaken by orgasmic climax. He backed off, spun her round and rammed his stiff dick up against her bottom, pulling her tightly against himself and letting his hands run up over the slightly abrasive texture of the nylon which covered her front until they rested firmly on her breasts. Without any action of the wrists or movement of his spreading fingers upon the surface of the fabric, he found he could produce a kind of suction by contracting and relaxing his palms. Already hard, the teats responded by lengthening like a pair of little cocks which pressed into the ticklish centres of his palms through the thin material.

Leaving his left hand in place over Gina's left breast, he lifted the right one, tweaked the bursting nipple it had covered and trailed his fingertips down her quivering belly until they found the hot mound at the base of it. After a few preliminary prods, he placed his palm over the convexity, just as it had rested on her right breast. The only difference was that his fingers, instead of being spread out like the legs of a crab, were squeezed together as they curled downwards and back between her thighs. As his palm replicated the contracting, sucking rhythm with which his other hand was palpating her left breast, his fingertips, bunched together, tried to press her knickers and their gauzy black covering up into the cleft.

To begin with, the plump outer lips seemed to resist the pressure. His tongue flicked out to tickle her right earlobe and cheek; she threw back her head and parted her knees, and suddenly the vulva gave way. The Captain felt dampness straining through the cloth to spread on his fingers and milled the heel of his hand in a circular motion over the mound as she pushed forward to meet him. He felt the whole ripe fruit split apart so that the ball of his thumb sank inwards to crush the pulsing pip of her clitoris. And yet his own swollen, stretched-out cockpiece was still unlodged. This was intolerable.

Once more he spun Gina round so that they were now face to face. He clutched her under the arms and then, hooking his fingers under the edges of the body stocking, pulled it towards him until the breasts sprang out at either side and it was gathered together into a black band passing down between them. Each nipple received a fleeting kiss and lip-bite. Then the fingers that grasped the two sides of her garment together at the front slipped inside. The Captain was conscious of the coarse hairs on the backs of his hands and fingers scratching against the youthful smoothness of Gina's belly as they worked their way down, until the surface over which they slid gave way to a wiry bush.

At that instant the romantic spell was very nearly shattered by the prolonged report of what he took to be a fart. He drew back instinctively and was relieved to see that the offensive sound had been caused by the ripping of fabric as the impractical garment was dragged forward over her hips and its only seam, running from the small of her back to the midpoint of her crotch, gave way to his tugging. Gina unfastened the bow at the back of her neck and the Captain pulled the tattered remnants down to her feet so that she could step clear of them. And now she stood before him in nothing but the saucy little lime-green knickers, the base of their V adorned with a dark, pungent stain. He shoved her roughly back on the bed.

Gina's hand moved to her crotch as her thighs sagged open. 'Oh no!' she cried. 'Sod it! I must rinse these out and put them on a radiator to dry.'

While she was in the bathroom the Captain slipped out of his robe and luxuriated on the bed, gently wanking himself into hard rigidity with one hand while using the other to sip his champagne. He could hear the sound of running water. A moment later his darling returned, gloriously naked. Stunned with her beauty, at first the Captain was so preoccupied with the way her moist lips pouted pinkly through the neatly trimmed triangle of auburn scrub that he was unaware of her scornful anger.

'Who's the ladyfriend?' she snarled.

'What ladyfriend?'

'Or have you taken to using mascara and lipstick? And wearing these?' She held up a lacy black bra.

In his enthusiasm at the thought of receiving Gina he must have overlooked these items when trying to conceal any traces of Gloria. Denial would have been futile in the face of such damning evidence. 'Well,' he admitted, 'I have got my PA with

71

me, but she's just — you know, an academic person. She does a bit of research for me.'

'Oh, I see; she's just here to hold your hand, is she? What kind of research precisely does she go in for?'

Experience told the Captain that argument was useless in a situation like this, so he toppled her backwards on the bed and stopped her mouth with his lubricating cockhead. Gina choked and spluttered. He prised apart her cuntlips and slotted three fingers into her quim, opening them to stretch it tight while his thumbnail scratched at her clit.

Soon it was evident that her anger had given way to sexual frenzy. He lifted himself from her tensed body, reversed his position over her and drove his penis home into the eager cunt. Staring down into the green eyes that gazed back in some puzzlement, he addressed her. 'Look,' he said. 'It's true. I hired her to work for me.'

Gina's cunt muscles contracted. 'I'm surprised she left her things here after doing the work you paid her for,' she remarked.

'You don't get it,' replied the Captain, commencing a slow but steady corkscrew motion as he supported his weight on outstretched arms. 'I've got a job in an American university and she's a research student who's come over here with me to help me set up a promising business scheme I have in mind. I'm directing her dissertation, you see, and she's got a lot of faith in my judgment,' he added, inconsequentially and rather incoherently, as a great head of semen built up in his loins and he doubled his rate of poking.

'No,' cried Gina. 'Not inside me. No — you've got to pull out — quick!' Almost out of control, he drew back the full length of his foam-flecked member until the knob sprang free and her distended labia were sucked together by the spasms rippling through her abdomen. 'Up here!' she gasped. 'In my — oh! — in my mouth!'

With one leap he had brought his knees forward to straddle her chest. His erect cleaver, wet with Gina's juices, hung throbbing above her. She reached up and curled her fingers round the slippery stem. Feeling their touch, the Captain lost all self-possession and spouted his pent-up seed in a succession of powerful gushing jets. The first hot package spilt over her forehead, hair and right eye. The second gob, by luck rather than judgment, was squirted clean into her open mouth, followed without a break by an eruption which splashed on her nose, left cheek, chin and throat. Only then did the ecstatic girl raise her head and take the pulsing organ deep between her lips, sucking firmly as the hot fluid issued in a steady and unremitting stream from her lover's bursting plum.

At this point a key turned in the lock and the door opened to admit a horrified Gloria. Prim in a simple white dress, she clasped her handbag in front of her and uttered a brief but poignant yelp of distress and disbelief.

The Captain did his best to exert a calming influence. 'Why aren't you still at the ballet?' he asked, as if to transfer the burden of guilt to Gloria and thus neutralise her anger.

'A police raid,' she wailed. 'These guys were jerking off all over the girls' faces right there on stage and I guess someone complained. The cops closed the show down but I split before they could get round to checking out the audience and asking for ID. But what the heck are you doing? You said you had jet lag.'

Spitting out his deflated penis, Gina intervened. 'His jets don't lag at all, lady. So you must be the academic person, the globetrotting PA.'

Sexual jealousy, almost palpable, was seeping into the atmosphere of the room from both women. The important thing, the Captain realised, was to maintain the initiative and not allow himself to become marginalised. He rose from the bed and threw Gloria down upon it beside the still-panting Gina. Not bothering with the buttons that ran down the front, he ripped open the American girl's white dress, forced her white bra up over her breasts and dragged her tights and panties down her struggling legs so that her own kicks sent them flying across the room. He seized a cuntmound in each hand, squeezing and shaking them violently as his fingers sank into the tender flesh, dry and resistant in Gloria's case but soft and oozing in Gina's. Having established a firm hold, he brought together the two mounds, the one auburn and the other chestnut. It was the work of a moment to drag his fingers out from Gloria's lips and substitute the thumb of the hand securing the other girl, so that he now held the two rivals clamped together by their sexual parts. As his thumb penetrated more deeply, it encountered the welling of oily exudations that told him his stratagem was succeeding with Gloria.

There was little doubt that Gina had recovered rapidly from her post-orgasmic lassitude and was beginning to enjoy herself and the new company. Their bosoms were squashed together, all antipathy forgotten, as the English lass lavished hot kisses on her new American chum. In her turn, Gloria seemed fascinated by the rank-smelling coating of ejaculate now starting to dry on Gina's face and by the salacious flavour of fresh spunk lingering stickily between her lips and gums and under her tongue.

The Captain churned his fingers and thumb vigorously round in the handful of juicy cunts that gloved them so excitingly. His free hand forced a way down between their bellies and into the intermingling hairpads as they ground together. Somehow he contrived with nails and fingertips to draw back the elusive hoods of flesh to expose the engorged clitoral buds and bring them into mutual friction. This proved too much for the young ladies to bear. Gloria Sweetbutts was the first to stiffen and thrash out wildly with arms and legs, but Gina was not far behind. The orgasms of both of them continued repeatedly for some minutes, until they gradually subsided in moans and whimpers and the Captain withdrew his helping hands. Shaking his aching wrists, he congratulated himself at having effected such a satisfactory introduction in rather unpropitious circumstances.

His next move was to mount the bed and lie face down on top of the girls, who were now stretched out side by side exhausted on their backs, so that each supported about half of his weight. He manoeuvred himself until his tongue was level with their fannies and his rigid prick somewhere between their faces. By pulling up his knees on either side, he was able to lift his loins slightly, allowing the girls to breathe and giving him more scope to dangle and thrust wherever the fancy took him.

Only a widely forked tongue could have explored both clefts simultaneously; the Captain was no innocent, but that was one attribute of the serpent that he lacked. He turned his head to the right to tongue through the tickling chestnut curls and down into Gloria's cuntlips, using his left hand to fondle those of Gina and soothe her internal twitching with a gentle massage of the outer parts. In contrast to the bout just concluded, this round was a peaceful, ruminative affair and the two girls had time to get to know each other a bit better as they idly licked the Captain's dangling balls and flicked their tonguetips up and down his shaft. In the process their lips and tongues came into frequent contact with each other but this did not prevent their owners from engaging in desultory conversation which the Captain was conscious of as a distant murmur.

Gina was the first to speak. 'What part of America are you from, then?'

'New Hampshire, but I go to school in Southern California.'

Gina gulped. 'School? I left school last year and went straight into personnel management, or human resources as we call it now. Surely you're a couple of years older than me?'

'Graduate school. The doctor here's directing my dissertation. That's good for me — you see, he runs the Reserved Collections department so it's real easy for me to get at the dirty pictures.'

The Captain judged from the breakdown of rhythm in Gina's manipulation of his testicles that she was having difficulty in processing this information. 'Dirty pictures?' she asked. 'So what's this — this dissertation supposed to be about?'

'It's called *Eros and the Camera: changing tastes in the photographic representation of female nudity, 1863–1937.* Well, that's the provisional title. I'm beginning to have serious doubts about its political correctness. Urrgh!' She wriggled her hips beneath the Captain as he curled his tongue into a tube and drove it deep into her vagina while his chin crushed her clitoris.

'What's political about that?' asked Gina.

'Aaah — that's *good*. Pardon me?'

'What makes — what makes this dissertation — I mean, what makes it political?' Gina's attention seemed to be wandering as a bold sweep of the Captain's middle finger split open her sex and paddled lengthwise between the lips.

'I guess we're talking about — aaah — we're talking about images, well, you gotta call them inflammatory images produced to arouse — whaddyer doing to me, doc? — to arouse male lust . . .'

'And to defuse it,' the Captain interrupted, lifting his head for a moment before burrowing down even more firmly into Gloria's spongy vulva.

'OK. To arouse it and defuse it. Wow! But they say you can't do that without degrading the girls and women depicted. That kinda worries me.'

The Captain was too involved in his tonguework to offer a further comment on what she said. But he reflected that Gloria's real worry, as he had gathered from casual remarks and from his observation of her reactions at unguarded moments, was that the lewd materials of her research had started to take over control of her emotional life. She found them irresistibly, addictively stimulating, giving rise to a conflict with her residual New England puritanism.

His train of thought was broken by a mildly stinging sensation as one of the girls used her teeth to nibble gently at the skin of his scrotum. At the same time her partner had battened on his truncheon, closing her lips as far as she was able around the thickness of the stem so that the purple head swelled out beyond the corner of her mouth. She too employed the gentle pressure of her teeth to stimulate the tender skin.

As a distraction from these rather alarming developments, the Captain squashed Gina's mound between middle finger and thumb while wagging his index finger insistently from side to side in her hot sheath, then swirled his tongue around Gloria's unfurled petals before pulling out of both girls. In a flash he inverted the arrangement so that he was fingering Gloria and tonguing Gina. But he had hardly started to do so when he became aware of a new disposition of forces around his own genitals. His bollocks were now being caressed by a cool hand, while the mouth that had been attending to them was transferred to the projecting head of his cock. He felt the tip of a tongue attempting to insinuate itself into the slot and the pair of lips wrapped round the stem, applying a powerful squeezing to its turgid length. But the *coup de grâce* was delivered by a rude finger thrust into his anus. His whole body shuddered as he went into spasm and emptied his freight of hot sperm in mighty gushes that swept aside the intruding tongue and flooded into whichever throat was so eager to receive it.

When the torrent was at its height, he believed the recipient's identity had been revealed, for it was Gloria's thighs and stomach that tensed beneath him and her cunt muscles that contracted round his probing fingers. But the conviction that it was Gloria gave way at once to renewed uncertainty. Even before he had finished ejaculating, Gina's cunt seemed to melt. She opened her thighs, throwing one of her legs right across both of Gloria's and hooking her hands behind her knees to pull them back as far as they would go. The Captain's whole face seemed to be swallowed up in a quaking, seething morass of pulsing girlflesh as he plunged into the tunnel of oblivion.

Both Gloria and the Captain were impressed by the old-world neatness and order of Miss MacDonald's cottage as they climbed out of their hired car. The April morning was unusually warm and still, and the strip of well-kept lawn between the lane and the front of the building was lively with narcissi. Their hostess welcomed them in a pink housecoat tied loosely at the waist, and ushered them straight through into the brightness of a small secluded garden at the back, gay with birdsong and pink and white blossom. Two white chairs and a matching two-seater were arranged at a round table.

'We're not overlooked at all,' Miss MacDonald remarked. 'and it's so sheltered. On days like this Melanie and I like to enjoy the sun.'

She untied the waist of her housecoat, slipped it off and dropped it over the back of a chair. Gloria gasped with admiration at the shapely, athletic figure standing before her. She saw a pair of generous but firm breasts, a flat stomach and hard, shining thighs. Where these joined, the pubic area was adorned with an extensive and dense brown thatch.

'So where is Melanie?' the Captain enquired.

'Oh, she'll be seeing to things up in her room. She'll be down soon. Take your things off, both of you, and I'll fetch some coffee.'

As she turned to the cottage, her long back gleamed in the sunlight, its pale perfection offsetting the blackness of the hair falling down over her shoulders. The tight, ripe cushions of her buttocks bounced springily to her tread. This rear view reminded the Captain of the time at Cunlip when he had taken her from behind in the shower. Even before they arrived at the cottage he had felt warm; without hesitation he now stripped off his clothes. Gloria was a little shy and stopped short at her high-cut red panties but her companion and research director advised her, as a point of etiquette, to slip them off. The visitors seated themselves on the garden chairs, thoughtfully padded with comfortable cushions, to wait for their coffee.

The Captain's attention was caught by a flash of reflected light as a little dormer window was opened and the familiar but sorely missed face and bare torso of Melanie Winspur appeared at it. She smiled and waved to them, and this movement set one of her pert, conical breasts jiggling in the sun. 'Be down in half a mo,' she called.

Closely followed by Miss MacDonald with the tray of coffee things, Melanie stepped into the garden, as naked as the others. Gloria was introduced to her and Melanie made a point of kissing her on the cheek.

Instead of sitting down, the English girl insisted on taking the Captain's hand and leading him back to the cottage while her older friend devoted herself to pouring the coffee and attending to Gloria. Reunited after so many months, the couple entered the coolness of the little kitchen. Melanie threw her arms round the Captain's neck. 'I just couldn't wait for a kiss, you old rogue,' she laughed, and proceeded to suck one from his willing lips.

After some minutes of passionate osculation, he became aware of stirrings in his genitals. The tip of his penis was climbing up the girl's firm belly. He drew back his head and looked at her. 'My turn to kiss you now,' he said, dropping to his knees on the tiled floor.

He had never known pubic hair quite the colour of Melanie's gingery thatch. The smell too, he remembered, had an unmistakable tang to it — something like hints of heather and lavender blending with a very faint aroma of seaweed freshly uncovered by the tide. But now his flaring nostrils caught a suggestion of something stronger. He turned his head sideways and with his palms on her buttocks pulled the plump cuntpad against his cheek, relishing the feeling of the soft wool on his skin. There was that smell again, growing in pungency as he pressed against the mound. Now he knelt back on his heels and watched, fascinated, as the pink lips appeared to swell outwards. A mass of whitish jelly slid slowly out. A thick globule was attempting to detach itself. Half-retained by a viscous thread it dipped lazily down towards the floor. Before it could land, Melanie crossed her right leg resourcefully over her left one, receiving, all in one go, a neatly decorative trail down the inside of the forward thigh and calf as far as her ankle. Still more of the substance was emerging from the moist labia; with the girl standing in her present posture it all rolled on to the smooth, inviting skin of her inner thigh. The Captain cast a querying glance up at her.

'Derrick's just been with me,' she explained. 'He often looks in on Saturday mornings on his way to the pub. Wipe it for me, there's a dear.'

If the discharge had been the product of his own sexual apparatus, the Captain would not have scrupled to run his tongue up her leg from ankle to groin. But its association with his memories of Derrick's stubby form caused his stomach to churn as he contemplated such a procedure. Instead, he tore a tissue from the roll on the kitchen wall and stooped to take hold of her ankle.

Melanie snatched the tissue from him. 'Not that way,' she objected. 'Smear it in. They say it's good for the skin, don't they?'

Kneeling once more, he fitted the palm of his left hand to the smooth back of her thigh to hold it steady while he used the fingertips of his right hand to spread the sticky trail as widely as possible. Particular attention was paid to the silky surface of the thigh, where the stroking action gave way to a rhythmic kneading. When the skin had at last lost its slick slipperiness, he cupped his right hand beneath the oozing pussy and with the fingers of the other one scooped into his palm the larger masses of spunk congealing round the opening. Melanie quivered at his touch. He patted his hand flat on her belly, which he now massaged with a circular movement until his rival's cold secretion was spread in a fine, silvery film all over the area between bellybutton and pubis. In response to this rubbing of the lower abdomen, he saw her nipples stiffen up and rose to lick them. The head of his hard cock nudged into her sodden mound.

A call from the garden reminded him of his responsibilities as a guest. Miss MacDonald was missing his presence out there. 'Come on, you lovebirds,' she cried. 'Your coffee's getting cold.'

Out in the garden the MacDonald was sharing the white two-seater with Gloria. They seemed to be hitting it off, for Gloria's head was pillowed on the bosom of her hostess, one of whose hands rested casually on the American girl's left breast while she poised her coffee cup in the other. The Captain, still shame-lessly erect, lowered himself into a chair. Without a word, Melanie straddled his thighs, facing him. But rather than impale herself on his member, she held her labia wide open and slid her hips forward until she could fold the sticky petals in a lewd, clinging embrace around the upright column. Then she reached across to the table and handed him his coffee.

Gloria giggled as Miss MacDonald's hand spidered down her stomach. 'Oh my!' she gasped. 'Whaddyer doing to me? And look − what's Melanie doing to Dr Haggler?'

The two Englishwomen laughed in unison, somewhat to the Captain's embarrassment. He had to explain that Haggler was the name he had adopted for professional purposes out in the States. He would never have landed his present position as departmental custodian in the Banesville University Library without a proper moniker and an appropriate academic qualification.

'But how did you get the job?' Miss MacDonald enquired. 'You'd never done anything like that before, had you? You were just a sort of honorary odd-job man the few weeks you spent at Cunlip.'

The Captain noticed that her hand had now insinuated itself between the tops of Gloria's thighs. As if bashful, the girl turned her face inward to hide it between the MacDonald's tits. 'Didn't take much,' he said. 'All I needed was a set of cast-iron refer-ences and a list of obscure publications. After all, I know my stuff well enough to teach it, don't I, Gloria? The business of being shortlisted, interviewed and appointed was a formality

— my plummy Brit accent simply wowed them.'

Miss MacDonald refrained from mentioning the slight taint of — Streatham, was it? — that discoloured the purity of his vowels. The general effect was, after all, one of plumminess, even if these plums had less to commend them to the connoisseur than the one now being crushed between his belly and Melanie's. The MacDonald changed the subject. 'By the way,' she said, 'I've got something for you. Here.'

Not letting the operation interfere with her sensual fingering of Gloria's private parts, she put her cup down and drew a sheaf of typed papers out from under the corner of the tray. The Captain reached forward below Melanie's arm and took them. While the girl gently frotted herself against the length of his shaft, he adjusted his focus to scan the pages he held beyond her right shoulder. Here, he saw, was the apocryphal chapter of *Middlemarch* he had commissioned from the Upchester ladies.

Perhaps it was unchivalrous to divide his attention in this way. But the pleasure was not entirely selfish. It was almost as if the input from the document he read was transmitted through physical contact to the young lady astride his thighs. There was nothing occult in this, of course. Where a particular passage excited the Captain, his already stiff poker swelled into yet massier solidity and stretched further up her stomach. Melanie in turn reacted to this stimulus. The leaves of her sex were forced apart even wider as the stem to which they clung thickened and throbbed. As each stroke of lewdness in the document spurred its reader to a higher pitch of arousal, this excitement was communicated directly to the sweating girl who jockeyed him, racking her body with a series of minor orgasms which had their own effect on him.

The Captain was well pleased with what he read and complimented the joint authors. Melanie leaned back on his lap to look up at him, taking care to keep her quim pushed right up against the stem of his cock. 'We enjoyed doing it,' she said. 'We even thought we might have a crack one day at writing porn without bothering to make it a parody. Just straight filth.'

He shook his head. 'No money in it. Not for authors, anyway — they die hungry and blind. I've heard they have to rely on fivers sent in by admiring readers. Now, publishing the stuff, that's another matter. That's what I might do in my next life. But while we're still enjoying this one, I want you to do me some more,' he said, hugging Melanie's panting torso in against his own so that his coarse hairs could scour her smoothness. 'I thought you could do the Crawfords seducing Fanny Price in *Mansfield Park*.'

Melanie, it seemed, had not yet sampled the civilised delights of Jane Austen's world, so the Captain and Miss MacDonald had to offer an explanation, disjointed by the parallel activity of pleasuring their partners. Fanny Price, they agreed, was a conscientious and virtuous girl, a paragon of retiring bashfulness who enjoyed Miss Austen's full support but tended to strike modern readers as an insufferable prig. Author and reader were at least able to concur in the suitability of her eventual marriage to the dull and pompous clergyman, her cousin Edmund. But before this happy outcome could be achieved, both Fanny and Edmund had to resist and survive the blandishments of a much livelier and more attractive couple, the siblings Henry and Mary Crawford. The Crawfords owed their specious polish to the corruption of London life which Fanny had been spared. Henry, lusting for Fanny's maidenhead but almost converted by her virtue, proposed marriage to her while his sister courted Edmund. But the eruption of scandal in the wicked city put paid to these plans, allowing the happy but unexciting outcome already mentioned. The Captain's idea, he explained, was that the Crawfords' campaign of seduction should succeed.

By this time his engorged penis was so sensitised and his gathering charge of sperm so heavy and under so much pressure that release was imperative. Yet he was reluctant to let his lust spill wastefully between Melanie's belly and his own. He observed that Gloria, whose attention had been centred on the hot place between her legs during the exposition of *Mansfield Park*, was now waving those legs in the air as her partner's fingers brought her to a jolting climax. Melanie was quivering in his arms, and Miss MacDonald seemed to be the only player in this harmonious quartet who had not yet approached a crescendo.

Placing his hands in Melanie's moist armpits he hoisted her to her feet, at the same time rising himself. He moved his chair a couple of feet and set it down right in front of the two women so that its front edge touched that of the two-seater between them. Then he resumed his place upon it and stretched his legs, inserting his feet between the MacDonald's right flank and Gloria's left one. Melanie lifted a leg to straddle him again as he reclined back stiffly to let his prick stand free, but he made her turn round so that she faced the others as she slowly and voluptuously sheathed its length in her dripping cunt.

The other couple took their cue from this move. They reached forward and drew Melanie towards them. Gloria's lips opened wide and closed over the girl's right breast, sucking the whole cone-shaped prize right into her mouth and forcing the nipple back into the surrounding softness with the tip of her tongue. In reciprocation, Melanie used her left hand to massage Gloria's right tit and her left one to masturbate the pussy that had so recently exploded to the older woman's touch.

Miss MacDonald now knelt on the grass to the Captain's right. She wedged her right hand down between his thighs and wriggled her fingers until she somehow contrived to put her thumb-pad on Melanie's clitoris, her index finger up her cunt alongside the Captain's thick stem and the other three fingers under his testicles to tickle and scratch. The Captain let a lazy right arm hang down behind her kneeling form. He fondled the groove of her bottom, working right down between the buttocks. After teasing the tight rear entrance, he slid the finger she thought he was about to stick into it down and forward; she moved her knees apart to facilitate his probing. Suddenly his broad thumb burst up into her vagina and two fingers were scrabbling furiously at the hardening tip of sensitivity at the upper end of her sexual cleft.

All four friends were simultaneously giving and taking and well on the way to collapse, but even now half-jocular attempts were made to preserve the conventions of polite discourse. It was Melanie's clear voice that interrupted the ragged panting. 'Got another idea,' she announced, 'What about *Jane Eyre*?'

'That's great,' commented Gloria, letting the other girl's flushed breast with its alarmingly distended teat flop out of her mouth as she spoke. 'Everyone knows about mousy little governess Jane and how she just idolises that fierce, sulking

Mr Rochester with his mad wife shut up in the attic.'

'Every schoolgirl's wet dream,' laughed Melanie, playing with her own stiff nipple. 'When I first knew the Captain here I thought he was like Rochester.'

Gloria continued. 'Jane calls him her master all the time. Anyone can see she wants to make out with him. But I guess she just can't let go.'

'That's it,' agreed Melanie. 'But in our version he'll make her. He'll rape her and *really* master her.'

The two young women, far gone in erotic excitement, concluded their conversation and clamped their mouths together in a passionate kiss. The multiple engagement was becoming serious. Each participant tried hard to take note of the state reached by the others, straining forward or holding back in a supreme attempt to hit the high spot in one great heave. At the very core of their concerted efforts towered the Captain's great column of flesh, boring up into the heart of Melanie's being in blissful reunion. It was the essence of this enterprise that his precious chalice should not be allowed to overflow until the three females were already clenching their cunts in orgasm.

It was Miss MacDonald who was in overall control. Her cupping fingers sensed the tightening of the Captain's balls and a preliminary convulsing in the shaft of his penis. 'Now, girls!' she cried. All three abandoned themselves to the overwhelming tide that swept over them from the complexity of collaborating stimuli. The MacDonald's left hand was free; she brought it down in a resounding whack on the Captain's behind. Her finger was nearly forced out of Melanie's contracting cunt as the prick plugging it swelled enormously and hurled its hot burden into the tight confinement. Finding no space there to receive it, the spunk was forced in a bubbling torrent out of the girl's cuntlips, to spill all over Miss MacDonald's hand and soak the Captain's crushed bush. His chair tipped backwards. All four, interlocked in orgasm, rolled on to the grass, gasping and groaning in prolonged ecstasy. A tabby cat dropped from the branches of a cherry tree and clawed its way over their nudity to leap on the table and attack the milk jug.

FIVE

WHAT PRICE FANNY?

After their successful collaboration on the *Middlemarch* chapter, the fabrication of a rejected draft of an episode from Jane Austen's *Mansfield Park* required no more than a week of the Upchester ladies' attention. The attention they devoted to the project was not undivided. Miss MacDonald, to be sure, was on holiday from the college. But she and Melanie found that the more closely they worked together the more they were tempted to neglect the task in hand and to abandon themselves to the delights of their growing intimacy. Soon, however, they devised a way of combining business with pleasure. Sitting side by side at the garden table when the days were warm enough and at other times in the small kitchen, one of them would send the tip of the ballpoint pen zipping across the paper while the other used all her imaginative talents to arouse the writer and inspire her to greater efforts. Whenever this input of inspiration overloaded the productive capacity of its recipient the writing was put aside for a few minutes and the demands of Eros attended to. Then the work was resumed, but with the frigger now taking over the writing and the writer the frigging.

At Miss MacDonald's suggestion they had agreed to adapt that part of the novel in which the young people were flouting propriety by engaging in amateur theatricals. This was without the knowledge or permission of Edmund's father, Sir Thomas Bertram, who was absent on a perilous voyage to his slave plantations. The play which the less responsible members of the party had chosen, *Lovers' Vows*, was considered quite unsuitable by the strait-laced Edmund and Fanny on account of its theme of illegitimacy, but Edmund accepted the part of the parson Anhalt when he realised that doing so would allow him to flirt on stage with the coquettish Mary Crawford. Fanny Price, lacking both the inclination and the ability to act, withdrew into herself and her own room to nurse her affronted sense of decorum and her scarcely acknowledged jealousy of Mary.

Such was Jane Austen's contribution to this production. Once they had agreed on a general idea for developing the story in a way that would easily account for its abandonment in favour of the paler version now enshrined in the canon of English literature, Melanie and Miss MacDonald found that the episode almost wrote itself. A couple of days were spent revising the finished draft, which was then dispatched to the Captain at the Kensington Moorlands Hotel.

> Everything was now in a regular train; theatre, actors, actresses, and dresses, were all getting forward: but Fanny did not share in the busy eagerness of the others. She thought of the morrow a great deal — for if the third act were rehearsed, Edmund and Miss Crawford would then be acting together for the first time — this act would bring a scene between them which interested her most particularly, and which she was longing and dreading to see how they would perform. The whole subject of it was love — a marriage of love was to be described by the gentleman, and very little short of a declaration of love be made by the lady. She had read, and read the scene again, with many painful, many wondering emotions, and looked forward to their representation of it as a circumstance almost too interesting. She did not *believe* they had rehearsed it yet, even in private.
>
> The morrow came, but on Edmund's insistence the rehearsal of the scene Fanny dreaded was deferred until the following day; he desired more time to study the part, and begged Miss Crawford to indulge him. That evening Fanny made her escape to her beloved East room, where she worked and meditated, undisturbed, for a quarter of an hour, when a gentle tap at the door was followed by the entrance of Mr. Crawford.

"Am I right? — Yes; this is the East room. My dear Miss Price, I beg your pardon, but I have made my way to you on purpose to assure you of my continuing esteem for you as a young person of taste and principle. This scheme of pleasure — the play — has given rise; — yes, we all see it, we all *feel* it; — to sentiments of disapprobation in your charming bosom. I honour those sentiments, Miss Price. They do credit, if I may say so, to the snowy charms they animate, suffusing them with a roseate hue to rival the blushes of Hebe."

Fanny was overcome with sensations of involuntary gratification at these compliments, but these sensations were commingled with embarrassment and indignation. That Mr. Crawford — that any man — should so far forget the obligations of civility as to seek out her company in the absence of female companions, and that he should do so at a time when the life of her uncle, to whom alone she might have properly applied for advice, was at hazard upon the high seas, — this was a consideration that filled her with alarm. Her bosom, from which Mr. Crawford had not withdrawn his gaze, quickened and heaved as the blushes came and went.

"Pray, Sir, what is your errand?" she demanded. "It cannot be merely to flatter and bring down confusion on a young girl who knows little of the world."

"As to that, my dear, it is the world's loss that you have lived so long in retirement. But no; you are right. It was no part of my purpose to distress you; and I declare myself a stranger to the arts of flattery. What brings me here, Miss Price — the pressing need that induced me to obtrude myself thus upon your maiden solitude — what brings me here is my wish to acquaint you with facts which will offer you no comfort."

"Then you are doubly my tormentor, Sir."

"Surely I was not mistaken? At our first meeting I determined you to be one of those rare creatures who take their pleasure not in comfort but in truth: a young lady who had rather suffer the knowledge of sin and shame in those she loved than dote on in ignorance of their trans-

87

gression. Oh, say I was not misled by these innocent looks.''

This speech had something in its urgency that persuaded Fanny to listen. Growing more animated, Mr. Crawford informed her that he had come to her direct from Sir Thomas's library, whence he had caught sight of his sister and Edmund privately rehearsing their scene of passion in the adjoining room. ''And so lifelike was their performance, that he had felt constrained to withdraw and deliver this intelligence to Miss Price without delay. There was no time to be lost, if she wished with her own eyes to behold what at that very moment was in hand.''

Thinking only of her dear Edmund's honour — how dear to her, the mortifying sting inflicted upon her sensibilities by Mr. Crawford's communication had shewn — Fanny accompanied her visitor as he raised his candle and led the way through long corridors to the billiard room. She followed him up the narrow stair that admitted them to the gallery running round the walls halfway between floor and ceiling. Mr. Crawford snuffed the taper as they stepped forward into the shadows cast upwards by a blaze of light from the improvised stage below. Fanny could not believe that Sir Thomas would have sanctioned such flagrant extravagance even if he had given his blessing to the play itself — no honest proceedings, she told herself, had aught to fear from the clear light of day.

She stood in silence beside the dimly perceived, upright form of Mr. Crawford, and they peered down at the scene being enacted. As Fanny recognised from her recollected perusal of the book, Baron Wildenhaim had prevailed upon the parson Anhalt, played now by her cousin Edmund, to persuade his daughter Amelia, in the person of Mary Crawford, that she should marry the insolent fool Count Cassel. Anhalt's subordinate station left him no choice but to comply, although he and Amelia had long harboured tender feelings of mutual regard which they had not dared acknowledge. This was the scene which had occasioned Fanny so much anguish; and even as she watched, the players, who seemed to her fevered vision

88

to be embodying their parts with more fervour and conviction than a mere rehearsal could require, had arrived at the crisis of their conversation; Amelia's unwomanly forwardness had beaten their shared secret from its cover.

"Why do you force from me, what it is villainous to own?" cried Edmund, falling to his knees and pressing Miss Crawford's hand to his lips. "I love you more than life — Oh, Amelia! had we lived in those golden times, which the poets picture, no one but you — But as the world is changed, your birth and fortune make our union impossible."

To Fanny's astonishment and horror, the passionate actress now snatched her hand from her reverend suitor's lips and tore open the front of her gown with its round, low-cut neck adorned with a double fall of lace. From the gallery it was plain to make out that Miss Crawford wore no chemise, no shift and no stay, not even that small, triangular "divorce corset" of padded iron she had shewn the blushing Fanny, with which she kept her breasts pushed apart to produce the Grecian shape so admired by men of taste.

Fanny was now surprised by the composure with which Miss Crawford continued to deliver the lines of the chaste Amelia; the lines themselves were impassioned, but the delivery controlled. "It is my father's will that I should marry. It is my father's wish to see me happy — If then you love me as you say, I will marry; and will be happy — but only with you." As she declaimed these words of defiant love, Miss Crawford dropped to her knees so that she was of a height with the kneeling Edmund. They kissed; his hands sought the alabaster globes of her bosom.

As the embrace grew warmer and more agitated, Fanny became aware that Mr. Crawford, too, was on his knees; his cheek rested against her hip, his shoulder pressed the back of her upper thigh, and — still worse! — his arm was around her waist. Despite the admonitions of conscience, despite the precept and example of her dear Edmund before his head had been turned by the attractions of their guests, despite herself, — her heart thrilled to the amorous discourse of the stage lovers. Miss Crawford withdrew her lips from Edmund's and continued:

"I will tell my father this. — At first he will start; then grow angry; then be in a passion. In his passion he will call me 'undutiful:' but he will soon recollect himself." Even as she spoke these words, she rose and led Edmund to a sopha, upon which she sat while he stood before her. "He will soon recollect himself," she proceeded, "and resume his usual smiles." Her fingers appeared to be fumbling at the buttons of Edmund's breeches. "He will resume his usual smiles, saying, 'Well, well, if he love you, and you love him, in the name of Heaven, let it be.' — Then I shall hug him round the neck —." As the flap of the nether garment fell open, Fanny was horrified to see what she at first took to be the ruddy-crested head and white neck of a common farmyard cock spring out into the brilliant light of the stage candles; her horror was augmented when Miss Crawford seized and shook this plump prodigy between her fingers; — it was no "tame villatic fowl" that she now pillowed between the naked hemispheres of her breasts, but the strangely enlarged manhood of Edmund himself, a rigid limb the like of which his cousin had never before beheld. Fanny now felt Mr. Crawford's hand slide down from her waist to the front of her thigh, where it lingered, pressing the tender flesh through her skirts; then down again to her knee, and right down to her ankle.

Miss Crawford, meanwhile, seemed to be struggling to recall her part. After some false starts and protestations she resumed. "I shall hug him round the neck; kiss his hands, run away from him, and fly to you," she assured Edmund, who stood before her, perfectly enraptured by the attentions he was receiving in her bosom. "It will soon be known that I am your bride, the whole village will come to wish me joy, and Heaven's blessing will follow."

Fanny quivered as Mr. Crawford's hand raised the hem and stole up under her skirts. It slipped up the outside of her leg, hurrying over the silk of her stocking until it found the yielding smoothness of her flesh above her garter, then proceeding higher, to rest for an instant upon the warm hardness of her hip before wandering downwards and passing round to work its passage from behind between her reluctant thighs just above the tops of her hose. At this instant Edmund's cry arose from the stage below as his blessing (if not the blessing of Heaven) burst from his throbbing affair, and was sprayed in the form of a thick, creamy effusion over Miss Crawford's delighted countenance and throat, flowing slowly down to bathe the flushed breasts and their ruby teats. Astonished at the novelty of the performance, Fanny wonder if this splattered fluid were the "milk of human kindness" which Lady Macbeth had accused her husband of harbouring to excess; — and what, (for the emotions provoked by Mr. Crawford's usage of her limbs had thrown her mind into confusion,) were the strange verses in which the regicidal queen spoke of plucking her nipples from his gums? — As if to enlighten her on this head, and to act out the mysteries alluded to so darkly by Shakspere and never explained to the girls in their nursery readings of his sublime productions, Miss Crawford took Edmund's now wilting and dripping staff in her hand and conveyed it to her open mouth.

Try as she would, Fanny was quite unable to keep her trembling thighs pressed together. As they parted, she could not but be aware of Mr. Crawford's hand rising between them until his palm was lodged firmly against the moist flesh of her most private place; — the tips of his four fingers lazily teazed the curls with which Nature had been pleased to conceal her parts of shame; at the same time, his thumb, bold beyond all measure, rudely sought to violate and breach the *sanctum* enshrined between her posteriors. No word, hardly an indignant sigh, passsed her lips. She could not believe that Henry Crawford, a man whose behaviour, she could not deny, had sometimes distressed her by transgressing the bounds of propriety, but who had never until to-day descended to carnal grossness, was now abusing his position as a guest at Mansfield Park. Assuredly she did not chuse to be handled in this way without protest; but something in the way the length of his first finger was rubbing between the soft and pulpy lips she had never herself looked upon, and tickling a small excrescence which, though she had never *seen* it, she had often *felt*, rendered her speechless and transformed her words of reprimand to little gasps and sighs of joy.

Upon the lighted stage below, Miss Crawford, too, was uttering such sighs and gasps. To do so, she had perforce removed her lover's member from her mouth. Fanny observed with interest that the red-tipped rod was quite restored to the vigorous condition it had displayed before the recent spillage. Miss Crawford now seemed to have forgot the *rôle* she had been playing as Amelia, and was bent quite simply on playing the whore to Edmund's parson, the seed-bed to his rake, the furrow to his plough, the mark to his musket, the barrel to his bung. She twisted round on the sopha so that she knelt on the seat with her legs splayed apart and her head and elbows supported by the back-rest. Poor Fanny realised with a pang that her beloved cousin Edmund, that cynosure of virtue, was by no means at a loss when faced with this new turn; — but whether his amatorial proficiency had been learned at some Covent-garden school of Cupid or arose direct from the instinctual promptings of Nature, she could not determine. Without waiting for further encouragement from his mistress, he threw her skirts and petticoats up over her head, and presented his magnificent, gleaming weapon to her rear. Brandishing it triumphantly, he clove the ripe, dark mossed fruit that bulged between her thighs. He grasped her by the haunches and lunged deep into Mary Crawford's body; his thrusts were reciprocated, and the shameless girl let out a cry of gratitude for the dear wound he had thus inflicted.

So absorbed was Fanny in the dramatic and emotional scene enacted below her, that she was scarcely aware of the tricks being played on her by wild young Mr. Crawford. A warm and comfortable glow suffused her own centre of attraction; — but leaning forward over the rail of the gallery, she was so far lost to the world, so far gone in her involvement with the action on stage, that it quite escaped her notice that her clothing was being drawn with slow and deliberate care up over her legs and thighs to reduce her to the same state of indecent exposure as Miss Crawford. Moreover, as Henry's hard bluntness began to batter her bottom-cheeks in his eagerness to force the passage, all her attention was taken by the turn of events down there in the candle-light. Edmund was ramming furiously into Miss Crawford's quivering loins — but now, with a great groan, he drew back. Inch by inch the mighty instrument emerged into the flickering light, until Mary's open flesh, no longer stuffed to bursting by it, presented to the gaze of Fanny's curiosity a vista of shady close-hedges embracing a rosy, dew-drenched bower, from the midst of which a dark cavern offered forth its liquid tribute. Yet this precious flood was the merest trickle when measured against the torrent of pearly foam which gushed spouting from the tip of Edmund's stiff stake to inundate Miss Crawford's back, thighs, and posteriors, not sparing the delicious grotto whence it had been so peremptorily snatched.

Fanny, pinned fast against the railing by her suitor's body and increasingly agitated by the friction caused by a wand of flesh, slender but rigid, working itself against the moist flaps between her thighs, blushed with horror and admiration at her cousin's performance. Her blushes took on a still livelier hue when it was borne home to her that she and Henry Crawford were not the only spectators of the scene; — from the darkness below rose sounds of applause, vulgar whistles and loud huzzahs of appro-bation. She turned her eyes from the dazzle of the stage and peered into the shadows. The pallor of their naked skin just visible, two couples were writhing, with limbs entangled, upon the great billiard table. Fanny could scarce bring herself to gaze upon the shameful spectacle, but her eyes fixed on it and were held as if by the force of animal magnetism. Mr. Yates was coupling with Maria

Bertram, while her sister Julia was wantonly anticipating the delights of matrimony with Mr. Rushworth. Crouched above them like some malevolent satyr, Tom Bertram threated every unoccupied opening in their bodies with a prodigious horn springing from the dark forest at the base of his belly. He moved, marauding, from one to the other until every one had received his attentions in rapid succession; — and while the horn was ravishing one lodgement, his tongue lashed into another and his lascivious hands were far from idle.

For the first time since they had stepped on to the gallery, Mr. Crawford spoke to Fanny. "Are not you pleased with the play, Miss Price? — Pray, how do you like our London ways now?"

Fanny was speechless. — Indeed, she had little breath left in her body for rational discourse, even had she desired to give utterance to the confused sentiments of excitement and disgust now coursing through her veins as the swollen head of her questioner's member probed the outer defences of her maiden shrine. The assault was painful, and nerved her to protest. "Desist, Sir, I charge you!" she cried. "What can it be that you want from me?"

With a violent lunge the intruder tore up into the core of her being. "My dear young lady," he gasped, "all I desire is *Fanny*."

SIX

THE WIDOW'S FRIEND

Torrential rain blurred the great stone-mullioned window of the drawing room; as May approached, the weather seemed to be deteriorating daily. There would have been nothing for Mary Muttock to see out there in the grounds that morning even if the leaded panes had been dry and clean, nothing but unpruned laurel bushes and funereal yew. But dark as the exterior prospect was, at least it outshone the cavernous gloom behind her. She sat down in one of the high-backed chairs, drew the eiderdown more tightly round her, sipped her gin and gazed out at the streaming blankness. In her imagination she swept aside the watery veils cascading down the window and populated the dull shrubbery with the sylphlike forms of the girls who had been her charges less than a year ago. Gauzy robes did little to conceal their lissom limbs and budding charms. Local youths with the legs, tails and horns of goats pursued them in and out of the bushes, ripped their garments to ribbons and buggered the squealing victims lustily. She awoke with a start.

A susceptible person might have attributed the sighs, groans, shudders and clanks with which the Victorian—Jacobean apartment resounded to the presence of some sinister visitant from beyond. To Miss Muttock the sounds were just now the only reassuring thing in this great house, for they indicated that, at the bidding of some grimy menial down in the cellars, the antiquated, fierce and probably dangerous coal-fired heating system was beginning to pump boiling water through the pipes and huge finned radiators. Soon the room would be so hot that she would be obliged to open the window and let in the rain, but as yet she still had to hug herself under the eiderdown. Oh yes, as she felt around between her legs she found (didn't she?) that — that *thing* once more. The Captain's manly stem, now grown unbelievably long, projected forward and upward through her thighs. Each time she folded her hand round the swelling head the length increased and the slippery head pushed out beyond her grasp, stretching up her stomach, burrowing between her breasts and nudging its way into her mouth and down her throat. She choked, opened her eyes and reapplied the glass to her lips.

In a few months' time, no doubt, Miss Muttock would have herself established in some comfort here in Cunlip Hall, the decaying mansion, forty-six miles north of Upchester and about twice that distance from London, which had been bequeathed to her so recently. If its acquisition after her disgrace and dismissal as principal of Cunlip College could be described as providential, this was true only in the sense that it had been brought about by her own foresight. An array of glum portraits glaring down on her from behind deterred her from lingering at length on what she knew of the history of the Cunlip family, which was little enough. Nevertheless, she recalled the relevant details briefly. They were never far from her mind.

Sir Julius Cunlip, venerable founder of the asylum which had later become the notorious Cunlip College, was the last bearer of the family name. After him the Cunlip Hall estate had passed in its decline to a series of obscure relatives until finally, the windows shuttered with corrugated iron, its true ownership was a mystery to all save a dusty Upchester solicitor with whom Mary Muttock had brought herself to sleep. And during that non-event, of course, the mystery was revealed to Mary Muttock herself.

Her discovery confirmed the rumour that her ancient bursar at the college, old Grote, who decades earlier had reputedly fulfilled some function in the original asylum (warder? inmate?), was indeed an illegitimate descendent of Sir Julius. What nobody realised was that Grote had inherited the entire Cunlip estate, though whether that legacy would turn out to be an asset or a liability still remained to be seen. Grote had lately fallen into a condition of advanced decrepitude. Miss Muttock's simulated concern and affection for this repulsive person had rapidly achieved two results: Grote had made a will in her favour and then died, exhausted. The timing could hardly have been more convenient.

If only the sun could shine, the clouds vanish and bare-bottomed girls cavort freely through the grounds pursued by their amorous, capriform swains! If only she herself could frolic among them enjoying the slow erosion or abrupt overturning of their modesty! And she herself could offer up the supreme sacrifice, taking the place of whichever coy maiden had been seized by the lad with the heftiest, meatiest goat-ram.

Perhaps it was association of ideas that reminded her: the Captain and his American assistant were to pay her a visit this morning. Mary Muttock hurried upstairs to the high-ceilinged bathroom, a powerhouse of gurgling pipework and once-white tiling now discoloured and crazed. Leaning over the bath, which stood high on lion-clawed legs, she applied both hands first to one brass tap and then to the other. A livid flame exploded up inside the rusting geyser and hot water gushed unevenly over the green stains on the porcelain.

While waiting for the bath to fill she laid aside the eiderdown still wrapped round her and took from a shelf a small packet labelled

THE WIDOW'S FRIEND
Empire Made

containing a pair of silver balls connected by a short length of chain. Mary Muttock put one foot on the edge of the bath and parted her long labia. The balls slipped into her easily.

Now she stood and examined her tall, goose-pimpled body in the mirror before the steam had time to mist away any blemishes. In fact she had none. Her thirty-odd years had been remarkably kind to her in that way. Her prominent breasts showed no signs of sagging, not even when she began the dancelike undulations that activated the Widow's Friend and provoked the onset of delightful sensations in her cunt. On the contrary, the tits maintained the kind of uptilted well-separated disposition one might expect if, instead of standing, she had

97

been lying on her back with her hips raised above the level of her head. Maybe she owed their firmness to the amount of time she had actually spent in such a position for the amusement of her lovers, especially the succession of paying beaux in her pre-Cunlip days out on the Arizona Raunch Ranch. Yes, her boobs had made her many friends and would continue to do so. Neither could the unmarked flatness of her stomach be faulted, with its neatly dimpling navel and the triangle of dark pubic hair. The cellulite-free tightness of her buttocks was supported by narrow hips – a dancer's hips, she told herself as her body writhed and rippled against the surrogate partner whose entire substance had been swallowed up inside her belly. Her legs, of course, had always been admired and her features were as handsome as ever. Even the mouse-coloured hair that tumbled down as she unfasted the tight bun in which it was usually confined was so lustrous and wavy that it was accounted one of her major attractions.

This rhapsody on the liquor-defying preservation of her charms continued as she lay soaking in the bath. The images of her own body blended into a reverie of gleaming, youthful flesh wallowing in a tropical watering hole and submitting to the ravages of rampant, pachydermatous wildlife.

When Miss Muttock opened her eyes, two figures loomed above her. Through the mist she recognised her old associate the Captain, his experienced body encased in a tight suit of washed denim. He stooped to kiss her and introduced Gloria Sweetbutts, explaining that finding the front door open they had simply passed from room to deserted room until they came to this place of ablution.

Gloria was casually dressed in damson-coloured cord trousers and a loose sweater of cream angora with a pink chiffon scarf at her throat. Mary Muttock took to her immediately. 'It's so good to see both of you,' she purred. 'But you must be hot in here. If you're going to be hot, why not make the best of it? Come here, Captain.'

He bent over the bath and she whispered something in his ear. At this cue he unzipped his tight pants and peeled them off. The long, dangling prick began to stir lazily as he fumbled at Gloria's waistband. The girl's scandalised protests were overcome when he took her in his arms and kissed her before resuming the operation of tugging off her white trainers and laying bare her lower parts. The bathwater rippled to the pounding of Mary Muttock's heart as first Gloria's pretty bottom was revealed and then, as the Captain spun her round, the fluffy bush of brown hair.

The Captain, his prick now projecting horizontally and angry-headed, positioned a handy wooden towel-horse beside the bathtub. He made his assistant bend over this piece of equipment with her legs apart (cheerleader's legs, Miss Muttock told herself with enthusiasm), grasping a rail just above the floor. The Muttock had a clear view not just of her behind and the neatly bisected sexpouch fringed with chestnut curls, but also of her inverted face, dark with the rush of blood. Even as she watched, the hem of the loose sweater fell down to Gloria's armpits. Although the nipples remained covered, the white underbellies of her breasts were exposed.

Clutching the girl's hips, the Captain flexed his knees to present an inflamed knob ready to hammer at the proffered entrance. He was already nudging the plump lips.

But Mary Muttock ordered him to stand aside. 'She looks so tight and dry,' she observed. 'Come here, Captain.'

Rather annoyed at the interruption, the Captain stepped to the side of the bath. Miss Muttock raised herself in the water and took the tip of his erect member between her lips. Her tongue swirled around it and her visitors could hear the saliva churning in her mouth. Then she swallowed the whole length for a moment before releasing it glib with spittle.

Once more the Captain laid his hands on Gloria's bare hips. The appearance of tightness and dryness turned out to be deceptive, for the girl's vulva split literally at the moment the cockhead touched it and he was able to move in, without force, to take possession.

Miss Muttock's professional experience in Arizona alerted her to the anomaly. She addressed the bare-bottomed Gloria. 'When did this gentleman last do sex with you, my dear?'

'Oh, I don't know. This morning, I guess. Yeah, that's it — on the way here, at a gas station on the freeway.'

'So recently? One would never have known,' remarked the

older woman, 'not from the way you stood there so innocently at first. But look, Captain — it's perfectly obvious now.'

The unsheathing of the thick cock had, so to speak, turned the girl's pussy inside out. The inner surfaces shone wet and pink. As the senior couple watched, the morning's earlier deposit began to flow heavily, clinging to the inside of Gloria's left thigh, sliding down it and filling the bathroom with the unmistakable and irresistible rank odour of sex.

Mary Muttock was fired to action. 'Come here, miss,' she cried, rising to her feet and standing at the end with the taps. 'Step into the bath.'

The girl pulled off her white socks and stood in the warm water, the hem of her cream sweater reaching to just above the triangle of pubic hair. She was made to turn and place her hands on the end of the bath with her feet as far apart as the tub allowed. Briefly Miss Muttock succumbed to the temptation of trailing her fingertips up the backs of those cheerleader thighs. 'Glorious!' (or possibly 'Gloria's!') she was heard to exclaim.

Resting his stiff rod in the palm of his hand, the Captain watched with interest as she then turned and lifted from its cradle the heavy shower head which resembled an antique brass and ivory telephone receiver. She turned on the taps and the geyser whooshed into action. Once the temperature of the water was adjusted to her liking she declared, in tones acquired during her pedagogical career, that she meant to correct the sorry state of affairs she had discovered. 'This girl is presenting woman's best gift to man in a condition unfit to be used,' she said. 'Just let me sluice away her shame and she will be yours to enjoy again, Captain.'

Considerable pressure threw the broad stream of hot droplets up between Gloria's thighs and all over her soft bottom. The water splashed into the cavity now gaping between her labia, drenched her bush and shot up her stomach to spill over the angora sweater. But whichever way Miss Muttock aimed the shower, the jets of hot water failed to shift the coating of spunk that clung to the inside of the girl's left thigh. She turned off the water and scraped away the surplus with the edge of her hand, which she swiftly sucked clean. Then she knelt behind Gloria and licked up the thigh to remove any remaining traces,

100

finally curling the tip of her tongue and raking it upwards between the slick lips of her fanny.

At a nod from Mary Muttock, the Captain stepped into the bathtub between the two women. Gloria had straightened up to remove the sodden sweater; now she leaned forward once again and rested her cheek on the end of the bath. The Muttock lowered herself down on her back with her feet towards the taps so that she could gaze up at the coupling from underneath as the straining shaft slid into its juicing receptacle. Her hands wandered over Gloria's dangling breasts, her belly and her soaking cunt-thatch. With one hand she tickled the girl's clitoris and with the other the swinging testicles. And now a hard nipple reached down into her mouth as the couple groaned and ground together above her.

Having sucked the teat into a tough, leathery toggle, Miss Muttock reached to grasp Gloria's hips and hauled her mouth up to the region of pistoning conjuncture. The musky odour was overpowering. She used her tongue as a broad brush to sweep backwards and forwards over the whole length of the region, starting with the Captain's taut perineum, dragging over his scrotum, savouring the foaming root of his prick as it slipped in and out, then moving from the thick stalk to lay wide open Gloria's inflamed cuntlips and finally flattening her hard pleasure pip before swooping forward again in the other direction.

Gloria was quite unable to withstand the combined titillation of this tonguework and her boss's fucking for more than a few strokes. Her knees gave way as the waves of delight overtook her, and Miss Muttock's weight hanging from her hips brought both her and the Captain splashing down on their backs and sloshing displaced water over the bathroom floor. Luckily the bathtub was sufficiently capacious to contain all three of them, but the Captain's denim jacket was even more thoroughly soaked than Gloria's sweater had been. He took it off, revealing the mat of dark hair which was all he wore beneath it.

Only Gloria had come; the Captain was still in a state of virile excitement and keen to unload his freight in any handy harbour. Mary Muttock rolled over on her right side and raised her left leg so that the calf rested on the edge of the bath. The Captain, who now lay facing her, floated both his thighs over her right one and lost no time in lodging the head of his cock among the tender leaves and hairs that waved in the water like the fronds of some luscious sea anemone.

Feeling the snout of his killer whale delve maddeningly into the fleshy folds, Mary Muttock turned her head to speak to Gloria, who lay half-floating and still half-stunned beside the rutting pair. 'Know what you remind me of, dear? One of those fresh-faced clean-limbed cheerleader types. Had a couple of them working with me when I was out in Arizona — hard at it all night and still looked wholesome as apple pie come morning. Now why don't you just give us some encouragement from the sidelines while the Captain here plays ball with me?'

Gloria complied with dreamy abandon, reaching across and between the lovers to stimulate all the erogenous zones she could locate, tweaking and plundering protuberances and concavities indiscriminately. Miss Muttock had forgotten all about the Widow's Friend, and thus a new slant was given to the ball game. Full penetration was prevented by the device, so the sensitive cockhead was confined to the tight sleeve of her lower cunt. With each manly thrust she could feel it jam the silver spheres even higher and harder up against her womb.

The orgasm soon achieved by the couple caused them to leap up with so much violence in the buoyant bathwater that they crashed down on Gloria and all but drowned her. Everyone felt more than satisfied with these watery transactions, so they climbed out of the bath and dried each other.

By this time the heating system had been stoked up to such a pitch that the Captain and Gloria were happy to go downstairs topless while their wet clothes were hung up to dry. Gloria tied her transparent pink chiffon scarf loosely at her throat so that the ends flopped down over her breasts without concealing them. Not wanting to appear overdressed by comparison, Miss Muttock put on a pair of elegant black and gold striped silk pyjamas. She left the jacket unbuttoned.

While the friends sat in the cavernous kitchen enjoying a bottle of wine and the refreshments prepared by an unseen servant inherited from old Grote, the Captain explained to Miss Muttock, as he had previously done to Gina, how he had come

102

by his Californian job and how he saw the nature of the mission that had brought him back on this visit to England. Mary Muttock expressed surprise that it had been so easy to pull the wool over the eyes of a scholarly community, but he explained the insights that had given him the confidence needed to carry off such a trick. After all, what prim academic was going to check out his supposed contributions to knowledge in little-known or nonexistent journals? And even if they had done so, at least half the titles on his list of publications were genuine — it was just that those articles and monographs had been written by other people. In this area of research, he had reminded the interviewing panel, the matter of reputation could be a bit dodgy, career-wise. Pseudonyms were, occasionally, essential if one were not to bugger up one's chances of preferment, especially in the fundamentalist colleges of the Deep South. But there in Tampoon County, he had declared with a wink and gesture that brought a blush to their faces, the Banesville folks were more broad-minded. Wasn't it out of deference to Political Correctness rather than to prudishness that Dean Frolander in the chair was carrying with him a copy of *The Christian Science Monitor* and not *Playboy*? Well, that blew his chances with old Frolander, but the others just loved it and gave him the job. After all, he knew enough about dirty books and pictures to talk the pants off these ivory-towered jerks.

Miss Muttock, very conscious now of the silver balls nuzzled inside her, listened intently to his plans for supplementing the Banesville collections with material of high quality but low authenticity and pointed out that she could provide an impressive provenance for these 'discoveries'. With Cunlip Hall she had acquired a Victorian gentleman's library in which experts might suppose many valuable curiosities to be buried — there might even be some genuine ones there. In high spirits they finished their lunch and set off with another bottle to inspect the Cunlip literary inheritance.

The dark, tunnel-like room with heavy velvet curtains, massive baize-covered table and floor-to-ceiling bookshelves showed every sign of neglect. Miss Muttock admitted that she had wandered into it only once before and had no idea of what it contained. Gloria tried unsuccessfully to amuse herself by

103

leafing through the earliest volumes of a bound set of *Punch*. The Muttock perused a weighty leather-bound tome entitled *Bedford's Scripture Chronology*, dated 1730 and containing an elaborate calculation of the precise tonnage of dung that Noah had to shovel overboard daily to keep the ark afloat. Meanwhile the Captain, versed in the ways of nineteenth-century bibliophiles, made straight for a roll-top desk and opened it. The first thing to catch his eye was a small stack of brown-spotted unused bookplates bearing the arms freshly granted to Sir Julius Cunlip and his motto: '*Sobrietas Custos Virtutis*'. These, surely, would prove useful in their planned enterprise. A swift examination of the desk soon found a key concealed in a secret drawer. The Captain marched the length of the library, dragging with him a little ladder on wheels, unlocked a closed bookcase and climbed up to examine the contents of the highest shelves. These he brought down in armfuls to the table, uncovering as he did so a number of empty brandy bottles of antique appearance. A grin of triumph lit up his face.

Soon the books were spread out open at their title pages, and the ladies were able to see at once that he had unearthed quite a respectable assemblage of erotica. These were not just classics of the genre but also lesser-known productions, all of them such as the Victorian paterfamilias would have kept under lock and key to spare the modesty of female members of his household. Mary Muttock and Gloria needed no such protection. As they leaned over the table examining this inflammatory material with avidity, the Captain observed their nipples tightening and growing darker. He came round to their side of the table, stood between the two women and placed a hand on the bottom of each. Miss Muttock felt the hand slip inside her pyjamas and a finger come to rest in the warm groove between her cheeks.

Gloria was turning the pages of a shabby, dog-eared volume bearing the title *Bedroom Confessions of a Lady's Maid*. Every now and then she paused to giggle and read a short passage aloud. The Captain moved his hand from her bottom and brought it round to her bare belly, sliding it up until it could support and steady the jiggling breasts as she laughed.

'Listen to this, guys,' she tittered. ' "Major Drummond forced Edwina's head down on the pillow and threw her petticoats up over her head. He drew aside her drawers and laid into the superb alabaster hemispheres with his riding crop before parting the gigantic globes and presenting his mighty affair, angry in its manly pride, to the entrance of her bottom-hole''. What kinda crap d'you call this, Doc?'

The Captain declared himself unimpressed as his finger slipped unopposed into the pouting bottom-hole of Mary Muttock. 'They were big on big bums in those times,' he explained. 'Me, I prefer tight little ones any day. But look, there's something hidden between the pages.'

Gloria extracted a folded sheet of notepaper masking a sheaf of postcard-sized sepia photographs.All three moved over to a lumpy old sofa with its back to the window. Miss Muttock pulled off the dust sheet covering it and they sat down, the Captain in the middle, and went through the interesting find, picture by picture.

The most innocuous showed a youth rigged out as Cupid, holding a bow and arrow and with a pair of wings attached to his back. He was taking aim at a naked maiden who squatted on a couch with her legs wide open to receive the wound of love. Gloria wondered aloud whether that supposed virginity was about to be pierced by the arrow or by the lad's standing weapon, almost as long and many times thicker, which was also aimed at the juicy target.

Mary Muttock uncrossed her legs thoughtfully, feeling the Widow's Friend stir inside her. 'Captain, what's the point of going to all the trouble of dreaming up new products when we've got the real thing here?' she suggested. 'Negotiate on behalf of your university to buy all these books and pictures, and we can split the proceeds between us. A legitimate transaction, almost.'

A moment's thought convinced the Captain that though this idea was good enough to merit a wet kiss and a quick frotting of his old friend's bosom, it was not the best plan. He agreed that some or − why not? − all the Cunlip Hall material should be included in the sale, to lend dignity and authenticity to the home-made articles supposedly found in the same place. But even if some of these articles were rare and valuable, and some of them not already duplicated in his Palace of Fantasies back

105

in Banesville, none of them could compare with the new literary outtakes he had commissioned in terms of the sensational impact they would make on the map of high culture. And, indeed, on the market.

Nothing remained to say on this matter, so the three of them turned their attention to the next photograph Gloria passed to the Captain. In it, a bewhiskered hussar reared up in full ceremonial uniform, including plumed helmet and burnished breastplate but minus his breeches. His legs were muscular and hairy; a dusky organ swelled stout and upright from a dense bush of black curls. He was on the point of inserting this fearsome tool into one of the two receptacles being offered to him by a young lady. She stood with her back to him, bending down with her skirts and petticoats hitched up over her back to expose a pair of generous white buttocks.

'I've seen so many like this,' the Captain complained. 'They're so static. You just can't imagine he's going to touch the whore after the picture's taken. He'll probably go and sell his arse to some top-hatted toff in St James's Park.'

'That's right,' Mary Muttock agreed. 'Of course, they had to pose a long time with their slow exposures, didn't they? You couldn't get the mid-air come shots we're used to today. But look, Gloria's found a better one for us.'

The proffered print showed a pretty girl spread in a state of nature upon the lap of a virile young man, also naked, on a wooden chair. She had her back to him and faced the camera. Her legs were wide apart to straddle his thighs, between which hung a bulging scrotum. Her right hand reached down to fondle his balls while she was caressing her own left nipple to rigidity with the other one. The girl's head was thrown back in lustful abandon. But the centre of interest, as the Captain pointed out, was surely that central rift dividing the patch of black hair between her legs. The lips were stretched apart by the man's cock, which appeared to be as thick as a wrist. It looked as if the girl was just lifting her bottom at the moment of mutual climax; although his glans was securely embedded in her flesh, several inches of penis were visible between his scrotum and her distended cuntlips. The root of the cock gleamed wetly. Below the point of ingress, creamy sperm had already leaked or spurted from that tight-crammed cunt to hang in heavy globules from the girl's drenched hairs.

'Notice a resemblance?' the Muttock asked in a throaty voice. 'They look just like the two of you. Come on — get on the chair over there and let's have it for real.'

Flushed with uncharacteristic enthusiasm, Gloria got to her feet and hauled the Captain up on his. He, of course, was eager enough to oblige and they both removed shoes and socks, trousers and underwear. Whether from negligence or perversity, Gloria retained the chiffon scarf around her throat. She placed the palm of one hand on his matted chest and pushed him so that he fell back on the chair. Unusually, the tube of flesh between his legs curved down over his bollocks with the foreskin closed over its tip.

Nothing could induce Miss Muttock to let the Captain disappoint the cheerleader. She directed the girl to sit well back on his lap facing her, as in the picture, and to fondle his flagging member. She herself stood before them, licked her lips and began to hum a waltz tune, partly remembered and partly improvised. The Captain gave some evidence of his masculinity by contributing a lusty if off-key bass accompaniment. To the bizarre strains produced by both of them, she started swaying her hips and performing an expressive, vaguely oriental routine with her arms and hands.

The tempo was steadily increasing and elements of limbo dancing were brought into play as Mary Muttock bent lithely backwards and shook her loins. As she did so the pyjama jacket fell wide open; even when she straightened up again her breasts remained exposed in their rhythmic juggling. She was finding now that the slightest movement of her pelvic region was enough to activate the Widow's Friend. The metal balls jostled together inside her and generated delicious ripples which coursed through her whole body but were felt more intensely in the tight knot of flesh at their epicentre.

As she swayed and writhed, she eased her pyjama bottoms down little by little. All but the inverted apex of her dark triangle was now visible to the couple on the chair. Mary Muttock was conscious now of the hard eyes of Sir Julius glaring down at her from a portrait. She was also conscious of the elastic waistband biting into the furry outswelling at the base of her belly. She laid a finger on the critical point at the top of the rift just opening above the waistband and swayed her hips even more lewdly. The elastic worked a little further over the curve of her buttocks and this was enough to let the pyjama bottoms slip silkily down to the floor. Stepping clear of them she brought her undulations closer to Gloria and the Captain, whose penis had now grown fat and long between the girls's fingers but still appeared to be too flexible to justify attempts at insertion.

Sensations so powerful as to be almost unfriendly if not down-right hostile even to the merriest of widows were now ripping through Miss Muttock's insides as the silver balls jolted together. A few more flicks of her pubis and she would explode. Afraid of anticipating her companions and thus missing out on the full, shared enjoyment she had proposed to herself, she dropped to her knees in front of them.

Merely by aiming a narrow stream of breath at the cocktip Gloria stretched out towards her mouth, the Muttock was able to bring about an immediate invigoration of the glans. Fresh blood distended its spongy tissue, stretching the skin to shining, purple smoothness. But once her lips were closed to form a seal around the stem, a dramatic lengthening and thickening took place in that already proud organ. And the Captain was no longer sitting passively under Gloria. Rising right off the seat, he started heaving up and down as his pent-up emotions were released and brought to bear on the task of driving the machinery of his sex to its inexorable goal.

Tactfully, Mary Muttock backed off and used both hands to assist in parting Gloria's soft, oozy petals and forcing the Captain's stiffness back and up into the throbbing sheath. When the couple were solidly joined, she stood up and resumed her swaying dance, maddened by the jouncing of those balls inside her. Her hands were pressed flat into her breasts and she never allowed her eyes to wander from the scene being enacted just a few feet away. As she watched and swayed, this scene suddenly acquired the finishing touch which brought it into full consonance with the picture that had fired her enthusiasm. Gloria cried out in rapture, overtaken by her climax. At that very instant the Captain stretched out his legs, the muscles tense, and poured his offering into her. His thighs slackened. And there at the point of juncture, as Mary Muttock's eyes widened and her own cunt contracted in the pre-spasms of orgasm, thick spunk issued from the pretty cheerleader's clinging pussy to coat the cockroot and balls beneath it before detached gobbets slopped over the front edge of the leather seat and eased themselves down to the dusty carpet.

Overpowered by this sight and her own emotion, Miss Muttock wriggled her tummy for the last time, parted her thighs and thrust her mound forward at the seated lovers. The release of contained energy was shattering. She felt her viscera tighten and her vagina clench like a crushing fist around the Widow's Friend. Her whole body convulsed. Like of brace of chainshot the toy was cannonaded out of her. With a heavy double thud it landed in the reeking puddle on the carpet between the Captain's feet.

The Captain reached for her hand and raised it to his lips. 'My dear madam,' he said, 'you are the hen who has laid silver eggs for us. But by joining our team you will gain the means to lay golden ones. Welcome!'

SEVEN

MASTER, MISTRESS AND MADWOMAN

A brief note from the Captain told Miss MacDonald and Melanie that he was pleased with their travesty of Jane Austen. He now urged them to do the same with Charlotte Brontë and suggested that they should take up the story somewhere around the point at which Jane Eyre gets to meet Mr Rochester, her master, for the first time, shortly after being installed as governess to his young ward Adèle. This could be quite an early draft, he explained, in which Charlotte Brontë had used material that was eventually to be scattered through later chapters of the cleaned-up final version of the novel. The two friends set to with a will and soon produced an episode which satisfied their growing sense of professionalism.

> The kindly housekeeper led me forward. I had brushed my hair very smooth, braided the locks, and put on my black frock — which, Quaker-like as it was, at least had the merit of fitting to a nicety — and adjusted my clean white tucker. Two wax candles stood lighted on the table, and two on the mantelpiece; basking in the light and heat of a superb fire, lay Pilot — Adèle knelt near him. Half reclined on a couch appeared Mr. Rochester; he was looking at Adèle and the dog. The fire shone full on his face, with its broad and jetty eyebrows, its square forehead made squarer by the horizontal sweep of his black hair. I gazed on his decisive nose, more remarkable for character than beauty; his full nostrils, denoting, I thought, choler; his grim mouth, chin and jaw — yes, all three were

very grim, and no mistake. His shape, I perceived, harmonised in squareness with his physiognomy. I suppose it was a good figure in the athletic sense of the term — broad-chested and thin-flanked, though neither tall nor graceful. His white buckskin breeches clung tightly to a pair of muscled thighs, at the meeting of which I observed a bulge which seemed inexplicably to stir and swell at my approach. I averted my gaze.

"Here is Miss Eyre, sir," said Mrs. Fairfax. He bowed, still not taking his eyes from the dog and the child.

"Let Miss Eyre be seated," said he. The housekeeper withdrew, but the master did not leave his couch.

In considerable discomfiture, I knelt down beside little Adèle and began to tidy the redundancy of dark hair that framed her pale, small-featured face and fell in curls to her waist. Thinking the moment propitious for making a request in my favour, she cried out —

"N'est-ce-pas, monsieur, qu'il y a un cadeau pour Mademoiselle Eyre dans votre petit sac?"

"Who talks of *cadeaux*?" said he gruffly. "Did you expect a present, Miss Eyre? Are you fond of presents?" He searched my face with eyes that were dark, irate, and piercing; as he stared at me I could not but notice his great hand close over whatever was swelling in his lap.

"I hardly know, sir; I have little experience of them; they are generally thought pleasant things, though it would shame me to accept anything *substantial* from a gentleman with whom I had not been long acquainted."

"Miss Eyre, you are not so unsophisticated as Adèle: she demands a *'cadeau'* clamorously, the moment she sees me: you beat about the bush. Come to the fire."

I ensconced myself beside my master; Adèle wanted to take a seat on my knee, but she was ordered to amuse herself with Pilot. Mr. Rochester quizzed me on my past eighteen years; and although his manner was rough and graceless, half sitting, half reclining, and looking preciously grim as he cushioned his massive head against the back of his chair to receive the light of the fire on his granite-hewn features and in his great dark eyes, it seemed to me that something in his tone and in the sparkle of those eyes betokened a regard not called for by my lowly station in his household. In spite of myself, I forgot my timidity, and answered his questions boldly; nor did I protest when his weighty palm came to rest on my knee. Encouraged, he took my hand and carried it to the strange mass that stirred at the base of his trunk.

Adèle, who had been a sly witness of these untoward proceedings, now stood up and stamped her foot in a little shew of pique. To appease her jealousy, my master directed her to search beneath the hanging cloth of the table.

"*Ma boîte! ma boîte!*" exclaimed she.

"Yes, there is your '*boîte*' at last: take it into a corner, you genuine daughter of Paris, and amuse yourself with disembowelling it," said the deep and rather sarcastic voice of Mr. Rochester.

Adèle was already busy untying the cord which secured the lid. Having lifted certain silvery envelopes of tissue paper, she exlaimed —

"*Oh, ciel! Que c'est beau!*" and then remained absorbed for some moments in ecstatic contemplation.

My master, meanwhile, sought diversion by insinuating his rough fingers into the snowy tucker at my breast and feeling out one of the little pink tips. I blushed deeply —

"Sir," I began, "I am not used —"

He stopped me short, and squeezed the breast masterfully. "Pray do not be alarmed, my dear little Janet," said he. "Hitherto you have lived a life of decent retirement; and it is not to be denied that your life at Thornfield Hall will be one of confinement and loneliness, for which the company of old Mrs. Fairfax will be but small consolation. To be sure, you may come to find in Adèle a more stimulating companion. But in those brief periods when my affairs permit me to sojourn beneath this roof, you and I are destined to partake of delights that would eclipse the brightest entertainment society can offer. Do you know, Miss Eyre, what is meant by *fucking*?"

112

I had never before heard this word spoken, and could only infer from my master's piercing look that something of a shameful nature was to be understood by it. The blush spread from my cheeks and throat down over the bosom now fully exposed by his ravages; but at this point our intercourse was interrupted by young Adèle, who had removed the long-awaited "*cadeau*" from her "*boîte*" and was eager to shew it to us. Her guardian (or, as I was beginning to suspect from something in the way Mr. Rochester had been eyeing her, her natural sire) might, for all I knew, have expended great sums on this piece of frippery: for all that, it was nothing more than a length of gauzy, saffron-coloured lawn. The girl had slipped out of her clothes while my master and I were so taken up with each other that we had quite forgotten her presence in the room, and she had swathed her slight form in the transparent veil. With the assurance and address of some houri, she stepped before us and swayed her narrow hips as if to the strains of an exotic dulcimer.

During my recent interrogation, Mr. Rochester had let slip that Adèle Varens was the child of an actress and dancer he had known in Paris, and of whom he could no longer speak without pain; in a spirit of uncharacteristic philanthropy he had undertaken to see to the girl's education upon the mother's decease, and was faithfully carrying out that commitment. Adèle, Mrs. Fairfax had told me before I was engaged as the child's governess, was a well grown seven years old; yet her childish prattle, her backwardness at her lessons, and her seeming inability to heed the voice of reason, had proved insufficient to persuade me that she was indeed so young. And now, as she danced for us with the firelight revealing the form of her supple body through the scant yellow covering, I judged her to be at least twelve or thirteen years of age. My master's eyes were staring; his fingers tweaked my hard, extended dug remorselessly; whatever strange device he concealed within his breeches was now towering upwards and threatening to burst the buttons of the fore-flap. I seized my opportunity to challenge him.

"What," I demanded, "were those blood-chilling screams and maniacal laughs I heard penetrating the stillness of the upper floors last night? Was it, as Mrs. Fairfax declares, nothing but the wretched servant, Grace Poole, the worse for too many jugs of black porter?"

The tower reared itself up, shuddered under my hand, and collapsed. For a moment Mr. Rochester's lofty, tormented brow slumped upon my bosom and his tongue traced a liquid trail down the valley between my naked breasts. Adèle spun to a halt and stood facing the fireplace. She bent, with feet apart, to touch her toes; her mass of curls spread themselves on the carpet, and she gave us both an inverted grin before flicking her gauzy, insubstantial garment up over her shoulders. The pale legs, it seemed to me, were more womanly than childish. Of the shining hemispheres they supported, I prefer not to speak. I gasped at the immodest sight, and some degree of stiffness was restored to the inmate of my master's damp breeches. Rising to his feet, he bade me a civil good-night, took Adèle by the hand, and led her silently from the room.

There being nothing further to detain me, I retired to my little bedchamber, where I drew the sheets tightly around my shoulders and endeavoured with small success to dismiss the recent disturbing events from my mind. The moon was full; and the blue chintz curtains, which endowed the room with such a cheerful aspect by daylight, were now ineffectual in excluding her pale beams. An eerie, livid radiance shimmered upon the walls. Far off, I fancied I heard those wild laughs that tallied so ill with the placid, bovine features of Grace Poole. Sleep would not come for a long time, and when at last it came it was shallow and fitful.

A light tapping on the door aroused me from my slumbers. I opened my eyes: a slim form had slipped into the room and hovered at my bedside. As my eyes grew accustomed to the dim blue light, they recognised the young houri, Adèle; an Adèle almost naked, her abundant tresses furnishing a dark contrast to the shining whiteness

114

of her limbs and body. No longer was the candour of those parts half-concealed by saffron gauze — instead of the veil, her only garment was a scarf of the same flimsy stuff, tied loosely around her hips and hanging down between her legs. In the blue dimness I thought I saw her smile; she swayed and stuck out her belly, as if dancing without moving her feet. She tossed her long hair back over her shoulders, exposing a pair of small but perfectly formed breasts, hitherto unseen and unsuspected by me, that bounced up and down elastically, in time with her movements: and now she pivoted round to turn her little bottom towards me. It, too, quivered lewdly like her breasts; there was something lasciviously suggestive in this exhibition that caused me to hide my head beneath the bed-sheet.

In a trice, Adèle was in the bed beside me. She hugged me and pressed a shower of kisses upon my closed eyes — I felt her cool, firm body cling to mine. The restlessness of my shallow slumbers had allowed my nightgown to ride up to my waist, and I was now aware of the girl's hands moving over my flanks. At the same time, she insinuated a sly foot beneath one of my legs and pushed it right through until my thigh was clasped high up between both of hers; and, indeed, the pressure those thighs exerted on mine spoke rather the vigorous young woman than the callow schoolgirl. Such thoughts were shockingly confirmed when Adèle drew herself up to me in an even closer embrace, so that the front of my imprisoned thigh was forced against the clammy heat of open female flesh; and, as this flesh slid stickily down over my own skin, the juices deposited by it were wiped or smeared, I could feel, by a pad of hair luxuriant enough to give the lie to my revised estimate of her age. Diminutive of stature and backward in both intellectual and moral attainments, Mr. Rochester's supposed ward was surely a grown woman posing as a charming, childish dunce: an imposture to which her French nurse, Sophie, must have been privy, and — oh, horror! — in all likelihood the woman-child's guardian himself. — On this reflection I stiffened in the bed, and tried to push the provocative fairy away from me. Rather than resist, she arose at once and, seizing my hand, exclaimed urgently, "*Venez avec moi, ma chère Mademoiselle Jeannette! C'est notre maître qui nous attend!* — our master, he wait on us!"

I allowed myself to be dragged from bed and out of the room. I knew not what to expect; Hope cried out in my heart, "Nought is amiss: your master plays strange, freakish pranks to test your spirit." But even ere the final word was inwardly heard, the voice of Hope was shouted down by the brawling tones of Vice: "Your master has imposed upon you, Jane Eyre. Rejoice, for he means to bend you to his evil will."

I followed Little Adèle, her bottom bobbing in the moonlight; she hurried along the gallery and up to the dark, low corridors of the third storey. Here the walls were hung with tapestries crusted with thick work now half effaced by time, wrought by fingers that for two generations had been coffin-dust. Thence we passed up a narrow staircase to the attics directly beneath the leads of the roof.

A small door stood open; muffled sounds of tussling and laughter came from somewhere within. Adèle led me first into a bare, dungeon-like apartment, in which a narrow, grated window admitted moonlight that weirdly illuminated chains secured to rings in the walls. We trod gingerly across the filthy straw that covered the floor, and passed into a smaller chamber containing copper pans and a great tub of steaming water. A profusion of wet towels and cloths, all of them direly needing to be boiled clean or burnt outright, testified to recently performed and long overdue ablutions; while the wetness of the bare floorboards and dripping walls persuaded me that the salubrious operation had been forced upon an unwilling subject.

Flushed with excitement, Adèle opened a door opposite to the one by which we had entered; as she did so, the sound of a woman's groan was distinctly heard from the room beyond it — a groan that was stifled as if a hand had been laid over the mouth that uttered it. I followed my little companion, and we stood side by side peering through a curtain of beads at the proceedings within: this room was windowless, but lurid illumination was furnished by a great fire of coals burning on the hearth, so that the scene rivalled the horrors of the Inquisition, or the Popish imaginings of an infernal torment which magnify those horrors into an eternal nightmare, worse even than the hypocritical rantings of Mr. Brocklehurst. Reader, I know not if this thought be the product of an overheated fancy, but I was reminded also of my ordeal as a small child in the terrible red-room at Gateshead.

In the middle of the firelit chamber stood a bed, its foot towards us, upon which the naked body of a woman lay supine. Her wrists and ankles were secured by cords looped tightly over bars that ran horizontally between the posts at the head and foot of the bed; the loops were stretched to their widest extension, so that the victim was displayed in the form of a saltire cross. The woman was lean, muscular and somewhat dusky-skinned; at the base of her straining belly sprung a great bush of wiry black hair. But the things that chiefly caught my attention were two. A white object such as I had never before seen had been thrust into the pink opening in the midst of that scrubby bush: a device of marble or alabaster, the hither end of which just projected above the distended lips of female flesh, and terminated in a pair of balls resembling two polished eggs. Of her face I could see nothing, for — and this was the second thing that astonished me — the top of her chest was straddled by a man, as naked as herself, whose shaggy mane of black hair was unmistakably that of Mr. Rochester. The nervous thews rippled on his broad back, and the woman's teats stood up hard and purple against the whiteness of his posteriors. Averting her gaze, I now took in the final touch of this most curious picture: on a stool beside the bed sat the square, placid form of Grace Poole, fully clothed and knitting.

Adèle pressed her slender body against me, as if seeking reassurance; we both held our breath, waiting for the next

117

transaction to occur. At that instant, my master brought his right hand behind him to impart a resounding thwack upon the woman's flank. His deep voice resounded in ire —

"Bite me, would you, hot-blooded, diabolical bitch? Ha! It is well, Bertha, that I anticipated such vicious freaks and took steps to secure myself against them."

He swung his knee across the woman's straining form and stood beside the bed. I now beheld plainly her mad, animal features, framed by a tangle of raven hair streaked with white, and distorted into a hideous grin. Her mouth was stretched wide open, the pink gums mercifully devoid of teeth through my master's foresight. Grace Poole laid aside her knitting and rose to remove the alabaster instrument from between the raving creature's legs. It was a thick cylinder some eight inches long; at the far end from the two ovoid balls, it widened into an obliquely sloping shelf which formed the lower edge of a plum-like bulb of formidable dimensions. Grace now stuffed this bulb into the toothless mouth without ceremony.

My master turned, presenting his noble, tormented profile to my gaze. As he stood thus, my heart leaped at an undreamt-of sight; from the close thicket of curls adorning his lower belly sprouted the very twin of the object now stopping the wild delinquent's mouth; but instead of lifeless alabaster, this proud device was moulded from throbbing, living flesh; the stem was a creamy white, netted with pulsing blue veins, and the crowning bulb shone like purple satin. Even as I watched, a drop of clear fluid oozed from a small opening at the tip; it grew, until its own weight bore it slowly to the floor, drawing with it a tensile thread of moisture.

At Mr. Rochester's direction, the servant loosened the loops of cord and moved them from the corners of the bed to the centre of the bars to which they were attached. My master rolled the woman called Bertha over on her front and held her while Grace returned the loops to their former position. The prisoner lay extended on her belly, her head forced up by the object projecting from between

118

her lips. Grace Poole then handed my master a riding-crop, with which he belaboured the back, thighs and posteriors until they were criss-crossed with crimson welts. Horrified as I was, I consoled myself with the reflection that this person must have been truly evil to merit such severe punishment, and I prayed that her sins would be forgiven her in a future life.

The crop was lifted to shower yet more blows upon the trembling form; but the tender-hearted Adèle sprang forward through the bead curtain to stay her guardian's arm. Seeing her, he softened, and laid his great hand on her head as I followed her into the room.

"Ah, my dear little Jane," he began, looking up at me. "Or let me once more call you my dear Miss Eyre, for ere long that maidenly domination shall be swept aside. Yes, Jane, you are to be my wife. Let us hasten forward the nuptials. Adèle, *tu vas jouer la petite demoiselle d'honneur de Mademoiselle* — you are to be her brides-maid."

Adèle, already instructed in her *rôle*, took from the table a piece of stuff that I recognised as the saffron veil in which she had danced for us downstairs. She seized my nightgown by the hem, and before I could protest had whipped it up over my head and left me standing as naked as the wretch upon the bed. The flimsy gauze was thrown over me so that it hung from the crown of my head to the level of my thighs; I felt indeed the awkwardness and embarrassment of a bride as I stood before my master's piercing scrutiny.

To my surprise, he turned from me, and with Grace Poole's sturdy help raised the bound woman up on her elbows and knees. Her breasts swung low, their teats grazing the sheet.

"Now," he cried, baring his teeth with a righteous frown, "as you have so long delighted in tormenting me with the allurements of your body, I shall take advantage this last time of your outlandish ability to rouse up my manhood, before I call upon the just gods to witness our divorce."

119

With that, he leaped up behind her and, before my astonished eyes, allowed little Adèle to place the tip of his bulging instrument within the soft folds of flesh between the creature's thighs; then, lunging forward savagely, he drove his supernumerary limb up into the recesses of her dark body. She writhed, as far as her bonds permitted, and, her mouth being crammed full with the alabaster simulacrum of the organ stuffing her belly, began to emit whining, whimpering sounds through her nose. I saw her eyes roll back until nought but the whites shewed ghastly in the firelight.

"No!" cried my master. "She shall not take her pleasure now. Heavens forbid that she should thus shame my wedding-night. With this curse" — and he uttered a mighty oath — "I nullify the unholy marriage into which you tricked me, Bertha Mason."

He pulled back from her loins; the great column emerged, seemingly twice its previous length and girth, dripping with sticky slime; the flaps of her flesh fell together with a sound as of wet fish flung down on a marble slab. He turned to his little assistant —

"Adèle: *ta langue; ce jus, c'est trop sale* — you must lick me clean for Mademoiselle Jeannette."

My "bridesmaid", unconventionally but attractively attired in the saffron scarf that still clung to her hips, sat on the edge of the bed while Mr. Rochester stood before her. She bowed her head as if in submission, and as the pink tongue ran repeatedly from root to tip in its cleansing mission, still more inches seemed to accrue to the already alarming dimensions of that member.

Grace Poole rolled up her sleeves, untied the cords from the bars at the head and foot of the bed, and secured the wrists of the former Mrs. Rochester tightly behind her back so that she could be marched from the room, her protestations still stifled by the dead and bitter fruit of lust on which she was forced to bite. The broad highway to my own wedded bliss now seemed open; but my master would have it that he had not yet attained the full pitch of his desire, and lying on his back upon the now empty bed, made Adèle squat over his loins. She flicked the strip of scarf hanging down between her thighs over to one side so that her tuft of fur was exposed, and the sweek pink lips projecting beneath it; nought remained but to lower herself with care upon the great blunt spike to which my innocent eyes were still unaccustomed. I was amazed to see at least half the length pass up into her delicate body, whereupon the girl threw back her head in obvious ecstasy, an ecstasy prolonged by the application of Mr. Rochester's thumbs to the top of the secret crease leading down to the point of entry. Suddenly she collapsed forward upon his darkly matted chest; he pressed her mouth to his and kissed her with passion.

All this time he had lain with his hips motionless on the bed. Only now, when Adèle flopped over limply on her side, releasing the great stem that had stretched her to such delight, did he rise to his knees: could it be possible that it had gained even more in size and rigidity? — Be that as it may, his ardent desire for me had no whit abated. As I stood at the side of the bed upon which he knelt, he reverently drew up my veil and lifted it over my head, so that it now hung down my back and left the entire front of my body shyly bare to his adoration. Chastely, he kissed my mouth; then less chastely, slipping a stiff tongue between my lips and teeth — teeth that would never have to be drawn for his pleasure and security. I closed my eyes, panting, and felt his mouth move down to my breasts. It lingered, licking and sucking the teats, loving them in turn until they ripened into hard berries of what I conjectured to be lust.

At this point he invited me to join him and Adèle, who lay in a dreamy state of exhaustion beyond him, on the bed. I demurred not. Prompted by Nature, I drew up my knees and let my thighs fall open. With eyes closed I awaited the battering that was, I knew, to be inflicted by that terrifying ram; but no — the assault, when it came, was at first no more than a gentle tickling. The tickling proceeded rhythmically: my loins were bathed in warm effusions, and I acknowledged to myself that the liquor

121

of love had at last been broached: my body was flowing with milk and honey.

Sighing, I opened my eyes; I expected to find myself staring up into my master's ebony orbs — picture my surprise, reader, when all I could see of him was his shaggy mane down at the meeting of my thighs. As he drew back with a look of ineffable longing upon his rough-hewn physiognomy, I understood why his penetration had felt so gentle: the insurgent organ had been his tongue. I noticed that my little bridesmaid had been less idle than I had supposed; she had one hand at the stem that stretched rigidly up under his belly as he knelt smiling at me. At last he spoke —

"It is time, Jane. The rites of Hymen must now be performed, and Adèle shall assist." His ward now became fully active: she bent over me and pulled my virgin flesh wide open while my master, rising between my legs, positioned himself above me. "There being no known impediment," said he, "I now declare us man and wife."

Even as these words fell from his eager lips, the bead curtain was swept aside and a dark stranger swept into the room. "Stop!" he cried. "An insuperable impediment to this marriage does exist, as you well know."

My master, though horrified, had been swept along too far by the tide of passion to resign his claim. I strained my head forward to look down at his purple-tipped weapon. I saw — I felt — a creamy flood begin to spurt from the slotted aperture in that throbbing tip, hotly filling the gap held open for it by Adèle's fingers. I say I witnessed the commencement of the passionate discharge — but not its end; for Mr. Rochester, *my* Mr. Rochester, lunged forward and pierced me to the vitals with that lance of stout English gristle. The highway to bliss had indeed stood open, but that highway proved a strait and narrow path; pain seared my inwards, but the pain gave way, instantly, to nuptial joy. The insolent intruder forgotten, I abandoned myself to my master's lusty heaving, returning it with thrusts of my hips. Just as my belly tightened and the core of my being shuddered convulsively to the unspeakable rapture that overtook me, I felt a hot torrent erupt from that other insolent (though welcome) intruder — the rampant staff which threatened to puncture my heart. Adèle squealed as the manly essence bubbled out from my split flesh to drench the hand cradling my master's oval reservoirs. The bond between us had been sealed — but without benefit of clergy. He had mastered me. I knew not what to think or to do; I bit my lips; I prayed. At once the scales fell from my eyes. Pushing Mr. Rochester aside from my naked body, I struggled to my feet, rushed past the stranger and fled from the chamber.

EIGHT

LABOURS OF LOVE

Melanie sat in the garden of the cottage, a tall glass of lemonade on the table beside her and her diary open on her lap. It was a very hot day and the cover of the exercise book felt pleasantly cool against her lower belly and upper thighs. Apart from the background drone of insects and frequent bursts of birdsong, the garden was steeped in silence. When she shifted the diary, Melanie could hear its cover being gently scoured by her gingery tuft. She set the book on the table and uncrossed her legs, spreading the slim thighs so that the sun could dry the dribble of Derrick's spunk which had been making intermittent appearances since his early morning visit. Soon Miss MacDonald would be home for lunch; Melanie would have liked to think her snatch would be ready by then to receive the older woman's kisses without any betrayal of her earlier bout, but there was something particularly thick and clinging in Derricks's deposits. Sometimes she had been embarrassed by a belated glob splatting on the floor between her feet a good twelve hours after he had screwed her.

The sun felt good on her body and the memory of Derrick so vividly evoked by the salty odour wafting up from her leaking sexlips restored her randiness almost to its early morning peak. Looking down, she saw that her nipples were standing stiff and casting long shadows down her tummy.

Nothing much would be achieved at this rate. The recent spate of playing first at Jane Austen and then at Charlotte Brontë had kept her so busy that nothing but the tersest record of comings and goings — especially comings — had been entered in the diary for the last few weeks. This morning she was resolved to make up for her slackness. She took up her pen, leaned forward to the table and wrote.

Had a letter yesterday from Captain. He went to see the Muttock at Cunlip Hall and took that Gloria with him — staying on there, he says, and making a start in writing out our *Middlemarch* chapter as a George Eliot manuscript. Explained how he did this. Seems quite a lot of effort needed to protect paper from flying sperm and female love juice — he's been having a nonstop fuck with Muttock and the glory hole and you bet he hasn't told me the half of it.

Says he was lucky to find a stack of Victorian writing paper in the desk of library up there. But thinks it would be risky to use same paper for other authors. Will tear blank pages out of old books, but wants Mac and me to do the Upchester second-hand bookshops, looking out for old albums, scrapbooks and so on — especially watching for paper watermarked with suitable dates. Ink going to be a problem with the other writers — says he's messing about with stuff like oak gall and gum arabic, whatever they may be. But for G Eliot he struck lucky again — box of unsold Victorian pencils in desk, genuine Cumberland graphite, whatever that is. For me, dodgiest bit would be imitating handwiting. Captain says he's had plenty of practice at that kind of thing, though not for such long stretches. Mostly just signatures and stuff. It was easy enough to get a life of GE from public library with plates showing writing. Gets to be quite automatic after a time. Best when he relaxes, so his Gloria and Muttock-chops laze about nude and keep him tanked up with Chablis while he's working. Quite a few pages got spoilt because though this treatment really relaxed him every time they began, after a while he'd get excited and tense up. They had a rule — whenever his dick got as long as the pencil, he put pencil down and let girls wank him off. But like I said before, with so much loose spunk around, some of it would end up on papers, so they gave up wanking and went over to sucking and fucking so it all went into their mouths and cunts. Ah well, it's all in the cause of Great Literature.

When Captain and Sweetbreads visited us here that time, he told us they'd seen snobby Gina Wootton in London. I think he's really gone on her, and the way Gloria blushed when it was mentioned I wouldn't be surprised if they all screwed around together. Anyway, in his letter he's asking if we know of any other old Cunlip girls he might be able to contact. Needs *models*, he says, to fake up some old-fashioned dirty postcards — wants a meet if poss weekend after next. He found a couple of antique cameras in attic, first one of those great wooden boxes on a tripod, then one of those contraptions with a leather thing like a concertina. Now that's just the sort of thing Derrick's into — wonder if Captain would like to meet him again? Must phone him to find out. Anyway, contacting possible models is what I'm going to look into today, but right now car's pulling up outside, so must spray some stuff round pussy to put MacDonald off the scent.

Whether or not Miss MacDonald was put off the scent of Derrick's spillages, she certainly made a meal of Melanie's tender flesh; and if, as is likely, she knew perfectly well what the rude yokel had been up to, and where he had been up, the scent didn't put her off her stroke at all.

Over the weekend Melanie addressed herself to the task of seeking out old chums. On the Monday morning she sat down once more with her diary. Her powerful recollections of the events she described soon had her dripping on the garden seat.

Mon, May 13
Well, I could have wasted a lot of time looking for names of girls in phone book — reason most of them are or were at Cunlip is because parents live abroad or in some godforsaken part of UK. Started wondering if the ones who left same time as me last year had got married and

changed names — that got me thinking about pretty little Susie Freemantle. We'd married her off in mock wedding to Darcy O'Flammery, so I thought he might still be in touch with her and maybe his people would be in the book as he was one of the local boys always pestering us. (Not that young Darcy could be called a pest — he was so tame we had to show him how to do it on the wedding night.)

Surprise! Found the father — Fergus O'Flammery, The Biggin, Downriders Crescent, South Upchester. But right above him a D O'Flammery, so couldn't help wondering if that might be himself, even though he'd be only seventeen like Susie. Dialled the number and who should answer but Susie! Told me she'd flunked her exams last summer, what with all the excitement — had left the college and made Darcy marry her properly. Seems both lots of parents all for it — S and D made out she was in pod — and set them up in a cosy little flat just off Market Street. Invited me over Sunday. I said if weather stayed fine I'd borrow Mac's car and take them for picnic on river. We agreed we'd both provide nosh and I'd bring bottle of something.

Thought Mac was going to be difficult about car. Wants me to take test before going more than a couple of miles without her. But I was lucky. That godawful Major Bruton with the nicotine-stained beard and grubby trousers picked her up and took her to watch cricket. She even left me car keys so I could collect skirt from dry cleaners for her. Slipped into lilac-coloured cotton dress, sleeveless and with buttons down front — lovely and cool for day like this. Arrived at flat.

Darcy's voice on entryphone sounded high-pitched and squeaky like before it broke. Asked me up. Lovely to see them both again. Susie had on skimpy white shorts and a close-fitting blue suntop with nipples poking up under tight material — her tummy was bare, all the way from just below tits right down to just above top of her fuzz. In fact, I could see the odd yellow wisp that hadn't been tucked into waistband. The yellow hair on her head was plaited into a thick pigtail down her back, just like mine.

On her feet she wore pink plastic flipflops and altogether she looked a real Lolita or whatever they call those jailbait types. Darcy was got up almost identically in little white shorts and blue vest, but proper sandals on feet and of course his hair's a sort of chestnut, cut short and neat. Also, Susie has fair skin while Darcy had a bit of a light tan on him, though not much — both of them freckled. Interesting to notice he's got hardly any hair on arms and legs, and I don't think he's started shaving yet, so the two of them look just like a pair of kids. But more like sweethearts than brother and sister — can't keep their hands off each other.

Noticed framed wedding picture on top of TV. Darcy a bit ridiculous in grownup morning suit, but bride quite lovely in long white dress. When I wandered into bedroom first thing I saw was another pair of framed photos on bedside tables — these ones were in colour. On side that must have been Darcy's, picture of Susie, and Darcy on Susie's side of bed, I suppose. They were from set of pix Captain took with flash at their first 'wedding', the one we got up for them in Palace of Sweethearts.

In these pix, couple rather less dressed up. Bride draped in veil hanging down her back from headdress of artificial white blossoms. At neck one of few non-white touches in outfit, that black velvet choker with red rosebud fixed at throat. Flimsy blouse, sleeveless and unbuttoned down front but not quite revealing the little breasts each side of opening, reached to just above level of tummy-button. Other touch of colour: two little red bows on ends of plaits falling forward over shoulders. White ribbon tied low round hips — I'd tucked into it, back and front, a pair of small white handkerchiefs. Legs bare, apart from saucy white-and-blue bridal garter halfway down left thigh. Feet pretty in white sandals and ankle socks. Glanced over bed at picture of Darcy. All he had on, of course, was choker with rosebud and the two-hanky arrangement. Front hanky beginning to lift a bit.

S and D followed me into bedroom and giggled when they saw what I was looking at. Darcy took my shoulders and spun me round so I saw enlarged picture hanging on wall opposite bed. This was from a bit later in ceremony — Susie's bum stuck up at camera. Her veil and back hanky had been pulled up to give full view of arse and tight little cunt, all lovely and smooth. That was what had given me idea of making bridegroom feel her up, I remembered.

Darcy must have remembered too. Felt him press into my bottom as he stood behind me. He backed off an inch, slid my hem up to small of back and shoved forward again. He was getting hard in his shorts.

DARCY: Oh no — Melanie hasn't got any knickers on!

SUSIE: Leave her alone — we're supposed to be having a picnic.

DARCY: This is enough of a picnic for me. Two lovely hard-boiled eggs and a little pot of sticky honey.

SUSIE: It'll keep till later, Darce. Wow, sorry, Melanie — I'm taking too much for granted.

ME: Not to worry, dear. There's going to be plenty for all of us. But you're right — best to get down to the river now while it's so lovely and warm. We can have a bedroom party any time.

Out to the old Morris Minor. Young Mr O'Flammery got in the back and pulled his wife in after him. I drove off towards Market Street, watching them in mirror. Car seemed sluggish even with foot right down. Halfway down hill remembered to take handbrake off. Rocketed forward — Darcy was hurled back, squashing Susie. Just before main road I stamped hard on brake pedal. Now Darcy was thrown down between front and back seats. Could see he'd rolled Susie's blue top right up under armpits, but I had to concentrate on traffic.

Easier when we got out of town, but D was all over her, so not much to see but plenty to imagine. Enough to distract me, anyway, so I took bend between high hedges on wrong side of road — at least, I think it must have been wrong side, because police car popped up out of nowhere and flashed lights for me to stop. A burly sergeant came over and stuck head in through window, breathing all over me. He saw what was going on in back seat and called to mate in patrol car — 'Over here, Jives. No wonder they was out of control.' Jives was busty young WPC with pretty grin. The sergeant stood behind her while she stooped to get eyeful. I'm sure he had hand up her skirt — she seemed to be encouraging him.

SERGEANT: I've a mind to run you in for dangerous driving, miss.

ME: You can see what they were up to in the back, officer. They distracted me.

SERGEANT: And I ought to be having the two of them there for causing a public nuisance, like.

ME: No law against what they were doing, is there? They're married, after all, believe it or not. You can't say they were doing it in a public place — not while we were moving.

SERGEANT: You're lucky this is an old banger without seat belts in the back, mind, or I'd be getting the pair of them for being unbuckled. May I see your licence, miss?

ME: Afraid I left it at home.

SERGEANT: Hear that, Jives? She left it at home. You reckon we oughter go along with her to get a sight of it?

WPC JIVES: Think I've seen her before. Wasn't you one of them Cunlip College girls, dear? Now then, sarge — remember how as old Hardbuckle warned us to lay off? Ouch! you're stretching me regulations!

SERGEANT: Right. Just give us your name and address, miss, and we'll determine what further action do be called for if any. All in the line of duty, you understand. Drive careful, now, and keep well over on the left. Duty calls, Jives.

WPC JIVES: I can't hardly wait, Albert Raddles.

They zoomed off. I drove in second gear all the way to the Black Swan at Mallows Bridge, where we hired a punt. Darcy was doing the punting — Susie said he was really good with his pole — and I made sure I was lying with head towards what would have been sharp end in normal boat so I could watch him doing it. Susie foot-to-foot with me on cushions. Darcy kept letting water drip

130

down on her from pole as it slid through his hand, and she'd squeal and try to grab at his ankles. He got hot and took his vest off. Loved watching sun gleaming on smooth chest with its tiny nipples. Each time he lifted pole I got view of cute brown tuft in armpit. Susie put hands behind her head, giving me view of similar on her, but yellow.

Darcy couldn't help showing off, holding on to pole as long as poss and crouching right down before pulling out for next thrust. Occasion for bawdy repartee. Tightness of shorts a problem, so he took them off. Now he had on nothing but tiny black silk G-string. People in other boats looked a bit shocked, especially when they got rear view, but he looks so young they didn't make a big thing of it (from my close-up position I could see his thing must be bigger than they suspected) — they just passed stuffy remarks. I lay back admiring the *litheness,* I suppose you'd call it, of those smooth, agile limbs.

Susie wanted a go. She kicked off flipflops and wriggled out of her shorts — under them she had a G-string the same as his. Looked round and saw there weren't too many boats coming our way, then pulled suntop off over her head. She stood up, rocking punt, and got up on platform beside Darcy to take pole from him. Side by side with their backs to me for a moment, the only difference I could see was Susie's plait — otherwise they made perfect unisex couple.

Darcy came down on cushions opposite me and grinned. I unbuttoned dress from hem to waist, drew knees up and let them fall open slightly so he got a bit of a view. He stuck his tongue out and licked his lips. Susie too involved in punting to notice stiff boner trying to burst out of his G-string. But if his pole was too confined, hers was all over the place — she couldn't control it, let alone the boat. We were going round in circles and she kept staggering and making us rock from side to side. How fresh and lovely she looked, though, standing there so awkwardly, tensing all her muscles and trying to keep her balance. Her little tits quivered like kiddies' birthday jellies. Wolf whistles from bank as yobs sat up and took notice.

131

Then she lost footing on slippery platform and fell, wetting my dress. Darcy grabbed paddle and reached it out for her to get hold of. Boat nearly overturned when she climbed in, dripping cold water everywhere. He retrieved pole and took over punting again, crunching metal claw at end of it on hard gravel and shoving athletically to make us shoot forward. Every time he rose up to lift puntpole right out of water his cuntpole stuck out as strong as ever in the black silk. Front of little pouch forced forwards by hard-on so I could just see side view of left bollock. Sound of water rushing past sides of boat kept me cool — bright sunshine helped Susie to get warm again, but then we came to narrow, gloomy, uninviting-looking backwater with chain across entrance and sign saying 'PRIVATE: KEEP OUT'. O'Flammerys had been there before. Darcy crouched down and we eased punt through under chain and between overhanging bushes and undergrowth. Then backwater opened out into sunny pool. He brought us alongside bank, stepped down to middle of boat and stuck pole in muddy bottom (not mine or Susie's!) to stop punt drifting away. We all climbed out and I spread blanket on grass for picnic and sunbathing.

After eating the sandwiches and stuff we sprawled in sun, eyeing each other. I'd unbuttoned dress all the way down front by now and lay on back with it open, very conscious that the mauve cotton made me look even more naked than if I'd had nothing on. Same true of S and D with their tiny back pouches. D's stretched by erection, especially when they rolled over on tummy. In that posture, with D lying on S's right, he started stroking her bum cheeks and running finger round crease between bulge of bottom and smooth skin of thightop. Had his right cheek resting on small of her back while doing this and I could feel his eyes burning into my bare crotch. Brought my left hand down to cover pussy, pretending to be shy — he blushed. But then I parted fingers to open outer lips and stuck finger of other hand into quim. The bad boy blushed redder and grinned. His hand slipped between Susie's thighs.

132

Just to tease them and make things last longer I stood up and slipped dress off, then stepped gingerly into water. Struck chilly at first but swimming a few strokes warmed me up. Floated on my back to give that young scamp good view. Hard nipples and sodden thatch stuck up above surface.

Darcy tore himself away from his missis and plunged into pool — she followed a bit more timidly. I wanted him to catch me, and he did. But now they were properly married I somehow felt it would be a bit off to let him go all the way with me. So while he held me I beckoned Susie over. We were just in our depth. I stood beside them and got them into belly-to-belly clinch. Dragged Darcy's sexpouch down to let his stiff pole spring out, and pulled Susie's G-string to one side. Working by touch I put his tip between her cuntlips. He shoved in and I showed them how they could sort of drift apart in water so they were plugged together at waist level but with a gap between upper bodies. I floated on my back again and worked myself forward on surface so one of my legs came in between their faces while other one slid past back of D's neck. Now his face was gripped loosely by my thighs. He got the idea, took a deep breath and nosed bubbling into my pussy. So what did Susie do? Well, there was only one thing she could do in that position. I squirmed with the shock as her finger pierced my arsehole.

No point in pretending I hit height of bliss. Earth didn't move for me though I shipped quite a bit of water — at both ends, probably. Felt a bit out of it when those two lovebirds hit their underwater peak. We climbed out. The happy couple discarded their bits of black silk and after rubbing each other down with towels we stretched out again in the sun. Susie quite lovely panting on her back with nipples all hard and puckered up and cunthair dark and damp. But I couldn't keep eyes off Darcy with limp cock curving over his pink scrote, the bluish (spelling?) tip just peeping out of foreskin and neat little chestnut bush just asking to be teased and twitched. Funny I get the hots for a kid two or three years younger than me when I usually go for older men like the Captain.

SUSIE: Poor old Mel — you were rather the odd one out, weren't you?

ME: Not to worry, love. It's great for me just to watch you two enjoying yourselves.

SUSIE: Look, I'm a bit fussy about where Darce shoots his load but I don't mind where he sticks his dick as long as he keeps it clean. What you can do, you can suck him up hard again and let him poke you and frig your clit while you lick me out. Then he can shove it up me for his orgy — you know, his orgasm — while you lick his balls. OK?

I didn't bother to answer but knelt over his rivery naughty parts, rubbed my cheek on his fur and took his whatsit between my lips, wrapping the length of my tongue round it. It had already started to straighten out when he heard what Susie said, and now it swelled and swelled like a balloon was being blown up in my mouth. While I sucked him I felt Susie's tonguetip licking round my rear and lapping up and down groove. Her hands were milking my tits that hung down like udders.

By this time the famous puntpole was at full stretch and I let it pop out of my mouth. For a moment I held it between finger and thumb and drooled over it. First time I'd seen it like this since the mock wedding — it seemed to have grown since then. Practice, probably.

Stayed on all fours but swung round so Darcy could kneel up, grab me by hips and split me. Lovely feeling as cock ran right up cunt, stretching it and ramming up against end. Susie got down on her back in front of me, legs wide apart. I put hands under her buttocks and squeezed. My tongue prised her open and plunged into salty broth of male spunk laced with female lovejuice. Felt Darcy's hand slide round my front to work clit like S had said. Soon started quivering. Must have been too much for the boy — all of a sudden he bucked and I felt him creaming inside me, all hot and bubbly.

And what did the cunning devil do? Forced himself to stay up on his knees, though he must have been ready to flop, and stayed right there like a dog stuck to a bitch.

134

Because I'd had my own climax at same time as Susie was having hers, she didn't notice he'd broken her rule. I reached round behind me and slapped his bottom two or three times to jolly him along. That made him perk up again. Cock grew and hardened in my cunt, stewing in our mixed juices. I nearly climaxed a second time when he pulled it out.

He pushed me aside rather roughly. Still kneeling, he seized Susie's open legs and dragged her towards him, then lifted her hips and brought her sopping pussy up to his spike. She arched her back and pushed herself forward to swallow him. Meanwhile I got behind her so I could play with her little titties and give her a long, upside-down kiss. Could tell her taste on my tongue was driving her crazy. Darcy was foaming at mouth. When he threw back head and *wailed* I knew he must be foaming at hosepipe too. Susie juddered so violently his prick slipped out, still spouting. Sperm splashed down her front. I bent right over her and licked her clean from throat to bush. What a picnic!

By the following weekend Miss MacDonald, at Melanie's persuasion, had invited Anne Amory and Carla Merryweather to accompany them to a photographic session at Cunlip Hall. The O'Flammerys were packed into the back of the Morris Minor with the two young friends, but the squeeze was too tight for much misbehaviour to take place. Things got a bit livelier when they stopped to let Anne move to the front and sit on Melanie's lap. Derrick, whom the Captain had invited on account of his technical skills, accompanied them on his motorcycle, often riding beside them and peering down at the lewd writhings in the car.

The Captain had set his heart on this supplementary project. It had occurred to him that, since Sir Julius had already assembled the modest collection of pictorial porn they had found in the library (though modesty was not its most obvious attribute), he might enhance its value and academic interest by adding some tasteful compositions of his own. Besides, it would be fun to do so.

He had been surprised when Melanie's shortarsed fancy man Derrick had phoned him to offer his services both as a technician and as a stud. The Captain had not enjoyed harmonious relations with spotty-faced Derrick in the past, but now the past seemed to be forgotten in the excitement of this scheme. When Derrick undertook what kind of equipment was available, he understood to bring a supply of alcohol — the Captain smiled approvingly when he heard this — ether, and something called pyroxylin, in order, he explained, to mix the collodion with which the glass negative plates would have to be coated. He would also get hold of the requisite chemicals to produce, on the antique paper found with the wooden camera, sepia-tinted prints that would survive the closest scrutiny. In this case, the Captain reflected, it would be the subject matter of the prints rather than their technical specifications that would attract the really close scrutiny.

Mary Muttock had accompanied him and Gloria to the attic in search of suitable props of Victorian or Edwardian vintage. They found a number of likely items, such as a dusty adult-sized rocking horse and some pieces of statuary dating from a more licentious age when such artefacts had been displayed in public rooms. A dented hat box contained a wide-brimmed straw hat decorated with a profusion of artificial flowers and a pair of stuffed robins; a similar box contained a top hat, while a third one was crammed with assorted wigs. Another brassbound Victorian camera mounted on its clumsy tripod turned up in a cupboard. A collection of china dolls might prove useful in pictures with the emphasis on youth.

Then they stumbled upon a real find: a couple of large, battered trunks plastered with faded labels memorialising many a home and colonial trip in first-class style. When they opened the first of these, their nostrils were assailed by an odour carrying vaguely subterranean or mausolean suggestions. Beneath discoloured sheets of tissue paper among which spiders had nested and died they had found the attire of a bygone age — gorgeous costumes that once graced their wearers on the parterres and in the salons of Cunlip Hall. Miss Muttock lifted a ball gown, magnificent but hideously disfigured by the workings of time. It disintegrated into a cloud of foul-smelling, powdery dust. As they rummaged deeper into the trunk the task became even less agreeable and much to Mary Muttock's regret they were forced to abandon it, for fear of encountering the original wearer of these clothes at the bottom of the trunk. 'Where moth and rust doth corrupt,' she philosophised inconclusively, and the Captain could but nod in grave assent.

On prising up the lid of the second trunk, however, their pains were rewarded. Instead of the stench of corruption, they inhaled the reassuring, sanitary pungency of camphor — the garments and bolts of unused cloth were perfectly preserved and as brightly coloured as on the day they had been packed away. This treasure chest promised rich inspiration for the weekend's labours — labours of love, they agreed these would be. All they had to do, the Captain reckoned, was get everyone kitted out in this gear and the tableaux would emerge of their own accord.

The weekend visitors were received with excitement and much ribaldry. Derrick was rather out of it; the Captain directed him to a closet that was to serve as his darkroom and left him to get on with his chemistry. The rest of them trooped into the kitchen for a naked and largely liquid lunch. Melanie and Miss MacDonald were impressed when shown the manuscript in which the Captain had copied out their version of George Eliot. After a sprinkling with vinegar and a suitable time in the oven on a very low flame, the paper had become foxed and brittle, crumbling authentically at the edges. Melanie read aloud from the Brontë episode she had brought with her for copying, and Darcy got so excited that he nearly came in his hands as he tried to hide his hard-on under the table.

Towards the end of their snack the Captain whispered something in Melanie's ear and she led Susie from the room. When they returned some minutes later a round of applause went up — Susie's pubic mound was now quite bare and shining, denuded of its cloud of yellow fluff and divided by a neat pink line. She raised her arms to display equally pristine armpits.

They finished eating and wandered out into the hall just as a sports car pulled up at the door and Gina Wootton got out accompanied by her uncouth, long-haired boyfriend from college days, Joker Jennings — despite his distaste for Joker, the Captain had asked her to bring him along so that the photos he planned to take would not be monopolised by a tiny handful of models.

After a brief exchange of kisses and gropes they all trooped into the library, which was to serve as a studio for a few indoor shots. Down at the far end a window, though dusty and birdshitten, admitted sufficient sunlight. The rocking horse stood ready for action, its nostrils flaring. Gina was persuaded to don a pair of polished riding boots, a beautifully tailored hacking jacket and the top hat, under which she sported an artificial chignon. A lacy cravat tied at her throat emphasised the nudity of the flesh stretching down to the tops of the boots — a smooth, curvaceous tract of white skin dimpling in at the navel and shading down to the neat little triangle of flaming copper where the convexity of her belly gave way to the rounded thighs. With the jacket hanging naturally her nipples were covered but not the inside curves of her breasts. The flat space between them was constellated with freckles.

Derrick stood behind the large mahogany camera and pulled the black cloth over his head as the Captain directed Gina to stand beside her steed. One hand rested on its proud neck and the other held a riding crop. As soon as he was satisfied with the arrogance of her stance he gave the word to Derrick, who emerged from cover to insert a glass plate into the back of the camera, remove the brass cap from the lens, count aloud, remove the exposed plate, return it to its lightproof container and replace the cap. The photo session had begun.

Gina mounted. Selected on account of his rough and ready appearance, the stalwart Joker was made to tie a spotted handkerchief round his throat. His only other garments were a working man's flat cloth cap, into which was stuffed the tangled mass of yellow curls normally falling to his shoulders, and a shabby leather waistcoat revealing his chest and belly shagged with a mat of fair hair. As Gina's groom, he stood holding the bridle while she stooped slightly and lifted his limp prick on the end of her crop. It was not clear whether she was living her assigned role or speaking in her own person when she opened her mouth.

'You pick them up as rough as they come,' she remarked, 'but get their pants off and what do you find? A kiddy's winkle.'

'What you after, then?' demanded the indignant Joker.

'Nelson's fuckin' column or summit?'

When this rather innocent picture had been taken and yet another plate inserted in the camera, Miss Muttock stepped forward to kneel in front of him. Cradling his balls in both hands, she took the flaccid organ in her mouth and sucked it up to full size. The previous shot was then repeated, with the difference that the mounted lady was now twisted sideways in the saddle and leaning down towards her groom. The front of her hacking jacket hung open to reveal her pear-shaped breasts tipped with nipples like drops about to detach themselves and fall to earth. With one hand she applied the riding crop to the youth's behind. With the other she handled his huge tool (a veritable steeple of lust, the Captain mused) and drew it up towards her. To complete this series with its equestrian theme, the horse was unsaddled and Joker was hoisted up and made to lie balanced on his back, his head resting on the rump and his feet almost touching in front of the neck. Gina mounted and stood in the stirrups. Reaching up, her lusty stable lad parted the soft ridges of her sex and pushed up with his hips as she lowered herself and allowed the purple knob to lodge at her entrance. The camera was brought forward to give a closer view of this lascivious conjunction. As soon as the lens cap was replaced, she sank right down to take the strain off her thighs.

'Sorry, love,' said the Captain. 'You'll have to get off him – we can't afford to lose any spunk in these long-exposure shots. Got to save it for the other camera.'

Taking all their equipment with them the party trooped out to a secluded, sunny part of the grounds, a sadly neglected and overgrown rose garden. The next composition, the Captain hoped, would convey a hint of postmodernism at least a century before its time. Four models were selected: Miss MacDonald, Gloria, Darcy and this time Derrick, who set up the camera on its tripod and saw to the focusing and loading but left the removal and replacement of the lens cap to the Captain. As a precaution against the possibility that they might be recognised, the appearances of Miss MacDonald and the two boys was transformed by the use of wigs chosen to contrast with their usual hair styles but to tone in with their pubic curls. Melanie supervised the MacDonald's dressing. The unfortunate woman was squeezed into tightly laced stays stiffened with whalebone and wire; her breasts threatened to burst from their confinement, and the nipples were indeed just visible above the lace trimming the upper edge. The other three participants remained naked, except that Gloria was festooned with strings of beads.

Miss MacDonald was instructed to stand posed to the left of a plaster replica of the Venus de Milo which had been brought down from the attic. Her face was raised, smiling, towards the sky. Her hands were clasped behind her neck, allowing a clear view of the rich scrub adorning her armpits. She supported most of her weight on one foot, the knee of the other leg being slightly bent and her ankles crossed. As a result her slim hips were cocked to one side (Grecian fashion, the Captain said), making them appear broader, and her extensive thatch of dense brown pubic growth was displayed at a jaunty angle. She was supposed to be unaware of the presence, just behind her and not quite hidded by a rose bush, of the naked Darcy, even prettier than usual with his face framed by the ringlets of a Lord Fauntleroy-style wig. The lad stood grinning with his knees bent and his belly thrust forward towards the MacDonald's unsuspecting behind. Both his hands clasped a long, slender rod of flesh, the tip of which almost touched her nearest buttock. But what gave the composition its distinction was a second female figure, that of Gloria. She had been placed in the foreground of the picture and slightly to the left with her back to the photographer. This was where the Captain found a clever use for the second large camera. It had been set up on its tripod with the usual black cloth attached. Gloria now understood why she had not been kitted out with a wig — she was directed to stoop and shove her head under the cloth so that she appeared to be in the act of photographing the posing model and her furtive assailant. The cloth fell to just below her shoulders, contrasing strongly in texture and tone with the nudity of back, bottom and legs. The Captain asked her to stand with her feet apart so that the furry pouch of her sex was fully in view between her thighs. To add a final touch of humour, Derrick, who by now had finished tinkering with the active camera, moved to stand on his stubby legs at what he knew would be the left-hand edge of the picture, preparing his truncheon-like erection for an assault from behind upon this tender female photographer.

As soon as the rampant Derrick heard the Captain count and replace the brass cap on the lens he was galvanised into action like some victim of a Victorian anatomist experimenting with the restorative effects of electrical currents. The great club he had held immobile was now thrust forward as he seized Gloria's flanks and impaled the moist split ripeness. Taken by surprise she reared up with a shriek, upsetting the tripod. Down she fell to her knees, her head still draped with the black cloth. Derrick rogered into her briskly until his facial contortions and agonised groans announced that he had emptied himself. Unceremoniously he got up, dusted the loose grass from his knees and busied himself with the cameras.

An action picture was now called for, so the smaller and more sophisticated apparatus with the leather bellows was used. Derrick explained that a modern one would probably have served just as well, as long as the result was printed on what would pass for prewar photographic paper. But it would be fun for him to use this ancient model. Moreover, the pictures might stand up better to expert examination if the shutter speed and lens angle accorded with the state of the art back in the twenties. He had purchased a suitable film in Upchester. It was, he repeated, the paper for these prints that would present the challenge, but he was confident he could overcome it.

The players in this next tableau were to be Darcy once more, Susie (who was encouraged to help him maintain his erection throughout the run-up to the actual shooting), Joker and Gina. But when the role of the latter couple was outlined to her, Gina declined to cooperate, stuck up her nose and flounced off into the undergrowth, so the Captain called on Carla Merryweather to take her place.

As a necessary preliminary, Miss Muttock devoted some attention to Joker's hefty club, restoring it to full vigour by rolling it briskly between her palms and using her tongue to moisten the tip as it lengthened and projected beyond her hands. Darcy and Susie were then made to kneel facing each other at a distance of about a foot; the boy was told to play with one of his young wife's tiny breasts. Joker had to squat behind her, his penis curving upwards provocatively. He reached round

141

Susie's hips and held her hairless cunt open, which was the part of the operation Gina had objected to. To complete a symmetrical composition, therefore, Carla was positioned behind Darcy, her task being to hold his rigid cock in place. But she was not content just to hold it. Without any prompting, her little hand began to administer a brisk frigging which, at the very instant captured by the camera, resulted in ejaculation — a stream of white come fountained from the bulbous cockhead, landing sqaurely on its succulent target.

The Captain required Darcy's active contribution in yet another picture, but first the lad had to be made stiff again, so some unplanned action was devised in which this might be expected to happen. It was the available costumes that suggested the scenario. The trunk contained some school clothes that must have dated from the turn of the century. Carla and her little friend Anne donned voluminous white blouses and black woollen stockings; over these they wore black gym glips which reached down to below their knees. Darcy, however, made a less modest impression, rigged out in nothing but a black waistcoat and jacket with a broad white Eton collar. Miss Muttock, who was also to play a part and wore her black academic gown and mortar board for the purpose, carefully parted his hair in the middle and patted his bottom. He lay in the long grass, his feet pointing away from the large tripod-mounted camera and his recently activated prick resting limply on his testicles. Anne and Carla then got down on either side of him, their heads level with his genitals. They were told to pull their gym slips right up to their waists, exposing tempting expanses of white girlflesh. At the centre of these expanses were situated Carla's darkly fleeced delta and Anne's tiny triangle of blonde fur, too fair and fine to hide the pretty slit of her snatch. The girls lay on their sides and turned inwards towards Darcy. He placed his hands between their thighs, dug his fingertips firmly into their bottom-cheeks and pressed his thumbs up into their cunts.

And now the Muttock was brought into the picture. Facing the camera, she stood above the three youngsters with her legs wide apart and her gown hanging open to reveal her slim lushness in all its glory. Her hands slid up the insides of her thighs right to the top. She thrust her loins towards the lens and pulled open the lips of her fanny. Without removing his hands from the girls' parts, Darcy jacked himself up on his elbows and stuck out an eager tongue which almost reached the juicy vulva.

In the meantime, Anne and Carla had laid their cheeks on his thighs. They too now extended their tongues but in their case the tips actually reached the goal. As if supported by their feathery touch, Darcy's penis stretched itself up between them. The Captain, his own cock fit to burst, stared at an upside-down image of outrageous lust, but realised there was no way the whole scene could be encompassed in this one shot. Enjoining patience and self-denial on his models and doing his best to set them an example, he slid the plate into the camera, removed and replaced the lens cap, took out the plate and heaved the cumbersome contraption on its tripod round to the side of the group for a second picture. It was only when he had taken another three shots from different angles and used all but the last two of the collodion-coated plates that he finally grabbed Mary Muttock by the hips and drove his rod into her as she stood astride the other three. Immediately, he felt the hot juice welling up his stem and bursting against the neck of her womb. The sensation was exquisite but not to be lingered over − young Darcy's disproportionately large cock showed every appearance of being about to discharge, and it was needed, of course, for the final pair of photographs.

These, it had already been agreed, were to carry captions which Derrick said he could easily write on the developed negative plates. The captions were to read: 'Fanny's First Fuck: Before' and 'Fanny's First Fuck: After'. Miss MacDonald assured the Captain that Darcy and Susie O'Flammery, the models in these pictures, really did look several years younger than their seventeen years. A mere shading of downy fluff sprouted around the root of the boy's stiff-standing prick, and Susie's depilation had been ordered specifically for these pictures. He was laid supine on an artistically draped couch which had been brought out to the rose garden together with a jungle of potted ferns and other indoor plants for greater authenticity. His dark hair had been neatly slicked down on either side of its centre parting. Little Fanny — Susie — parted her lips in a wicked smile as she knelt straddling her partner's thighs and gazed down on him. The wide-brimmed straw hat decorated with a profusion of flowers and robins sat jauntily on the back of her head, and the corkscrew ringlets of a fetching wig cascaded down over her bare shoulders. She wore a frothy cravat forming an extravagant bow beneath her chin, and nothing else but a flimsy white garment trimmed with lace and held up by narrow shoulder straps. This item, which reached to her hips, hung open, pushed right back at the sides to show off the pouting little breastlets with their delicate, puffy nipples and areolas swelling up on either side of the foaming bow.

The Captain handed her a large china doll. Without being told, she cradled it in her arms and pressed its rosebud mouth to one of her teats. Her young lover's hands rested on the tops of her thighs, and framed the hairless split mound. With his index fingers the boy pulled aside the tender layers to allow the plumlike head of his cock to lodge between them. Susie knelt poised, resisting the urge to bear down on it with all her playful force. The Captain, who had snatched Derrick's black-furred bulk from under the black cloth and shoved him aside, took the first shot and winked at the lovers.

For the companion picture, penile insertion and ejaculation were effected. The supposed virgin's head was thrown back, her face contorted in agony or ecstasy, or perhaps a simulated combination of both, and the china baby was held negligently suspended by one foot. She cupped a breastlet, letting the nipple project upwards. Her cuntlips slid right down to meet the short fur at the base of her radiantly happy partner's belly while he heaved up his loins to meet her. The Captain caught his breath as he saw, welling out from the stuffed vagina and spilling into the creases of Darcy's thighs, streams of creamy come. At this point Miss MacDonald hurried forward with a little bottle of cochineal which she sprinkled around the inundated area so that the leakage appeared to be streaked with blood.

The sight proved too much for the Captain. He sprang up on the couch, straddled the dreamy Darcy and bent forward to lick his sopping prickroot. The flat of his tongue worked its way up the girl's slippery slit and lapped over the gleaming bare mound. Then the tip bored into the clitoris. Susie jerked up and subsided back, the top of her head resting on Darcy's knees.

At this moment the Captain too felt a shock as the knob of his erect dick somehow found its way into Darcy's mouth. The boy sucked it. It swelled up even more proudly but the Captain was not inclined to be baulked of his first fuck with Susie since her wedding night. Pulling out of Darcy's lips he moved forward on his knees and gently straightened the girl's legs so that they reached out over Darcy's shoulders. She was lying back on her husband's legs and his half-softened tool was still bathing in her wet sheath. Inflamed by the sight of it disappearing between the pulpy leaves of flesh, the Captain plunged his own manhood in, just above it. Both Susie and Darcy yelled out at the tight fit. As he lay savouring this novel mode of enjoyment, the Captain felt Darcy's cock growing beneath his own and striving to achieve an impossibly vertical angle. Susie's eyes stared up wildly. He could not allow her to be split agonisingly and maybe ruined for future pleasures.

The Captain thrust rapidly. His action at first threatened to be counterproductive, for the friction thus applied to the boy's stem made it even bigger. But suddenly the operation succeeded — both occupants of the young cunt discharged their hot loads simultaneously, even as the girl cried out in her own ecstasy.

NINE

SHE IS COMING, MY OWN, MY SWEET

The Captain had suggested that the new discoveries ought to include some verse, and set Miss MacDonald and Melanie to work on Alfred, Lord Tennyson. Miss MacDonald selected *Maud* as a suitable text. The obvious place for rewriting seemed to be the famous closing lyric of Part One and the opening section of Part Two. The hero would still leave Maud's brother for dead, thinking he had alienated his beloved forever by his action, but the action in the garden would be a little livelier than the perfunctory duel that had satisfied stuffy Lord T.

As a clever variation on what they had done with the other texts, the Captain was keen for this one to be printed rather than handwritten. He made a brief visit to an old accomplice based in Amsterdam who was usually known in the trade as Benny de Bok but sometimes addressed as Kenny. Benny had proved useful a few months back, he explained to Miss MacDonald, when that crazy feminist bitch from Tennessee had ripped three plates out of the unique Banesville exemplar of Aretino's *Postures* and disappeared. At least, this was the official explanation of a costly disaster. The truth of the matter was that the vanishing lady, an unstable scholar who made the headlines a few days later by falling from the Golden Gate bridge, had nothing to do with the theft. The Captain himself, using her visit as a pretext, had removed the priceless plates and arranged for their delivery to the retreat of a high-rolling presidential candidate before raising the alarm.

'And you never got them back?'

'Not the originals. But I was able to do the library a big favour

146

through old Benny. I told the library committee I'd arranged for the purchase of replacements — there are always a few loose pages torn out of rare books floating about if you know where to look — and had them tipped into our copy so expertly you wouldn't notice anything wrong.'

This again, he explained, was not the entire truth. The replacements were not genuine at all, but printed from plates engraved by his Dutch friend, who found such commissions even more lucrative than his usual occupation of running off banknotes direct on his clandestine press. The Captain had made a fair profit on the deal and the University President, the Provost and everyone associated with the library or interested in the integrity of its collections, even Dean Frolander, felt pleased with the outcome. There was, after all, no need to advertise the fact that this priceless volume had been, to use a technical term favoured by the Captain, *sophisticated*. The constituent parts, they all believed, were genuine; it was just that they had been put together to disguise the fact that the original plates had gone missing.

Benny de Bok reacted enthusiastically when the Tennyson project was put to him. He was always keen to get his hands on real greenbacks; whatever you said, they somehow felt more reassuring than the ones that fell from his press. The old bugger with the beard, he pointed out, was an ideal target because of his practice of having a few copies of a trial edition printed for each of his major works so that he could see what it would look like in print. *Maud* was no exception, but they would make it exceptional by producing what purported to be an *earlier* trial edition including the 'newly discovered' rejected passages.

The Captain left and Bent Benny bent his back to the business of typesetting, working carefully through the eight hundred and fifty genuine lines that detailed the hero's recollected infatuation with the desirable but haughty Maud. At that point he abandoned the copy he was using and proceeded with the Cunlip version.

Come into the garden, Maud,
    For the black bat, night, has flown,
Come into the garden, Maud,
    I am here at the gate alone;
And the musk of my manhood is wafted abroad
    From a limb that has quiver'd and grown.

For a breeze of morning moves,
    And the planet of Love is on high,
Beginning to faint in the light that she loves
    On a bed of daffodil sky,
As Maud will faint in the arms she loves
    After feeling my hand on her thigh.

All night have the roses heard
    The flute, violin, bassoon;
All night has the casement jessamine stirr'd
    To the dancers dancing in tune;
Till the dancers, hearing the waking bird,
    Are tranc'd in an amorous swoon.

I said to the lily, 'There is but one
    With whom she is yearning to be.
When will the dancers leave her alone?
    She is weary of all but me.'
But soon the guests at the Hall will be gone,
    And I wait, a-tremble, to see
My Maud dance out down the steps of stone
    On feet that are light and free.

I said to the rose, 'The brief night goes
    In revels that sicken and cloy,
O young lord-lover, what sighs are those
    For one thou shalt never enjoy?
But I alone,' so I swore to the rose,
    'Shall make her my plaything, my toy.'

And the soul of the rose went into my blood,
    As the dancers gyrated their hips;

And long by the garden lake I stood,
    And dream'd of your passionate lips;
I remember'd that time in the lakeside wood
    Where I kiss'd your bare breasts at the tips.

Queen rose of the rosebud garden of girls,
    Come hither on dancing toes;
Then lift your gown to reveal the curls
    Around your unopened rose;
My essence will spurt in dewy pearls,
    To moisten the bud that grows
And blooms when the flower of your lust unfurls,
    To tremble in passionate throes.

My breath will come bubbling fast and thick
    As my club rises stout and blunt;
I will stoop to the seam of your sex, and lick
    From the rear approach to the front,
Tickle the lips till they lie back slick
    And both of us gurgle and grunt.
Then at last my potent prince of a prick
    Will plunder the depths of your cunt.

There has fallen a shower of seed
    From my loins, aspersing her womb.
She bucks like a hard-spurr'd seed
    As my hot-blooded prick slams home;
The red rose cries, 'She writhes in her need;'
    And the white rose weeps, 'Will she bloom?'
The larkspur whispers, 'I see her bleed;'
    And the lily sighs, 'She has come.'

She is coming, my own, my sweet;
    Once more she is meeting my thrust.
She kicks with her dainty feet
    As she wriggles and squirms in the dust;
My pego is roused by her heat
    As I rip all the lace from her bust;
In purple and red this teat,
    And then that, will blossom with lust.

Before getting on with Part Three, Benny conceived a refinement of the scheme which he was sure the Captain would approve. His finer instincts and literary tact told him that Victorian scholars would have grave difficulty in acknowledging effusions of this colour as the work of the high-minded and squeamish laureate. Any danger of exposure would be avoided, and the market value might even be enhanced, if this trial edition were subtly got up to look like one of the forgeries of the notorious Thomas J. Wise. Wise's *Bibliography of the Writings of Tennyson,* published in 1908, was still valued as a tool of scholarship despite the known fact that Wise had tried to authenticate his own Tennyson forgeries by listing them in it. The absence of the Cunlip trial edition of *Maud* from the list, Benny reckoned, could be passed off as Wise's masterstroke.

Fearing eventual exposure and realising that a text as outrageous as this one might attract attention that would bring the whole edifice of his creative endeavours toppling down, the devious old rascal had deliberately omitted his *Maud* from the bibliography, thus dissociating it from his name. Either it or his other forgeries might be discredited, but hardly both. Benny, of course, had other tricks, of a typographical nature too technical to be briefly described, which would re-establish the link and bathe Wise's well-deserved posthumous disgrace in an even more lurid glow, without the need to disccredit Queen Victoria's favourite bard.

He returned to the labour of typesetting the remaining pages of the poem, in which Tennyson had portrayed the madness that overtook the hero on fleeing the country under the impression that he had killed Maud's brother — the evil brother who had been determined that she should marry the wealthy upstart lord whose wealth he coveted. Eleven lines into the text he switched to the copy the Captain had left with him.

. . . For she, sweet soul, had hardly spoken a word,
When her brother ran in his rage to the gate,
He came with the babe-faced lord;
Heap'd on her terms of disgrace,
And while she wept, and I strove to be cool,
He fiercely gave me the lie,

Till I with as fierce an anger spoke,
And he struck me, madman, over the face,
Struck me before the languid fool,
Who was gaping and grinning by:
Struck for himself an evil stroke;
Wrought for his house an irredeemable woe.
Then, seizing Maud, he ripp'd from her back the gown
With every shred that cover'd her maiden shame,
And tore and twisted the fabric into strips.
While he and the pamper'd lordling held me down,
They tied me securely, bidding me watch the game.
I cried out loud, but they threaten'd my Maud with
  whips,
Tickled the peeping tips
Of the milk-white breasts that had known
But the touch of one man, one man, and that man I,
Her destin'd love, who had fondled her free of blame.
Her brother tweak'd the flesh of each smooth-curv'd
  thigh
And wantonly laid his hands on her swelling hips
As trembling she stood with her back to the garden
  gate;
From the front of his breeches there leapt a monstrous
  wand
Which nuzzled and sullied the lips
Of love that pouted 'mid shadowy curls.
And now, with incestuous hand,
He open'd the sweet nether mouth to admit the beast
That gluts on the virginal juices of innocent girls
And gorges their fragrant flesh, a voluptuous feast.
His rod ramm'd home, and his unbutton'd breeches fell
From his flanks as his pamper'd friend, the effeminate
  lord
Stripp'd naked, flaunting a slender sword
Of flesh, which sprang forth to stand
At the base of a belly reeking of costly scents
Smear'd into its girlish skin to dispel
And disguise the ranker odours exhal'd
From a myriad pores, foul vents

For the festering lust within.
And now, as her brother invaded my dear,
And drove ever up her, filling the new-broach'd flask
Of desire with the boiling, bubbling seed of sin,
His sleek accomplice stoop'd to the task
Of boring open her brother's tunnel of vice
That slyly wink'd from between the globes
Of lard which heav'd as he hammer'd and fuck'd
And ravish'd my Maud, and I knew that two lecherous
   probes
Were pumping, one slender but deeply trench'd
In unspeakable soil, the other manly and thick,
Embedded within the cunt I had lately drench'd
With a passionate flood from my own unsullied prick.
I burst my bonds in a trice
And rose, and launch'd a furious, forceful kick
At the lord's backside, sending him howling in pain
Out of the garden he never would enter again.
The brother turn'd, still dripping with scummy seed,
And bending, from one of my feet I pluck'd
The only weapon I had, the trusty shoe,
Which I aim'd at the lecher's astonish'd head, and threw.
He fell to the dust with a cry; I saw him bleed.
Then, pierc'd by the look in Maud's eye, at once I
   knew
I had quench'd the light of my life with this vengeful
   deed.

On receiving the slim pamphlet, fresh from Benny's press, the Captain pasted one of Sir Julius Cunlip's bookplates on the reverse of the title page. That evening he lay in Mary Muttock's bed perusing this forged trial edition with her, Miss MacDonald and Melanie. They found both the concept of the production and its execution so sexy that the four of them linked together in an oral-genital chain to celebrate its completion. The Captain's prick was in Melanie's mouth, the MacDonald's tongue in Melanie's cunt, Miss Muttock's lips and teeth gripped the MacDonald's plump pussy, while the Captain licked along the Muttock's sexual cleft. By using their hands to lash the buttocks of the partner nearest their faces they contrived to regulate the speed of this operation, driving each other inexorably to a simultaneous orgasm. Unfortunately, Miss MacDonald's ministrations to Melanie were so effective that the girl, in her moment of crisis, allowed the Captain's spouting cock to slip from her mouth. Several large slugs of semen landed on the open pages of the pseudo-*Maud*. The Captain merely laughed, cynically pointing out that Sir Julius Cunlip might well be supposed to have left such marks on what he would have considered the jewel of his collection, had it existed in his time. In any case, he added, whatever scientific checks the Banesville experts applied to these pages were unlikely to include tests for DNA.

TEN

PARTY TIME

Preoccupied with a rather ill-tempered diatribe that had just been forced on him by his superior, Dean Frolander, the Captain wandered back to the Department of Reserved Collections. It was now late May and he had been back in Banesville for several weeks without having raised the question of the Cunlip discoveries with the dean. Frolander was a larger-than-life bookman of the old school — a bull-necked, bullet-headed bibliographical bully of choleric temperament, who saw all issues in terms of black, white and red. With careful management it was to be hoped that the red might be thinned down to rose-tinted pink. It seemed, however, that the Captain's only common ground with Frolander was their shared belief that access to the Reserved Collections should be restricted to a few hand-picked students and scholars. To be sure, they would have picked quite different ones and on quite different grounds. And their reasons for wishing to keep the doors of the department locked were in sharp contrast. The Captain took a perverse interest in the way those selected for admission to his Palace of Fantasies reacted under the corrupting influences to which, under his private supervision, they were exposed. Frolander, on the other hand, was simply ashamed that his fine library harboured such depraved material, and resented the extent to which the fame of the university itself rested on these embarrassing holdings.

'Any developments?' he asked Gloria Sweetbutts, now installed as a semipermanent fixture in his office.

'Two freshers with written permission from Professor

Packard. One of the girls who gave you the eye down in the cafeteria yesterday. And a guy who must be her boyfriend.'

'Her boyfriend? How do you know that?'

'I guess I could tell from the way they kept kinda touching each other. Like they were so attached they couldn't even go to the john by themselves? I wanted her to wait while he went into the stacks to fetch their books but she insisted on going along with him.'

'I thought I told you,' the Captian said, laying a hand on his assistant's bottom and peering intensely into her eyes. 'Unless there's a very special reason, which I alone can decide, you ask all readers to wait in the reading room — the Palace of Fantasies. Then you fetch their books or pictures for them. That's entirely consistent with the dean's policy — calls it his CHI.'

'His CHI?'

'Cultural Hygiene Initiative.'

'And which dean would this be?'

'Why, Dean Frolander, of course. I've just been in conference with him. In fact I've just invited him to our party to soften him up for the big one.'

Gloria smiled and kissed his cheek. 'Dr Frolander's no dean. You been with us two semesters and you don't know that? Deans are heads of faculties. It's his name, like we have guys called Earl and Dook and Prince and King? They're just regular guys, not like your royals — we're a democracy, I guess, a free country.'

The Captain wondered whether the uncalled-for familiarity this misunderstanding must have sometimes occasioned in his dealings with Frolander had been harmful or beneficial to his own standing. Most Americans went straight into first-name terms to ingratiate themselves or make you feel obligated, as they would say. Frolander had always treated him with cool or blustering formality, but maybe that was just because the Captain was careful to keep his own real name to himself. So as not to lose face, he decided he would stick to his habit of addressing the university librarian as Dean.

Pinching Gloria's behind, he winked down at her. 'Yes, I've noticed this is supposed to be a democracy. But not so demo-

155

cratic, I hope, that we've no respect for what those in authority decree. Where do you think those kids have got to now — what books did they want?'

'Well, that's the problem. This is why they didn't want me to go fetch them? Professor Packard had told them to look at something called *The Altar of Venus*, but then to browse round all the novels in that section to see what they could find for the paper they're writing.'

Pausing only to slide his flash gun into the hotshoe of the Leica already slung round his neck, the Captain marched off into the narrow aisles between the stacks with Gloria hurrying along behind him. Soon they reached a place where it was possible to remove a couple of books from the shelves and peer through into a wider and brighter space.

The tussling couple silhouetted against the window were already partially undressed; clothes were scattered on the floor. Both still wore their baseball caps, and the tall young man sported a sweat shirt emblazoned with the glorious name of the Banesville Butchers. His long legs and white buttocks were bare, and a red-capped club stood up sportingly from the dark scrub at the base of his belly. His girlfriend's lower limbs were hugged by snugly-fitting pants of green cord, the bottoms tucked into white boots. Above the waist she was palely naked apart from the flaming red hair that tumbled down over her shoulders and pert little breasts. The Captain registered that, although she was in no sense fat, her arms were graced with an inviting roundness and the waistband of her pants cut slightly into the flesh. She was defending herself valiantly as her partner tried to pin her against the window.

'Give me a break, Warren,' she was gasping. 'I told you — you could do it over my boobs or have me give head. But no way do I get to take these pants off.'

The Captain heard Gloria's hushed voice at his shoulder. 'I guess that's outright sexual harassment he's laying on her,' she breathed. He turned to look at her and was amazed to see her already stripped to her black underwear and stockings.

'Get in there,' he whispered, 'make sure the story has a happy ending.'

Gloria needed no encouragement. Her knickers were peeled

off even as he spoke, leaving her in black bra, suspender belt and stockings. He was grateful for the peck on his cheek before she ran off up the narrow aisle, disappearing at the end as she turned to hurry back on the other side of the shelves. And there she was once more, right in front of him. The couple were too taken up with each other to notice her until she was right on them, and the rampant Warren was thrown off his guard when she grabbed his shoulders and threw him sideways against the bookshelves.

Her next action, though, was even more unexpected. Standing with her back to the red-headed girl and her feet apart, Gloria reached her arms straight up above her head. Then, with consummate athleticism, she leaned right back until her hands found and supported her on the girl's hips. Framed by white flesh and the black suspenders and stocking tops, a chestnut-coloured thicket of hairs was thrust towards the youth, whose nostrils widened with desire. As Gloria strained back and up, her outer labia fell apart and even from the Captain's distance the scarlet slit of the inner petals was visible as they too divided. Warren grabbed her by the flanks and plunged his lance into her. Then, without further ado, he began to stab it furiously in and out.

The rather bewildered girlfriend, who had been vaguely toying with the black silk cups of Gloria's bra, reached forward with both hands. The fingers of her left one closed round the base of the young man's cock, now slippery with cuntjuice, to squeeze it as it rogered Gloria. With her right one she rummaged through the chestnut curls until she located the little hood at the head of the slit, and began to work the hardened bud of flesh hidden beneath it.

This onslaught was too much for Gloria, who threw her head back even further in wild abandon. In doing so, she transferred so much of her weight to her hands that she started to drag the other girl's trousers down over her hips and buttocks. The zip at the front was forced open, revealing lacy white panties, but these too were dragged down with the outer garment. A fiery red triangle of close-trimmed hair came into view. Because the girl's feet were slightly apart, the downward slide stopped halfway down her rounded thighs. Gloria hung there with her braided hair touching the ground. Already at full stretch and tensed in anticipation of her approaching climax, she made the supreme effort and pulled herself up the couple of inches needed to lodge the tip of her tongue in the pussy just above it.

For some minutes the Captain's flies had been open and his tool pumped up to bursting point in his hand. Just in time, he remembered his responsibility for the safekeeping of the books in front of him. He was relieved to see Gloria's discarded black knickers draped where they had fallen, over the spine of a hardback limited edition of *Adventures of a Naked Girl* on the bottom shelf. He sniffed the skimpy garment and wrapped it securely round the bulb of his prick, holding it in place with one hand as a precaution against uncontrolled spillage. His other hand was sufficient to operate the camera. It made a welcome change to be photographing for fun, for his private collection, rather than for profit.

Warren roared out as his seed gushed into the convulsing Gloria, whose licking and sucking simultaneously brought the redhead to tumultuous orgasm. At the selfsame moment the Captain flooded thickly into his PA's panties, and a blinding flash left the surprised trio stunned on the floor.

The party had been progressing fairly quietly for about half an hour. The Captain was throwing it in his spacious downtown apartment. Some twenty guests were boring each other in pairs and little groups while they tried to absorb enough alcohol to lower their own thresholds of boredom. Informal dress was the order of the day, but the denim-clad Captain observed that most of the men were wearing suits, or at least immaculate and expensive leisure wear, like that stuck-up Wayne Packard rigged out in his pathetic, sanitised affectation of English squiredom. And as for the women, well, they certainly looked attractive − but the dresses they were wearing were not the kind of thing they sported on campus.

Most of these people were casual acquaintances on the faculty, including, of course, Packard and Frolander, the latter being the Captain's target on this occasion. He had also invited a sprinkling of students, mainly so that the couple who had behaved so entertainingly in the library the other day would not

feel out of things. Their names, he had ascertained, were Warren
S. Buckmaster Junior and Coralmay Connochie. Unlike the
faculty members, most of students had turned up in their worka-
day clothes. It struck the Captain that with the exception of
Wayne Packard, who was staring intently into the eyes of a
sultry sophomore, the teachers showed no inclination to
fraternise with their students.

The Captain moved round the room filling glasses. He had
mixed large quantities of cocktail − a sidecar, so stiff it could
have supported his Harley-Davidson − and hoped that a constant
trickle of this potion down Frolander's throat would soften him
into amenability.

Right now, though, Frolander was tied up in some sort of
intellectual brawl with a sharp-faced woman from Social
Anthropology. The Captain's eyes swivelled and came to rest
on Wayne Packard, who by this time was holding forth
magisterially to Warren and Coralmay. By pretending to listen
to the drivellings of a deaf old trout standing next to them, their
wily host was able to overhear this lecture. Packard seemed to
be discussing the paper he had set both of them on the books
they had looked for in Reserved Collections.

'But these reprints of older works are honeycombed with
typos,' he was saying.

'Excuse me?' interjected Warren.

Packard rolled up his eyes at the boy's ignorance. 'Typos are
misprints. Take *The Altar of Venus*. If you remember, there's
an interesting textual crux at the foot of page one hundred. The
narrator has been watching that blue movie showing the rape
of the virgin Eva, right? At the end we're told the screen is
darkened. Then − and I quote from memory − ''The
spectators, impressed by the terrible realism of the representation, whisper hushed commentaries. The cheer is again
illuminated, and before us, bowing and smiling, we see the
characters.'' How can a *cheer* be illuminated? You could
imagine the audience cheering if they weren't hushed like that,
right? But I've used a statistical wordcount analysis to . . .'

'It must be *sheet*,' Coralmay interrupted. 'They used a sheet
to screen the movie. How does the next bit go, when the
characters disappear one by one, leaving Eva until the last?'

Somewhat taken aback, Packard consulted his cerebral data bank and continued. ' "Smiling, she raises her dress waist high. There are no undergarments to obstruct the view. With her dress elevated fan-wise on either side of her, she undulates her hips with circular, rolling movements, projecting her gentials outward voluptuously. Then she drops her skirt, kisses her fingers to us daintily, and disappears.'' Strong stuff, I guess.'

Packard sipped his sidecar and gazed into Coralmay's eyes, making a point of ignoring Warren. He needed to regain the initiative he had come near to losing. 'An interesting problem on page one hundred thirty-eight,' he enthused nasally, letting his eyes drop to the nipples now poking up pertly through the thin stretch of Coralmay's pale blue T-shirt. 'Irma and the narrator pick up the little flower-seller Lucille and have her round to their apartment. Now there's a rule in the British reprint trade that everyone has to be at least sixteen. But here we have an anomaly. Even allowing for the later onset of puberty in those days, the hairless smoothness of Lucille's . . .' (he looked round, lowered his voice and allowed the back of his free hand to brush against the plump mound that seemed to be pleading for the zipper of Coralmay's green cords to be eased down) 'the smoothness of her, um, *pudendum muliebre* – or should I say *puellare*? – could indicate that she is quite a bit younger than sixteen in the original version. And my suspicion that something may have been omitted from the episode featuring her is prompted by the description of her nakedness when she's been stripped for a bath. Reluctant to remove her panties before a male spectator, she's reassured by Irma, remember, who says, '' 'Never mind him, darling. He's a nice man.' – Off came the small garment, and Lucille was naked in the presence of her hosts. Like them, this child was immature''. *Like them?* But they, her hosts, were certainly not immature, as you appreciate. There must have been some reference to other young girls at this orgy, and I'm doing my durndest to unearth the original version. I'm writing this paper, my dear – *Emasculating the Text: Signs of the Censor's Scissors'*.

Warren had stood by resentfully throughout this spiel but now faced Packard squarely and addressed him. 'You been assuming some guardian of morality's gotten in there with scissors and snipped away the juicy bits, Professor Packard? Let me tell you something. These guys that write the stuff, when they negotiate the really hot passages they get the horn and go kinda crazy with it. And the same happens to the copy-editors who read it and the typesetters and the proof-readers. They're so steamed up they don't get to see these glitches. You need to be impotent to spot them!' He took Coralmay by the elbow and led her away. The Captain saw him fiddle with the latch of the sliding glass door and lead her out to the deck.

Frolander had finished with the social anthropologist and was toting an empty glass. The host hurried across to him to dispense another half pint of sidecar and raise the little matter of his recent 'discoveries', but his boss held a large hand over his glass. 'Whaddyer mean by it, Haggler?' he snarled.

The Captain was at a loss but not surprised to find himself once more at odds with this blustering intellectual lumberjack. His rage now, the Captain soon ascertained, was to do with his belated discovery that six thousand dollars had been charged to library funds, without consultation, for the purchase of the *Don Juan* fragment back in February. The Captain protested that he was supposed to control his own departmental budget, but his superior maintained that any disbursement over five thousand dollars had to be cleared by the Library Committee.

'Just wait a minute, now, Dean,' the Captain shouted above the background of bored conversation and forced laughter. 'This was a unique opportunity.'

'You could have asked the vendor for twenty-four hours' grace and come to discuss it with me, dammit.'

'I asked for forty-eight hours. She — I mean he — gave me ten minutes. *Ten minutes*!'

Frolander might be pig-headed as well as bullet-headed, but the concept of fairness was not totally alien to him, not when there was no way of dodging it. He stood pensively, sucking his lips and boring a finger into one of his ears. 'Well, in that case ...'

'And there's no question of the find's authenticity. It's Byron's hand, and the, er, paper's contemporary — it's, er, counter-marked *Joseph Coles 1818*.'

'No, I ain't questioning that. I had it checked out by Professor

161

Packard. He can sure tell a hawk from a handsaw. Yeah, he wanted us to display a photocopy of it — with the unacceptable words blanked out, of course — in our exhibit in the reception area. But I told him I couldn't sanction that. We have to think of the young unmarried women among the student body. And their parents, too — many of them are powerful and generous alumni. He saw that at once. Said we ought not to place financial considerations above the propagation of scholarly truth, but in his view the purity of American womanhood was to be prized above all else. Those were his words, Haggler.'

The Captain saw an opportunity for flattery. 'That's a very good point, sir,' he said, 'and one well worth making, I would have thought. You have my full support in taking a firm stand on such an issue. Yes, you demonstrated sound judgment there.'

That smooth operator Packard, he told himself, was nothing but a pompous, cold-hearted seducer who treated his admiring female students with sadistic contempt. In matters of scholarly discrimination Wayne Packard might be able to sort out his hawks from his handsaws, but when it came to bedroom behaviour (if it ever got that far) the chicks had better watch out for the chainsaw.

Frolander was droning on. 'Well, I certainly hope so, Dr Haggler. I may not have taken any of those new-fangled courses in personnel management you been telling me about, but I do see myself as something of psychologist. I know how easy it is to damage the minds and emotions of young people by exposing them to corruption? You and me gonna get on fine. Just fine. Birds of a feather. We'll get on fine just as long as you remember this: from now on, any acquisition over five thousand absolutely must be referred to me. That's mandatory. In an emergency just call me. If the line's busy, speak to Packard.'

Without bothering to ask, the Captain poured more of the potent brew into Frolander's empty glass and steered him out to the deck. As he had expected, the only people out there in the early evening sun were Warren and Coralmay and, as he had half expected, the young man had rolled up the red-headed girl's T-shirt to give his lips access to her large but well-formed

162

bosom. As he sucked, his hand was busy inside the fly of her pants and maybe inside what he found in there. Coralmay caught sight of the new arrivals, pushed her beau away and adjusted her clothing. The couple were about to slink back to the party without a word but Frolander raised a hand to detain them.

'Hey, you guys, don't let minor interruptions take the wind out of your sails,' he bellowed. 'Get to my age, there won't be no wind — leastways, not that kind. Wanna be private? Well, I'm sure Dr Haggler here will have locked any rooms he don't want his guests fooling around in. Go geddit, baby. Enjoy.'

Dean Frolander appeared to be mellowing. It proved quite easy to engage his interest in the momentous find at Cunlip Hall and he listened attentively when the Captain related how he had negotiated favourable terms for a private sale to the university. His answers to Frolander's predictable questions were well rehearsed. The current owner, he explained, shunned publicity. If she took the goods to auction it would be difficult for her to maintain anonymity, as their authentication depended on the Cunlip connection. Moreover, since an export licence would be unobtainable for what would surely be seen as a kind of national treasure (even if it was in reality more of a national disgrace) the price reached at auction would be well below Banesville's capabilities.

'So we're talking what kind of figure, Haggler?'

'Two million dollars.'

Frolander seemed relieved and immediately undertook to set up a commission of scholars who would accompany the Captain to England to scrutinise the new find. The Captain objected to the choice of Professor Packard as leader of this commission, suggesting that an outsider might be more suitable.

'I got just the lady,' said Frolander, clapping him on the back. 'Dee Dee Burdle from UCLA? She's a fine bibliographer and a cute cookie. You'll get on real dandy together. But I just thought of something. You say we couldn't get an export licence. So how we gonna get the stuff out of the country?'

'No sweat. Our commissioners bring it back in their baggage. Discreetly. We'll book them on different flights.'

'OK. But when everything's set up here we need to go public, eh?'

163

'I've worked out a story to cover that. We'll say that before he died Sir Julius Cunlip sold his collection to an American connoisseur who shipped it over here. We bought it from the great-grandson, who chooses to remain anonymous.'

After drinking to their understanding the two men returned to the party. Spirits seemed to be flagging, or perhaps people were just getting too hungry on the diet of insubstantial snacks and powerful cocktails. Most of the students had already slipped away. Now that their host was back in the room, everyone else, led by Wayne Packard, took turns to utter slurred thanks before slipping out into the summer evening. Repeatedly calling the Captain Dr Haggler in a loud voice to dispel any impression, however correct, that she might be cohabiting with him, Gloria justified her failure to depart with the others by audibly offering to remain behind and help clear away the glasses. Most of the male guests of all age groups were keen to stay and assist her but the Captain was emphatic in showing them to the door.

Left alone with Gloria he told her of the promising developments with Frolander. While explaining what had been agreed, he unzipped her close-fitting black dress and peeled it off her. Gloria reached behind to unclip her transparent black bra while her dissertation supervisor knelt and drew the matching panties down. The dark shading between her thighs sprang out as a fluffy bush of brown hair and her lithe body stood before him, its bareness exaggerated by the black girdle and stockings he left in place for his pleasure. The odour of freshening cuntflesh assailed his nostrils but, instead of diving into the pouting cleft she offered, he stood up. In a flash he was out of his own clothes and held her in his arms. His tumid knob nuzzled her belly; he forced it down so that the shaft pressed into her moist trench.

Gloria broke away from him and skipped out of the room. The Captain followed and entered the bedroom. He found her standing at the foot of the bed, unseen by the naked couple already on it. Warren Buckmaster lay on his back with his feet dangling down to the floor. He was being ridden by Coralmay, who knelt astride his hips. As she dipped her head to the lad's lips and her bottom rose in its pumping, Warren's thick white cylinder of flesh, slick with her seepings, could be seen slipping

164

in and out between his balls and her sexlips. The Captain winked at Gloria and gestured to indicate what he had in mind.

So as to evade the notice of the mutually engrossed couple, Gloria kept her distance as she moved around the bed before stepping forward and mounting it. Then she crawled on splayed knees until the only thing that prevented her from planting a cuntkiss on Warren's mouth was Coralmay's stooped head. The Captain stood between Warren's hanging feet and leaned down to feel for Coralmay's plump breasts; these he used as handles to pull her gently but firmly into an upright position. At the same time, Gloria edged forward, parted her chestnut curls and spread her moist sex over Warren's face.

If the youthful couple were astonished by these developments they did not show it. Perhaps, the Captain surmised, the act of fucking in which they were engaged attuned them to all the varieties of lechery, of which they had inherited an instinctive genetic memory. Be that as it might, the two girls now inclined their upper bodies towards each other, embraced and began a prolonged kiss. At the same time Warren's hand went up to rummage beween their breasts as they bounced and rubbed together. His tongue lapped thirstily at the pink petals of flesh which had already smeared their nectar all over his face. He alternated broad strokes with hard jabs up into the entrance of Gloria's vagina.

Still standing between Warren's feet, the Captain placed his palms on Coralmay's buttocks and pulled them apart. He could not help dribbling at the sight now exposed. A string of saliva landed right on the puckered pink arsehole. Enraptured, the Captain continued to drool. The tilted well could contain no more. His spittle overflowed and ran down the sexual gash until it coated Warren's bulging testes.

It was not an instinctive genetic memory that triggered the Captain's next move, but the recollection of something he had got Gloria to read aloud to him that same morning as she sat on his lap in the Palace of Fantasies, her skirt up round her waist and her knickers down to her knees – a passage from the Victorian classic *The Romance of Lust*. On a lonely beach the boy narrator had been screwing the elder of his young sisters. Just as he discharged he said to her, 'Did not that feel delicious, and was it not up to the hilt?' At that instant a stranger's voice was heard to respond: 'I should think so, with such a rammer as that up her cunt.' The stranger introduced himself and was soon fucking and buggering the three siblings in turn and together. When they all met the next day the elder sister was made to stand guard while the stranger fucked the younger one; at the same time the boy was told to drive his reinvigorated prick up the girl's back passage so that she was doubly impaled. This, according to the author, was the youngsters' first lesson in the 'double fuck'.

That example vividly in his mind, the Captain transferred some of the saliva to the shaft of his cock — the bulb was already well lubricated with his own oiliness. He now reached forward and placed one hand on Gloria's thigh to support him as he used the other one to guide his tool until the blunt tip pressed throbbing against Coralmay's anus. To get a better purchase he transferred both hands to the creases of Coralmay's crotch, pinching her clitoris between the joints of his thumbs as he bored into her. Suddenly the ring of tight muscle relaxed and his entry was unimpeded. Fully embedded inside her, his belly and chest in close contact with her firm back, he realised that there was no need for further movement on his part. Separated from it only by the girl's internal membranes, he felt the ridged thickness of the underside of Warren's cock against his own as he was forced up and down by Coralmay's preclimactic heaves. The youth's erect member was masturbating him.

But he had no more than a few seconds to savour this fact before the highly unstable quartet exploded in a succession of orgasms so rapid as to be almost simultaneous. The contractions of Gloria's cunt on Warren's tongue as she came caused the lad to shoot his load straight up into Coralmay's quim. The passionate fury of Gloria's kissing brought the other girl to climax just as she received her boyfriend's spunk. The combined effect of contemplating this train of events and feeling the final swelling and pulsing of Warren's huge rod against his own drove the Captain to a frenzy. Wave upon wave of hot come welled up his cock into the tight sheath that squeezed it so indecently. Coralmay shrieked with joy and rolled over on her side; Gloria and the Captain collapsed on top of her and Warren, and the foursome smeared the leaking semen over each other's bodies, wondering what the next move would be.

They slept before it came.

ELEVEN

HIGH FLYERS

Cruising at thirty-one thousand feet with a stiff tailwind behind him and a stiff cock in front, the Captain was on a high in more senses than the literal one, whichever that is. Only a week after Frolander undertook to set up his commission of authentication, here they were heading for Cunlip Hall, six sharp bibliographers (seven including the Captain, whose status on this mission was somewhat ambiguous) led by the tall, impeccably groomed Dee Dee Burdle. The Captain had approached Dee Dee as an old buddy when she joined the rest of them at the airport but Wayne Packard had elbowed him out of the way and laid claim to her possessively. Dee Dee now occupied a window seat on the right of the wide-bodied jet with Packard beside her and a lager-drinking heavy between Packard and the gangway. A few rows back the Captain sat on the inner side of the same gangway. On his left sat Dr Phyllis F. Carton, a dried-up old toad from Manuscripts and Rare Boooks. To his relief she seemed to be completely involved in scholarly disputation with her portly colleague Cameron Meldrop, who insisted on addressing her as 'my dear lady'. Right up front and over to the left he could glimpse Gloria Sweetbutts, a little bit out of things on this occasion as she was travelling with them in her PA capacity. Somewhere behind, out of the Captain's field of vision, were Randle Fargo and Lindy Simmering. These were possibly the sexiest couple in the party and it was to be hoped they had not already paired off irretrievably.

The cabin lights were dimmed as the in-flight movie began to roll. It seemed to be some sentimental crap about this visually impaired guy and his 'seeing eye' dog. The Captain rose from his seat and ambled up the aisle towards the toilets at the rear, glad to stretch his legs and uncramp his guts.

Surprisingly, only one person was waiting to relieve himself and this gentleman was able to take over the closet even as the Captain approached. No sooner had that door closed than the adjacent one opened. Framed in the narrow doorway stood the tall, distinguished Victorian scholar Lindy Simmering, a ravishing apparition at any altitude but now, grinning playfully at the Captain, the most desirable of heavenly bodies. She wore a cool linen costume of pale lilac. At her throat a frothy lace cravat repeated the scarlet of her lipstick, blouse and stockings. Only her fine flaxen hair, centrally parted and hanging straight to just below shoulder level, diverged from this theme of mauve offset by red.

'Hi!' said Lindy.

'Hi!' the Captain replied.

No further preliminaries seemed called for between these two kindred spirits sailing high above the clouds. Down on the ground they had never exchanged more than the most perfunctory of greetings. Yet the Captain's privates had stirred in anticipation when Dean Frolander named Professor Simmering as a member of the commission. And here she was, giving him the eye and wordlessly inviting him into the tiny closet. He stepped forward and reached behind him to shut the door.

The facilities provided on aircraft are so cramped that some agility is required to perform even the natural functions for which they were designed. To use them for the relief of other bodily needs presents a real challenge, as countless readers will have discovered. The Captain rose to meet this challenge but the very size of his erection, stretching out horizontally from his open fly, still further restricted his freedom to manoeuvre. He tried to turn round so that he could sit on the childishly low lavatory with the lady on his lap but found himself wedged between the walls.

Lindy, however, seemed to have been here before and pushed him back against the door. She lifted the hem of her pleated skirt, bringing it right up above her waist. Her bright red stockings were supported by a skimpy red girdle. The tops of her rounded thighs, her hips and her lower belly were now presented to the Captain's hands in all their gorgeous whiteness — she wore no concealing undergarment. Because the couple were obliged to stand so close together, the full visual impact could not be properly appreciated until she hoisted herself gingerly on to the stainless steel washbasin, wincing slightly at the coldness of the metal.

Her sex, the Captain now saw, was bare not only of knickers but also of hair. Between her thightops the fleshy mons asserted itself arrogantly, split by a narrow double line that matched the pale mauve of her costume. With slender scarlet-nailed fingers she peeled the leaves apart. The sticky inner moistness that now released its heavy fragrance was puffed full of blood, a glossier version of the colour of her stockings.

The Captain moved forward to close the couple of inches separating the tip of his prick from this open invitation. But Lindy placed her hands on his shoulders and pushed him down. His knees bent with a cracking of under-exercised sinews and he found himself squatting uncomfortably with his face masked by slippery cunt. This, he thought, was a moment he would remember the next time someone asked him to press the flesh.

Any discomfort in his knees and thighs was temporarily forgotten as he threw himself into the task of working Lindy up into a rapturous lather. When the wetness of her twat and the powerful squeezing of her thighs round his head indicated that she was beginning to experience the throes of orgasm, he dragged himself to his feet and stuck the head of his bursting cock in among the slackened folds of cuntflesh he had been ransacking with his tongue. The leaves closed hot around him and he nudged forward. Moving into her like a thumb pushed into soft butter his manhood doubled its thickness. His forward progress, boring through the pulsing pulp of her feminity, seemed endless; the deeper he probed the more tightly her living sheath was stretched as he swelled and swelled, a process which impeded the penetration and at the same time enhanced the sensations of exquisite pleasure. He paused a moment and felt the spasms of that tight-crammed cunt undulating along his member. Then he dug his fingers hard into Lindy Simmering's buttocks, braced his legs and lunged forward to sleeve his whole length. Just as his wiry hair was crushed against the shaven smoothness of her pubis, the delicious outer constriction of tight cunt on swollen cock was complemented by the inner distension of his urethra — a massive infusion of seminal fluid blasted along it in a jetting, high-pressure eruption demanding accommodation in the innermost recesses of her womb. The Captain had now joined the legendary Mile High Club.

Consciousness of the outer world began to return. Neither partner had uttered a word during this brief encounter after the initial 'Hi', but now the hammering of urgent fists at the door of the WC called for a plan of action to be formulated. 'Quick!' whispered Lindy. 'Geddouta here, lover, and create a diversion while I split.'

The Captain reached behind, released the catch and backed out of the narrow doorway. 'Hey — look there!' he cried, pointing across to the other side of the plane. Instinctively, the three impatient passengers lined up ready to bust swivelled their heads round while Lindy made her getaway.

On returning to his seat in the darkened cabin, the Captain was at first annoyed and then pleased to find Wayne Packard occupying it and imposing his distasteful personality on Dr Carton. Presumably this meant that Dee Dee Burdle was now free. But no — beyond the bulk of the lager lout, now snoring loudly, both seats were empty. The Captain stepped over the sleeper's legs and lowered himself into the window seat. After some minutes Dee Dee, who said she had also been to the john, returned and appeared to be glad to see him, or perhaps not to see Packard. The Captain half lifted himself to slide over to the middle seat but she motioned him back to the window and sat between him and the snoring drunk.

If Dee Dee Burdle had known that the decision to squeeze the commissioners into economy class on this flight had been forced on him by his own financial misjudgement, he would have been too embarrassed to apologise. But she didn't, so he sympathised with her and threw the burden of blame for their cramped conditions where she assumed it belonged, on Dean Frolander. Frolander was prepared to part with extravagant sums of the library's money in exchange for the Cunlip discoveries, if they proved genuine. But he had no intention of subsidising an expensive joyride which might turn out to be a wild goose chase, and had left it to the Captain to pay for the trip out of the Reserved Collections budget. Although as custodian of these collections the Captain had access to considerable funds, every cent had to be accounted for since the trouble over Dee Dee Burdle's *Don Juan* manuscript. To be sure, it was understood that in many cases the mode of accounting would have to be sketchy. This simply reflected the facts of life, and in particular the fact that the acquisiton of pornographic material sometimes entailed dealings with the criminal underbelly of the market. At this end of that unforgiving market the term 'hardcore' could evoke not just lurid bookjackets packaging sights of illicit pleasure but construction sites in which outbidden punters were packaged in concrete overcoats. Strictly cash in hand was the order of the day, and no nonsense about receipts. As a result of these various considerations, the Captain's budget had been all but exhausted when the time came to book the flight. He explained all this to his companion.

Professor Burdle, however, seemed to be impervious to her surroundings. Even the length of her legs was not bothering her in her present position. She had twisted over on her right side to face the Captain, hauled up the skirt of her pink woollen dress and now threw her left leg uninhibitedly over his lap. The leg, being encased in a fine black mesh, felt firm and slightly rough to his palm. As to his lap, the most obvious thing about it was the damp and pungent prick that now sprang to attention. Before leaving the loo he had forgotten to pull up his zip. In the heat of his encounter with Lindy Simmering he had also forgotten to relieve his bladder. At the moment the weight of the fluid in it seemed to be helping him to maintain a stout erection, but he hoped Dee Dee would not get an urge to sit on his lap.

But no — Dee Dee Burdle had something else in mind. She unfastened the top of her dress, which buttoned down the front. Unconfined by any restraining lingerie, the soft white hillocks tumbled out into the Captain's hands. Gently he pinched the nipples into hardening teats and bent his head to take the uppermost one between his lips. It lengthened into his mouth and he frotted the engorged end of it with the tip of his tongue.

As he did so, he felt a cool hand closing around the stem of his cock. It appeared that this impressive lady with her streaky black and gold hair wished to have sex with him. Who was he to deny her desires?

A dark figure caught his eye, moving across the front of the cabin towards this side of the plane. For a moment the upper part of the profile was silhouetted against the dog-dominated movie screen; it was Wayne Packard returning from a hike up and down the aisles. 'Look out,' the Captain mumbled to his partner. 'Packard's coming back.'

Dee Dee acted without hesitation. She dropped to the floor between his legs and pointed to the blanket the stewardesss had left on her seat. Her lips closed softly on his stiff tool. The Captain wrapped the blanket round himself and the kneeling woman, pretending to be asleep. Indeed, as the subdued roar of the engines and air conditioning lapped deep into his ears, reclining back with his eyes shut and his unsubdued spike cradled in the wet glove of Dee Dee's mouth, he suddenly found it quite hard to stay awake.

A hand clapped on his shoulders shook him out of his trance. His body bucked reflexively, almost throwing off the blanket. 'Well now, Haggler, how you doing?' demanded the intrusive Packard.

The Captain explained that he was just trying to get some much needed sleep. What motivated his distaste for this smooth operator was a combination of professional and sexual jealousy. Packard was thought to be brilliant, although in the Captain's view it was only in the States that anyone so lacking in humour and the capacity for self-disparagement could hope to maintain such a reputation. Packard was on the faculty of the English Department full time, but his accomplishments as an astute bibliographer — he had produced a detailed *Descriptive Catalog of European Literary Autographs in the Banesville University Holdings* — had secured him a special position within the library.

The university's collection of such manuscripts was not actually very large; it was even possible that Packard's multi-volume catalogue contained more pages than the collection itself. And much of the material was drearily unimpressive — romantic

173

novels and TV scripts by living authors of no substance and little merit. Wayne Packard's undisguised ambition was to break up the Captain's Reserved Collections on the grounds that their very existence depended on outmoded notions of impropriety, and to absorb all suitable materials into 'his' department of the library, making it many times larger. The Reserved Collections, of course, contained the most important and extensive repository of erotica on the Coast. Its destruction would put paid to Banesville's reputation as a Mecca for a category of scholar dear to the Captain's heart. The high-class pornography would still be there, of course, but most of it would be diluted and scattered among work of much lower intensity, while the unique manuscript material would be tarnished by association with the staggering mediocrity of the rubbish Packard had catalogued. Or something of the sort . . .

Either the grip of Dee Dee's mouth was tightening or his erection was growing dramatically in girth as the Captain tried to deflect Packard's barrage of questions about the Cunlip discoveries. He let his head loll on his chest and responded with grunts and simulated snores. What was not possible, though, was to create an appearance of relaxation, for Professor Burdle's subtle ministrations − mere variations in the tightness of her lips or flickerings of her curled-back tonguetip − had brought him to a state of expectant tumidity. He stretched back and his body formed a straight line from his shoulders to his toes.

Packard's voice was droning on. 'We need to get our heads round the whole question of the aesthetic of orgasm,' he seemed to be saying. 'How it bears on the fragmentation of the subject and the perception of confinement and closure. Would you say it offers escape from binarism towards Derridean deconstruction? Can we ever relocate − climb right out the inter-textual reticulation?'

Pressure was mounting in the Captain's loins. An unbearable sensitivity radiated from the base of his spine. It was as if the slightest touch would trigger his detonation and release the heavy charge accumulating in his spermatic reservoirs.

'That sassy little assistant of yours,' Packard was saying. 'That Gloria Sweethearts or whatever? Bust your buns all day grading term papers, you're gonna need a little R and R. Glad to see

174

she's along for the ride.'

The mouth gloving the Captain's cock began to suck and a pair of fingers pressed into the flesh just behind his balls. The heavy burden of bottled-up spunk was propelled along the constricted tube, squirting out into the unseen throat. Packard, growing ever more animated at the thought of Gloria, gesticulated expressively. His elbow caught the sleeping drunk to his left full in the mouth. Instead of lashing back at his assailant, the man rose to his feet, still snoring, and staggered towards the back of the plane. Wayne Packard followed, apologising profusely.

After an indeterminate period of slumber the Captain awoke to find Dee Dee Burdle asleep in the seat to his left and his bladder demanding instant relief. He stepped over Dee Dee's legs and headed up the aisle but seeing the length of the queue thought better of it and turned to pass round the front of the cabin and up the other side. The movie had now finished and most passengers were dozing fitfully. A few rows from the front he caught Gloria's eye, illuminated by the reading light above her seat. She seemed to be sitting up very high, as if on a pile of cushions – but no, he realised it was a man's lap she was sitting on. Gloria leaned slightly forward and he saw that this partner was the stout middle-aged nineteenth-century scholar Cameron Meldrop. The blanket draped over her from throat to feet fell away. Her white summer dress was unbuttoned all the way down the front and she appeared to be quite bare beneath it. A pair of pudgy hands, their backs bristling with black hair, were squeezing her breasts so that the nipples stood out between the fingers and thumbs. The Captain gasped at the sight, soft in the dimmed lighting, of her milky thighs spread wide and dangling down over Dr Meldrop's legs. Those legs stuck out stiffly in front of the learned doctor, the trousers down round his knees. A hairy ballsack bulged between his thightops. The root of a thick, shining stem was visible, pumping up into the chestnut-fringed gash that curved down from the girl's fluffed-up bush.

Meldrop realised his privities were under observation and removed his hands from Gloria's tits to grab the blanket and haul it up into position again. Affecting to be scandalised, and confident that his discovery would make Meldrop his pawn in any acrimonious negotiations when they got to Cunlip Hall, the Captain hurried on up the aisle to join the queue of only three men waiting for the toilet on the port side.

The closet door burst open. Wayne Packard emerged in a state of atypical confusion. 'Hey — look there!' he cried, pointing across to starboard. The three men in front turned their heads but the Captain kept his eyes fixed ahead. Out slipped a rumpled-looking Lindy Simmering, followed by the almost anorexic figure of Randle Fargo, and all three disappeared into the gloom of the cabin.

An exhausting train journey followed by a long ride in a couple of taxis brought the travel-stained party to the drive of Cunlip Hall. It was a cold and blustery June morning. Not even the spires and crenellations of the Victorian pile could fire them with much enthusiasm, although the male commissioners were favourably impressed by the figures of Miss Muttock and Miss MacDonald, who waited on the steps to greet them and to be introduced by the Captain.

The seven travellers split into two groups and lined up outside the small downstairs WC and the cavernous upstairs bathroom to attend to their most pressing bodily requirements. Packard, Meldrop and Fargo declined the offer of quick service in an outside installation when they heard that it was built to accommodate three defecators side by side. Eventually they all foregathered, considerably relieved but even more exhausted, in the kitchen, where they were plied with toast and coffee discreetly laced with cognac.

The Captain wondered what Mary Muttock had in mind when she announced that they should now accompany her to the hall to meet the 'indoors domestic staff'. Lined up at the foot of the great staircase he recognised an array of familiar faces: Melanie Winspur, Gina Wootton, Anne Amory, Susie and Darcy O'Flammery, Derrick (whose surname had never been mentioned in the Captain's presence) and Joker Jennings, as well as a youth who looked only half familiar. Derrick and Joker wore the usual gear of stage butlers; young Darcy and the other youth were got up like pages, or what the visitors might have called bellhops, in pillbox hats, tight, high-waisted black trousers and little bumfreezer jackets over their white shirts. The females were all identically dressed as maids in skimpy black and white outfits hired, like the lads' attire, from a theatrical costumier. Their skirts were outrageously short and it was hardly possible for them to move without flashing a band of bare flesh above the tops of their stockings.

Each of these young people stepped forward and bowed or curtsied as his or her name was called out; their names were prominently displayed on labels attached to their costumes. When it came to the turn of the mysterious second youth, the Captain's memory was jogged by the name: Carl. Of course. The boyish figure of Carla Merryweather, her black hair cropped short, was being passed off as male. Then Miss Muttock explained that one of the staff had been allocated to each guest as a personal body servant. She regretted that the dozens of bells connecting the rooms of the Hall with the servants' quarters were no longer functional. But if the distinguished visitors left their doors unlocked she would see to it that every hour, on the hour, their personal servants would quietly look in to see if anything was required. 'But don't overdo it,' she warned. 'Most of them aren't much more than kids. When it gets to night-time they'll need a bit of shuteye between the hourly checks.' Miss MacDonald was then asked to pair the Americans off with their attendants.

It was not clear whether the allocation was random or the result of some rapid calculation. Wayne Packard got Melanie; Derrick went to Phyllis F. Carton, on whom, in the Captain's judgment, he might well be wasted; Lindy Simmering seemed pleased enough to be paired with Joker; poor little Susie quailed visibly when introduced to the gaunt person of Randle Fargo; Anne had to conceal even greater horror faced with the lardy bulk of Cameron Meldrop; Dee Dee Burdle seemed quite happy with the pale and smooth-faced 'Carl'; Gloria and Darcy were already secretly acquainted, of course, although the Captain was not sure if they had ever fucked with each other. He was certainly relieved that either chance or MacDonald and Muttock had had the decency to reserve his favourite, Gina, for his own use.

The servants now withdrew and the Banesville contingent trooped into the library. All the supposed discoveries, including the genuine items from Sir Julius's private collection, were displayed on the long table, surrounded by tall glasses of a chilled white wine. The Captain noticed a new manuscript which must have been produced from conception to execution on the ladies' own initiative; it appeared to be a fair copy in the hand of Charles Dickens.

By this time the colleagues were already shagged, pissed and jetlagged out of their minds. They made noises expressive of interest, surprise and satisfaction. But their real interest was in the beds awaiting them, with or even without the promised room service. Soon they asked to be shown upstairs.

Miss Muttock tinkled a handbell and the servants filed back into the library. Each of them found his or her master or mistress and steered them up the main staircase and along winding corridors to their various quarters. If some of these pampered Americans were disappointed or even disgusted by the gap between the standard of accommodation to which they were accustomed and what was being offered here, they kept their sentiments as far as possible to themselves for fear of alienating their charming guides. Only the fastidious Professor Packard suggested to Melanie that she might be so good as to remove a family of fungoid growths the size of dinner plates that sprouted in the angle of the walls beside his bed. Coolly, she pointed out that whenever one of these was scraped off another two appeared in its place overnight. He tried to concentrate his attention instead on the two firm protuberances sprouting beneath the front of her maid's uniform, but even as he dropped on the bed and beckoned her to him his eyes closed in sleep.

Although as tired as the others, the Captain had deliberately abstained from the alcoholic refreshment provided with and after the welcoming snack. Gina escorted him to a room high in the attic and drew the dusty curtains against a flood of bright sunlight interrupted by racing clouds. Without a word they both stripped off their clothes. Gina stretched her long, freckled body on the bed. He flopped beside her and nuzzled his nose into her coppery bush, smelling, it seemed to him, of male secretions. He guessed that she was still being pestered by that uncouth Joker Jennings, but thought better of complaining. In the distance he could hear her pleading to be fucked and realised she must be addressing him as there was nobody else in the room.

But as he defied a gravity that seemed to have doubled its normal force and heaved himself up so that he could bring the head of his dick to bear on her slick lips, the door opened and two others entered. Melanie, in her maid's costume, and Gloria, in a filmy white negligée, threw themselves down on either side of the embracing couple. Screwing slow and hard into Gina, he arched his back up to get a view of the newcomers. Melanie wriggled her bottom and pulled up her little skirt. She had no knickers on. Below the gingery tuft her slit opened damply to his gaze. Over on the other side, Gloria's negligée had fallen open, exposing the creamy flesh. His eyes ran down the curving surfaces to the fluffy bush where her thighs joined. He laid a palm flat on the plump triangle. She opened her legs, paused and opened them wider. Then she brought her hands down to pull the pink petals apart. The Captain introduced three fingers, leaving his thumb free to tickle her clit and his little finger to worry around her arsehole. With his other hand he applied the same treatment to Melanie. Luckily Gina realised what was happening just in time to put both her hands under his chest to support his weight as he burrowed away in her cunt while pleasuring their two companions.

In spite of tiredness his control was superb. He varied the speed and strength with which he operated on the three young women until he could sense, from the tossing of their heads, the dark flushes spreading down their bellies, the tension of their abdominal muscles, the quivering of their thighs and the rippling of their tight, oozing cunts on his fingers and jousting prick, that all three were on the point or in the process of exploding. At that moment he closed his eyes and imagined their three pussies ranged side by side for his inspection. The thought was too much for him. He howled up at the cobwebs festooning the sloping ceiling and clenched his loins in rapture as he spilt wave after wave of foaming sperm high into the belly of his quivering darling.

TWELVE

PIP SQUEAKS, OR THE HAND-REARED BOY

A few hours of sleep restored the Captain to a condition in which he could no longer restrain his curiosity concerning the piece of Dickensiana he had seen in the library. He put on a dressing gown and made his way down there in the late afternoon while the other commissioners slept the day away.

The manuscript, which he quickly recognised as purporting to represent work on an episode of *Great Expectations,* was beautifully written and even smelt a hundred and thirty years old. 'Dickens' had indicated its unsuitability for publication by ruling a diagonal line across every page. Now the Captain was not an uneducated man, fraudulent though his academic qualifications were. This had been a favourite novel of his in his younger days, and he recalled very clearly how young Pip, 'hand-reared' by his nagging grown-up sister and indulged by her husband, the kindly blacksmith Joe, had been summoned to play at the house of Miss Havisham. He remembered how Pip, quite at a loss as to what he might be required to play *at*, was received by Estella. This snootily beautiful girl of about his own age, though seeming older in her self-possession, had shown Pip to the dimly lit dressing room of Miss Havisham, the strangest lady he had ever seen, who told him she had not looked on the sun since he was born.

The figure of old Miss Havisham, with her faded yellowish wedding dress hanging from her in its decay like grave-clothes, still haunted him, as did Dickens's description of the darkened room where the table remained set for her aborted wedding feast after all those years. He recalled the blotchy spiders running in and out of the heap of cobwebbed mould that had been the cake.

With these memories still potent, even if the details of plot had long since faded, the Captain began to read.

"I am tired," said Miss Havisham. "I want diversion, and I have done with men and women. Play."

I think it will be conceded that she could hardly have directed an unfortunate boy to do anything in the wide world more difficult to be done under the circumstances.

"I sometimes have sick fancies," she went on, "and I have a sick fancy that I want to see some play. There, there!" with an impatient movement of the fingers of her right hand; "play, play, play!"

For a moment I had a desperate idea of starting round the room in the assumed character of Mr. Pumblechook's chaise-cart. Instead, I stood looking at Miss Havisham in what I supposed she took for a dogged manner, inasmuch as she said, when we had taken a good look at each other:

"Are you sullen and obstinate?"

"No, ma'am, I am very sorry for you, and very sorry I can't play just now. I would do it if I could; but it's so new here, and so strange —"

She turned her eyes from me, and looked at the dress she wore, and at the dressing-table, and finally at herself in the looking-glass.

"So new to him," she muttered, "so old to me; so strange to him, so familiar to me; so melancholy to both of us! Call Estella. Call Estella," she repeated, flashing a look at me. "You can do that. Call Estella. At the door."

To stand bawling Estella to a scornful young lady neither visible nor responsive was almost as bad as *playing* to order. But, she answered at last, and her light came along the dark passage like a star.

When Estella entered the room, I caught my breath at the transformation in her appearance. She had changed her dress, and now stood before us clothed from head to foot in white raiment that was surely meant to set off the pitiful condition to which Miss Havisham had been reduced. For, although the skirts were somewhat shorter, as became her age, and her upper arms were bare in the light of the candles, Estella's attire also resembled that of a bride. She stood there as a youthful apparition of Miss Havisham herself, her body unshrunken and her rich clothes unyellowed by the flight of years. She was crowned with a chaplet of orange-blossom, and a little veil hung over her shoulders, leaving her exquisite but unfriendly features exposed. Miss Havisham beckoned her to come close, and addressed her in birdlike tones of suppressed excitement. "Fetch the cards from that cabinet. Let me see you play forfeits with this boy."

"With this boy! Why, he is a common labouring-boy!"

Miss Havisham replied in a rasping whisper not meant for my ears, "Well? You can break his heart."

Estella brought from the cabinet a pack of cards, dog-eared from use. "You know the rules, boy," she sneered; I had to confess that I was a novice.

"What card games do you play, then, boy?" asked Estella of myself.

"Nothing but beggar my neighbour, miss."

"Beggar him," said Miss Havisham to Estella, "not the way he knows, but with the game of forfeits; you must tell him what to do."

I began to feel that I found myself in a predicament in which I could hardly expect to win. Although pitted against but one opponent, and she of the softer sex, it was as if Miss Havisham's will, a powerful will issuing invisibly from a feeble corporeal frame, was urging Estella on to my defeat. Estella dealt out all the cards, face down, while she instructed me in the rules of what I judged to be a strange and daunting sport of hazard.

"It is wonderfully simple," she explained. "We each turn up our top card; the highest card wins. The loser pays his forfeit, and we then turn the next card, and so on, until the loser has no more to give."

I thought I saw her wink at Miss Havisham, but I could

not be sure, as she turned her face away from me at the same moment. I was puzzled: her directions seemed to have left something unexplained.

"But what are these forfeits, please, miss? I have nothing in my pocket, saving three new farthings Mr. Pumblechook gave me when he set me down at the gate."

"He doesn't know what we mean by a forfeit, this boy!" said Estella with incredulous disdain. "And what coarse hands he has! And what thick boots! But he will not keep them on for long. Boy, a forfeit is an article of apparel. One of your boots could serve as a forfeit. Or your jacket. Or your shirt."

I looked down, blushing and speechless.

"Do not fear," she added. "Before you are sent home you can have all your forfeits back."

I looked up, still speechless and blushing. Her reassurance had not allayed my fears one iota. She made me sit down on the threadbare hearth-rug, while she herself perched on Miss Havisham's foot-stool. Both females looked at me expectantly; I turned up my first card, which was the queen of hearts. Estella threw down the five of spades with a grimace, and pulled off one of her dainty satin slippers. My next card was the two of clubs; hers, the ten. I surrendered a boot. It was well for me that I had not yet seen enough of the world to feel shame at the much-darned state of my stockings.

The next five tricks were taken by my adversary. In payment I gave up my other boot, both my stockings, the red spotted handkerchief knotted at my neck, and my jacket. Then my eight of diamonds beat Estella's four of hearts. She peeled off one of her gloves. My ace of diamonds succumbed to her three of clubs; my waistcoat joined the heap of clothes beside the hearth. My leather belt paid for the feebleness of my five of spades against Estella's king of hearts. With the exception of my very first card, I had turned up no court cards. I had no recollection of seeing the cards shuffled before play commenced, and this led me to speculate on whether the drubbing I was receiving at her hands might be attributable not to ill fortune or my lack of skill but to guile and trickery.

I turned my next card; it was the eight of spades; Estella could do no better than the three of hearts. Off came the other glove. Her slender arms and hands were bare, but otherwise she might pass as fully dressed, whereas I was fast approaching the limits of decency.

"There," I said, revealing my next card with some surprise because I was convinced that it would be a low one. "The Jack of hearts!"

"He calls the knaves, Jacks, this boy!" said Estella with disdain. And she turned up the king of diamonds.

Increasingly alarmed, I now had to choose between my shirt and breeches as the payment for this latest debt. I began to unbutton my shirt, but thought better of it; the effect of nakedness would be less if I divested myself of the garment encasing my nether limbs. I stood up before the ladies, let the breeches drop to the floor, stepped out of them, kicked them aside, and finally resumed my place on the rug, taking care that the long tails of my shirt concealed as much as possible of my somewhat skinny legs.

"Hurry, boy," said Estella. "I am dying to see your—your next card."

It was the king of clubs. I had won a brief reprieve; but, however brief, the reprieve was welcome. It might even be the prelude to a run of better luck. Estella lifted her top card, held it face-downwards for a while and then turned up the ace of spades.

"Aces are high," decreed Miss Havisham.

"But that cannot be, ma'am," I protested. "I had to give up my waistcoat when I drew the ace of diamonds."

"You are mistaken, boy," Estella contradicted. "Mistaken and insolent. Aces have always been high. It is the rule of the house." And she denounced me to Miss Havisham as a stupid, ignorant labouring-boy.

"You say nothing of her," remarked Miss Havisham to me. "She says many hard things of you, but you say nothing of her. What do you think of her?"

"I don't like to say," I stammered.

"Tell me in my ear," said Miss Havisham, bending down.

"I think she is very proud," I replied, in a whisper.

"Anything else?"

"I think she is very pretty."

"Anything else?"

"I think she is very insulting." (She was looking at me then with a look of supreme aversion.)

"Anything else?"

"I think I should like to go home."

"And never see her again, though she is so pretty?"

"I am not sure that I shouldn't like to see her again, but I should like to go home now."

"You shall go soon," said Miss Havisham, aloud. "Play the game out. You owe a forfeit."

Smarting under a sense of injustice, I unbuttoned my shirt, rose to my feet, and pulled the patched white garment over my head. I stood before my tormentors, covered in nothing more substantial than confusion. Totally unused to such proceedings, and knowing not whether more shame attached to displaying my posteriors or the little diddler that hung down in front like a shrimp, I lowered myself once more to the floor and sat with my knees clasped before me. No doubt Estella was thus granted, quite unintentionally, an unobstructed view of the as yet unexercised cods for which I had never had much regard, having no notion of their function.

"Well," said Miss Havisham with a half-amused scowl, "you have no need to sit down again so soon, and will have small inclination to do so after you have paid your next forfeit."

"My next forfeit, ma'am?"

"Why, yes. You have lost the game, have you not? The loser owes a further forfeit to the winner."

"But I have no more forfeits," I stammered. "Miss Estella has taken them all away."

Miss Havisham smiled grimly. "The loser's forfeit partakes somewhat more of the nature of a punishment.

Estella knows what is required. See to it, Estella."

The haughty beauty brought a chair from against the wall and sat upon it right in front of Miss Havisham. She raised the hem of her bride-like dress so that the skirts were drawn half-way up her handsome thighs, and slid the white silk hose, one after the other, down to just below her knees. My heart throbbed with excitement as I watched, and so did my diddler, trapped between my own thighs as I sat there gaping. Estella spoke, and if I am not mistaken there was a hint of something akin to warmth in her accents:

"Come here, boy. Come and lie over my lap."

Oh, the sense of burning shame as I stood in front of them and displayed perforce the stiff stake which had caused me private discomfort and puzzlement on previous occasions but had never yet been exposed naked in its flaming arrogance before the eyes of witnesses. I essayed to cover it with my hands, but being too small, they merely drew attention to the wagging monster. As I approached Estella, the sight of her pretty knees and bare thighs made it grow still longer; it felt as if a straight bone were being pushed up its length from the base of my belly almost as far as the little slot in the head.

Oh, the indignity! I was made to lower myself so that my middle portions rested on Estella's thighs. My hands, touching the floor to her left, supported part of my balancing weight, and the humiliating picture was completed by my legs stretched out sloping away to her right.

Oh, the strange sensation as one of the girl's hands steadied itself on the small of my back! She brought her knees together. My stiffness was now trapped between her warm thighs, and felt as if it would grow and grow until it stretched right down to the dusty rug. She began to hum a romantic air.

Oh, the bitter smart as the palm of her other hand descended upon my expectant backside! My diddler now increased not just in length but in thickness, as if it would force her thighs apart. Again the hand fell on my tingling flesh, and again, and again.

My posteriors were on fire, but that extreme sensation was now supplanted by one still more potent, concentred, it seemed, on the root of my rigid spigot. It was a sensation of fullness, of gathering, of tightening. Again the hand fell, but this time it hurt my burning skin no more than the tender melody she hummed.

Oh!—oh!—oh!—o-o-oh!

I squealed aloud as the core of my enlarged member was stretched internally by an undreamed-of substance rushing down its length to burst in a rapturous cannonade from the swollen muzzle. Estella's thighs squeezed together in an even stricter clasp until the last gouts of this pulsing flood were finally spent. An odour of salt fish freshened the dank staleness of that sepulchral chamber.

Miss Havisham now summoned me to sit on the floor beside her. Standing and looking down, I caught a glimpse of the shameful, pearly mess on the rug between Estella's legs. My dominant sentiment, however, was one of relief, as I also saw that my rebellious diddler had shrunk to no more than twice his wonted dimensions. The skin that sheathed the shaft had assumed a shrivelled appearance, and the prepuce seemed reluctant to roll down to sleeve the empurpled head, which still dripped balm. When I took my place at Miss Havisham's feet, the rascal dropped out of sight between my legs.

"Let us have a song, Estella," croaked Miss Havisham. "Sing us what you were humming as you disciplined this young man;—that number from Mr. Balfe's 'Bohemian Girl', was it not?"

Estella rose and walked to the curtained window; since her dress was so short I was able to observe that her movements caused one of the lowered white stockings to fall right down to her ankle. To one side of the window stood a great harp, hitherto unnoticed by me. She sat facing us, lifted her skirts as high as when she had beaten me, and drew her chair forward so that the sloping sound-board of the instrument passed up between her legs. For a moment I thought I saw something winking in the darkness at the joining of those sweet thighs—I almost swooned at the vision. By the time I was somewhat recovered, the harp had obscured whatever it was that I might have seen.

"You will find that when she sings she becomes a veritable siren," Miss Havisham remarked. "Do you know what a siren is?"

"A kind of mermaid, ma'am. They lure poor sailors to their death with beautiful songs." I was fortunate to recall this information which my mentor, Mr. Wopsle, had retailed to me one evening when the booming of the gun across the marshes had taken on an unearthly, wailing modulation in the high wind. As I watched the pretty musician, it struck me that the spectacle reversed the characteristics of mermaids as emphasised for my benefit by Mr. Wopsle: her breast was not, alas, bare, and her lower parts were clearly divided as high as my eye could see—which was not, alas, as high as I might have desired.

The instrument lacked a number of strings and was in need of tuning, but when Estella's fingers swept over it, coaxing the most delightfully pathetic strains from its chords, my heart melted.

I dreamt that I dwe-elt in ma-a-arble halls,
With vassals and serfs at my si-i-ide,
And of all who assembled withi-i-in those walls
That I was the hope and the pri-i-ide.

Miss Havisham ran a bony hand through my hair and was asking me something about the circumstances of my life at home, but all my attention was on Estella's stirring performance.

I had riches too gre-eat to co-ount—could boast
Of a hi-igh ancestral name—

The seductive voice paused on a sustained note as the little hands executed one of the *arpeggios* that had accompanied the melody throughout. Miss Havisham stroked my cheek and mused aloud:

"Ravishing. This girl's *portamento* could vie for the palms with that of the divine Grisi."

Her words meant nothing to me (although it occurred to me irreverently that *portamento* might be what the harpist carried between her legs and appeared to be pressing into the vibrant instrument), so I simply purred like a contented cat as she continued to fondle me. Estella's amorous but plaintive tones became softer—

> But I a-also dre-eamt—which ple-e-eas'd me most,
> That you lo-ov'd me still the same,
> That you lov'd me,
> You lo-o-ov'd me sti-ill the same,

—before rising in a powerful *crescendo* to a triumphant, resounding climax:

> That you lov'd me,
> You lo-o-ov'd me sti-i-ill the same.

Meanwhile, Miss Havisham's questioning about my antecedent life had become insistent. As Estella warbled the second verse of her dream of suitors, telling of knights pledging their faith to her on bended knee with vows no maiden heart could withstand, I remembered dear Joe Gargery's parting words to me in the forge: "Boy, be for ever grateful to all friends, but especially unto them which brought you up by hand." Accordingly, I paid tribute to this manual upbringing; my words brought a smile to Miss Havisham's thin lips.

Estella, too, seemed to flash a smile through the candle-lit gloom as she declared in passionate tones how, in her dream, one of that noble host had come forth to claim her hand—

> But I also dreamt, which charm'd me most,
> That you lov'd me still the same.

As she uttered those closing words, she seemed to flash

189

a glance in my direction. Her fingers struck one last plangent chord; she rose to her feet and resumed her place on the footstool beside us. She sat, or rather squatted, in a most inelegant posture, her skirts once more up over her thighs, her knees parted and her hands dangling down infuriatingly to conceal from my curious gaze the embowered vista between them.

Miss Havisham spoke. "He tells me he was reared by hand," she said. "Let us see if you cannot use your hands to rear him up once more."

I was made to sit on the floor right next to Estella, facing Miss Havisham with my legs wide open. Mortification overcame me as the lovely girl reached a hand down between my thighs. Her fingers curled under and cradled my aching cods, while her thumb flicked rudely at my limp diddler. In no time at all, however, mortification gave way to sudden revivification; the puny appendage filled with blood like a sucking leech, then straightened and lifted itself to rub against my belly. Estella now released my purse, replete with treasures ready to overflow, and closed all her fingers around the mettlesome warrior. A heavy dew-drop gathered at the tip.

Eagerly, Miss Havisham ordered the girl to let me be. She was told to kneel before a chair and lean over it, hitching up her skirts and petticoats to reveal all the exciting and unexpected beauty of her hidden attractions. Never before had I bent my eyes on such a glorious spectacle. The white roundness of those plump hemispheres! The smooth curves of the denuded thighs! The enticing crevice that ran down between the globes, from which peeped out the little pink hole proclaiming the fallen humanity she shared with me!

But most of all, and quite eclipsing all these other delights, I drooled and moaned at the sight of something which declared unequivocally that not *all* the parts with which Nature had endowed her were common to both of us. Below the puckered bottom-mouth, the groove gave way to a puffy, pink pouch that pouted out, pushing aside the plump tops of her thighs just where they sprang from the undercurve of her buttocks. This pouch had the most tempting appearance. It was like a peach, covered in soft down and divided by a pink line inviting the hands to pull its yielding flesh apart.

I gazed in wonder, little doubting that Miss Havisham would impose on me the grateful task of belabouring that bottom in requital for the indignity and pain inflicted on my own. But I was mistaken. It was not my discomfiture that was to be avenged but Miss Havisham's, all those years ago, when her bridegroom had deserted her, consigning her to these dark apartments sealed as effectively from the light and business of healthy quotidian intercourse as her womb was to remain sealed from the fructifying irrigation of manly seed.

The withered bride tottered across to Estella and stooped, inserting a gnarled hand to force the girl's legs wider apart. What an inflammatory sight the haughty beauty now presented kneeling there, the upper part of her clothing still intact but everything south of the waist in "sweet disorder", the white stockings loose round her ankles and the skirts tossed up over her back! Cushions were placed on the floor between Estella's legs. I was instructed to kneel on them. Doing so, I found it needful to lean back to avoid rubbing my damson-hued rammer against her silky flesh.

"Nature has been denied too long!" Miss Havisham quavered. "Let that which was snatched from me be bestowed on this young girl. You have admitted that you find her pretty—but insulting. Very well. Her prettiness is now yours to insult. Her cunt is as pretty as her face, is it not? Let Nature prevail. Do you know how to fuck?"

She had availed herself of two words unfamiliar to me. Truth to tell, the second of these had sometimes been heard in the forge when Orlick (or occasionally even Joe) had brought a hammer down on his thumb or clumsily touched the red-hot iron; but I knew not what it signified. Now, from the circumstances in which it was used, the meaning of that imprecation became clear.

I viewed the pretty fruit before me, too overcome by

191

emotion and lust to make a move. As I watched, that central split widened and fell open to reveal moist layers of the softest pink. Suddenly and involuntarily my back straightened up and Nature did indeed prevail; I plunged my dagger in, up to the hilt, in complete disregard of Estella's yelps of protest and pain. For the second time that day—nay, the second time in my life—an almost solid load of boiling essence shot in scalding jets from my loins. The first time I had spent, it had spread wastefully over the rug. This time it drenched the virgin womb of Estella and forged an intangible bond which was to hang between us in years to come like the chains that shackled Magwitch to his fellow-convicts. "I love you!" I cried, scarcely aware of what I was saying. "Let me be your hope and pride even as in the song. Oh, you have captivated me. Squeeze harder—it's still pumping out."

"You may go now," wheezed Miss Havisham. "She is properly broken. Another time you may have her again."

The Captain replaced the manuscript on the library table, demolished half a cold chicken he had stumbled across in the kitchen and returned to his room. He was so tired that he fell asleep immediately, waking only when he found his already aroused cock nudging against Gina's auburn snatch.

THIRTEEN

BUSINESS AND PLEASURE

As hostess, of course, Miss Muttock had been left out of the process of pairing off guests with 'servants'. She had spent an agreeable night in the arms of her friend Miss MacDonald. The latter remained late in bed. Mary Muttock came down to the kitchen for breakfast in a cheerful mood and chatted with the mostly rather haggard Americans who wandered in from time to time in the course of a hot sunny morning, escorted by their charming minders. Several sightings of the ghost of old Sir Julius were reported; on the insistence of a strangely radiant Dr Carton, who now looked marginally less desiccated in a tight white sweater, Mary Muttock undertook to have these sightings investigated. Wayne Packard drew her aside and made an offer for the freehold of the Hall, which she promised to consider at her leisure.

If any of the guests had enjoyed carnal relations with their body servants during the night they did nothing to advertise the fact. Nevertheless, Mary Muttock inferred from various clues in their demeanour that their slumbers had not been of the chastest. Melanie lifted her maid's skirt to reveal marks on her buttocks which testified to the brutality of Professor Packard's lust. At a suitable opportunity Miss Muttock took aside the supposed page-boy Carla, curious as to whether Dee Dee Burdle had taken the girl to bed and blown her cover. Carla laughed and explained that by dint of a combination of simulated shyness and the use of a dildo she had managed to elude detection by the exhausted Dee Dee.

Miss MacDonald put in a late appearance and drew the

Muttock aside. 'I had a visitor up in our bed,' she confided. 'That weedy-looking Randle Fargo. Not so weedy where it matters, though. I'd asked young Susie Freemantle —I mean O'Flammery — what kind of room service he'd been getting from her. Said she was too revolted to do much more than let him have a good look up her cunt and stroke her little boobs. Something *creepy* about him, she said. Said it was like wanking a great fat salami sticking out of a bag of bones, except that he had quite a bit more juice in him that you'd expect to squeeze out of a skeleton. Anyway, when he burst in on me I can't say I minded. His cock was, well, gargantuan's the only word for it. But the rest of him's nothing. It if hadn't been such a fucking tight fit where it mattered the whole of him would have been swallowed up inside me. I can see what Susie means. Creepy.'

During what was left of the morning, and most of the afternoon, the band of scholars made their individual assessments of the exciting materials laid out for them in the library. From periodic peeps into that den of industry, Miss Muttock got the impression that it was not only their intellectual faculties that were being excited. In differing degrees, the facial expressions of all of them were coloured with indignation, amusement or lust as they contemplated the salacious texts and photographs.

Towards the end of the afternoon Miss Muttock rang the handbell and announced that, in accordance with their chairperson's request, the main ballroom had now been made ready for their all-important meeting. The commissioners trooped into this setting of faded grandeur, a lofty room where golden motes of dust swam in the bars of sunlight slanting in from high lancet windows. Across one end of the ballroom hung a great curtain which had mellowed from rich purple, still visible in shaded patches, to cobwebby grey. All who were not entitled to attend the meeting took up places silently behind this curtain, carefully positioning chairs so that they could peep through the many moth holes that gave the decaying fabric a somewhat netlike appearance from the back. Just in front of this curtain stood a long table and from its ends another two tables of similar length projected at right angles into the room so that an area of floor was enclosed on three sides. The tables were draped with cloths of crimson velvet hanging to the floor.

Dee Dee Burdle, chic in a Chinese-style trouser suit of turquoise silk, took the chair with her back to the curtain and Gloria beside her to keep a record of the meeting. Gloria wore a crisp white blouse, her pale blue wraparound skirt and matt black stockings. One of the projecting tables was occupied by Packard, Carton and Meldrop; at the other sat Fargo, Simmering and the Captain. All the places had been set beforehand with businesslike blotters and glasses of what might have been water but was in fact something stronger. Professor Simmering still wore her travelling outfit of lilac and scarlet, slightly rumpled but undeniably elegant.

Dee Dee called the meeting to order. 'Hi there, you guys,' she began. 'First of all I have to welcome you to this meeting called to determine the authenticity of certain items we have all been examining today and to get our heads round their suitability as acquisitions to your great library. Second of all I wish to put on the record our appreciation of Miss Mary Muttock's efforts in respect of our accommodations and the unusual arrangements for our comfort — that is, the arrangements for our comfort in her unusual and, er, venerable home. These arrangements, I have to tell you, extend to the provision of a little extra surprise this afternoon. Right now, boys and girls, we are about to witness the first act of a modest entertainment. It's the brainchild of Miss Muttock's talented, er, companion, Muriel MacDonald, who tells me she has spent some weeks putting the performers through their paces. These performers, friends, are by this time well known to us already. But before they do their thing for us, you will wish to know how they are slated to fit into our tight schedule. Well, we begin, as I say, with the first part of their show. Then we shall address the authenticity of Miss Muttock's remarkable literary acquisitions before passing on to the second part of the fun. Thereafter we turn to the photographic materials and finally, after a third terpischorean interlude, we have to get real and consider the reasonableness of the price being asked for this most desirable collection. OK then, guys — sit back and enjoy.'

Behind the curtain, Anne, Gina, Melanie and Joker were lined up ready to take the floor. Anne and Melanie, identically dressed in black leotards and with their calves and knees encased in

195

woolly pink legwarmers which emphasised the silky whiteness of their bare thighs, might almost have been mistaken for twins. Both were slim and shapely blondes and both had their shoulder-length hair tied back in a thick pony tail. Anne was only seventeen, two years younger than Melanie, and this age difference was reflected in their faces: Melanie, with her tempting upper thighs red-welted from their rough handling the night before, looked knowing, sophisticated and seductive, while Anne was all eager innocence. Yet from their figures a bystander might have remained convinced that their ages were the same. They differed only in their busts. Defying the flattening stretch of her leotard, Melanie's stood out as a pair of small, upward-tilted cones. Anne's were firm hemispheres tipped with prominent nipples. These two girls were cast as Gina's handmaidens in the ballet about to be performed.

Their mistress was got up differently. A headdress of flowers freshly picked in the garden held up a diaphanous veil of yellow muslin which hung down to her feet. This veil shrouded her face, body and limbs completely; as she stood there it was impossible to make out where it opened. Every intimacy was faintly hinted to the spectators' sight, yet nothing could be clearly distinguished.

The male lead, Joker Jennings, towered above the three girls, his yellow curls falling in a tangled mass to his shoulders. His bronzed torso was bare, apart from the pelt of matted yellow which luxuriated over chest and belly and grew denser and stiffer down at the edge of his low-slung waistband. Through the white tights which were his only garment his well-developed reproductive apparatus swelled out as an exaggerated bulge.

Taking her silver hip flask from her lips, Miss Muttock lifted the end of the curtain and the little troupe stepped out on to the floor, rather nervous to begin with as they filed round and took up positions within the space enclosed on three sides by the tables. The spectators took in their youthful attractions, especially the suggestively veiled charms of Gina, identifiable by the auburn curls on her head and pubis, their colour just showing through the pale yellow muslin. Ballet music by Delibes issued from a tape player operated by Miss Muttock. The dance commenced.

Intensive training under the supervision of Miss MacDonald had achieved creditable results in these young people. To be sure, not much in the way of point work had been attempted (in the end it was decided they were to dance in bare feet), and her heroic efforts to tame Joker, who hardly knew his *entrechat* from his elbow, had succeeded merely in whipping up his elephantine clumsiness until it was more reminiscent of the cavortings of a carthorse. There was no question of formal choreography plotted step by step and meticulously rehearsed. But the dancers had been given a story line and had worked out, with the MacDonald's help, a broadly blocked sequence of movements enacting the tale of courtship and ravishment now presented before the enthusiastic audience.

Gina remained in the centre of the square of tables, stretching herself languorously and gyrating with her arms raised to let her semitransparent covering fall open revealingly down one side. A little nest of curls adorned the exposed armpit, beneath which everything down to her ankle was bare. Every now and then she extended a naked leg sideways and lifted it high, momentarily bestowing tantalising glimpses of her intimate person. More active were her two attendants, who knelt before her, circled around her and ran their hands over her veiled form. In the background Joker appeared to be contemplating and developing his own physique in a succession of beefcake poses.

The music took a more frenzied turn. Galvanised into action, Joker leapt into the air and pranced into the centre of the arena. He kept throwing himself towards the disdainful Gina with gestures that spoke of longing and urgency. Each time he lunged at her, however, Anne and Melanie moved between them and restrained him with hands that ranged frustratingly all over his body. As a result of these attentions and his own exertions his tights worked their way ever lower over his narrow hips. The bulge just below the precarious waistband was swelling noticeably.

After each attempt on Gina's integrity he withdrew and performed a little dance of sulky defiance before launching another attack. The handmaidens now changed their tactics. One of them would interpose her body between his and Gina's, clinging jealously, not to say voluptuously, to her mistress. At the same

197

time her mate would try to distract Joker by engaging him in a close embrace. As he twisted and turned in his efforts to free himself, he only became more distraught and aroused. Then the girl would unwind her legs from round his hips and propel him away to the periphery of the floor to repeat his routine of sulking.

This pattern was gone through several times. Then Melanie and Anne each gripped one of Joker's arms from behind and held him rigid between them, bent right back with his manly appurtenance standing up in torment within the stretched white tights.

An audible sigh escaped from the audience as Gina, who stood facing him, leaned back to mirror his posture. Once more the side of her garment had fallen open; the whole of her right leg was on view, the yellow muslin that draped the other one hanging down to conceal the joining of her thighs. She edged forward in time with the music until her mound just touched the great swelling that throbbed in Joker's tights. As if stung by an electric discharge, Joker straightened up and cast the two handmaidens aside. Falling to his knees he lifted the hem of Gina's veil over his own head and stood inside it. The two lovers, united at last, swayed in each other's arms, enveloped in a gauzy tent that hung open down Gina's right and Joker's left flanks. Melanie and Anne now stood on either side of the couple, their arms encircling them and drawing them yet closer together. This lovelocked group began to whirl round, at the same time moving back from the appreciative commissioners and round the tables to disappear through the curtains.

A brief, stunned silence was followed by thunderous applause which brought the dancers back to take their bow. More precisely, the three girls curtsied while Joker executed a reverse bow, thrusting his loins forward towards the audience to flaunt an erection that threatened to split his overtaxed tights asunder. Then all four ran back to join their chums behind the curtain.

'And now,' said Dee Dee Burdle in an emotional, slightly strangulated voice, 'we come to the main business of this meeting. I shall call on you in turn to report your conclusions.'

As far as Mary Muttock could tell, and her impressions were supported by the MacDonald's whispered comments, the level of debate was crude and unimpressive. The minds of the speakers seemed simply not to be engaging with the topic as they shuffled distractedly through their notes. Whenever an apparently more penetrating remark was made, Mac dismissed it as an empty show of deconstructionist jargon with no practical bearing on the matter in hand.

So far, so good, thought the anxious Muttock. The only reservations regarding the collection's genuineness were voiced by Phyllis F. Carton, on whose features the spectacle of the dancing had called forth an excited flush but who was now reverting to her habitual pallor, and Wayne Packard, whose deepest nature it was to be obstructive. As the Chair and everybody else began to lose track of his rambling discourse, Packard really got into gear. Miss Muttock deemed it was time to act. She signalled to Derrick, Carla, Susie and Darcy, waiting behind the curtain in their servants' outfits, and Melanie, Anne, Joker and Gina, who had not yet got round to taking off their ballet costumes.

One by one they dropped to the floor and crawled out through the curtain. Because the centre table, occupied by Dee Dee and Gloria, was so close it was easy for these intruders to slip under the hanging tablecloth without being noticed by the disputing scholars. Soon they had all disappeared. Mary Muttock and Mac smiled at each other and waited to watch the visible results.

In most cases these were fairly subtle — a twitch at the corner of a scholarly mouth, the dropping of pens and wringing together of hands or the upward rolling of enraptured eyes. Presumably the sensations to which the commissioners were reacting were so agreeable that none of them wished to draw attention to what was happening and thus risk bringing the sensations to an end. It could also be presumed that none of the recipients of these unseen delights realised that his or her colleagues were receiving similar treatment. Starting with those seated furthest from the curtain, one by one they succumbed and adopted facial expressions indicative of quite unlooked-for pleasures.

Only the Captain seemed hesitant in surrendering to these joys. His problem was that unlike the others (with the exception of Gloria, who although she shared his inside knowledge was not bothered by it) he knew who was under the tables and realised there was a one in four chance that the lips fellating him belonged to Derrick or Joker. Darcy's unfledged mouth he had no objection to, but the thought of those two hairy brutes glutting themselves on his pork sword put him right off his stroke. This kind of Russian roulette, he realised, was not his favourite sport. He was somewhat relieved and invigorated however, when it occurred to him that such an encounter would be equally abhorrent to the young men, who unless their tastes were more eclectic than was generally known would surely have made a beeline for fresh cuntflesh. Fresh? Well, maybe his cock might attract a male whose only alternative was Dr Carton's minge. But what the fuck — he was hard and ready to burst anyway.

The effects of all this sucking and frigging were most conspicuous in the case of Professor Packard, who was still attempting to present his argument to the meeting. 'So where we at, man?' he was saying, beads of perspiration standing out on his brow. 'Confronted with an evidential challenge of this, of this magnitude and complexity, we need to get smart. Real smart.' He gasped, licked his lips and tried to continue. 'For Dr Simmering here the issue would seem to be one — pardon me — would seem to be one of feminist politics.' (In fact, the issue troubling Lindy Simmering at that moment seemed rather to be how far it was safe for her to lean back on her chair with her legs parted and stretched out rigidly under the table.) 'But clearly, the real issue relates to intertextuality and its implications. Guess you guys drive with your brights on, these days.' He raised his eyebrows and his eyes nearly popped out of their sockets. 'Remember all the hours we wasted trying to nail, nail, to nail plagiarisms in dissertations and term papers?'

Randle Fargo glared, remembering how shamelessly Packard had plagiarised an essay he himself had contributed to an obscure *festschrift*. Through their peepholes Miss Muttock and Miss MacDonald watched with amusement as Fargo loosened his tie while the glare was transformed into a bland and beatific smile.

Wayne Packard rambled on, fighting a gallant but unequal battle with whatever disruptive forces were assailing him beneath the table. 'In the world of intersexuality, er, that is, intertextuality, the author is dead, along with the bourgeois concept of literary proprietorship. Our words do not belong to us alone. Our bodies, too, our bodies . . .' For a moment he seemed to drift away into a kind of catatonic trance. Recovering, he went on: 'Dr Haggler wants us to find the Cunlip collection sexy on account of these pieces purporting to be by Austen, Eliot, Dickens or whatever. Now I'd say that's just Haggler's take on reality. Not even those authors' uncontested writings are truly the work of Austen, Eliot or Dickens. Copyright is nothing but a legal fiction. The idea that these embarrassing scraps of paper might be worth big bucks is just a wet − that is, a pipe dream. Every text is a mosaic made up of quotations from every other text. We all, all, we all belong to − *everybody.*'

Miss Muttock had never heard Packard address a meeting before, so she could not tell whether the treatment he was getting beneath the table was raising or lowering the level of his rhetorical powers. Nor could she follow the fine detail of the case he was presenting. But she understood enough to realise that he was arguing against the purchase of the Cunlip materials. Resourcefully, she took a swig from her flask, went down on all fours and crawled out through the curtain and under the table.

The interior of the dark tent created by the hanging tablecloths was hot, stuffy and overcrowded. She began to work her way along the table extending forward on the left, the table at which were seated first Cameron Meldrop, then Phyllis F. Carton and finally Wayne Packard. To move forward was far from easy as she had to squeeze past three upturned bottoms. The middle of these was that of Joker, whose white tights had somehow got dragged down halfway over his buttocks. To his left, attending to the stout Meldrop, the neat bum in skimpy black briefs and the white thighs between that garment and the tops of the black stockings must have belonged to Susie. To Joker's right knelt Anne Amory, identifiable from her leotard and legwarmers. The knees on either side of Anne were those of Wayne Packard; an inch or so of wet white cock extended from his open fly to Anne's lips, which were sealed tightly round it. He kept shifting his feet as his voice continued its nasal drone above the table.

Room to manoeuvre was very restricted down there on the

floor. But Mary Muttock managed to worm her way round so that her arse was sticking up alongside Packard's right thigh. Her skirt was well up over her back. She reached behind her and took the risk of lifting the tablecloth to let her hand emerge and find his elbow. Once contact was thus established it was a simple matter to bring his hand down and place it on her bum. No sooner was this contact made than he started to fiddle and fumble with her knickers, sliding his fingers under the edges and forcing his whole hand into their confines. So vigorous were the movements of his wrist as he explored between the soft buttocks and reached right underneath to rummage in the furry sex mouth that the elastic gave and the silk was ripped. The whole extent of her bottom and pussy was now bared to the lustful depredations of his fingers.

Even as the tip of one of these attempted to force her anal opening she scandalised her abuser by edging back so that her bum emerged from the tablecloth between his chair and that of Phyllis F. Carton. It is possible that the latter saw the shining white globes with Packard plundering their central division, but if she did so she was so lost in her own luxurious feelings that the inappropriateness failed to register.

The purpose of Mary Muttock's move, however, was neither to distract Dr Carton nor to please Packard but merely to bring her mouth into line with Anne's ear, so that she could whisper some instructions. The girl could hardly be expected to follow the nuances of Packard's speech, which was becoming increasingly incoherent up there above the tabletop. Muttock's idea, which she now put into practice, required Anne to be kept aware of whether what he was saying was favourable or unfavourable to their financial prospects. As long as it continued unfavourable, she told Anne to slacken the pressure of her mouth on Packard's prick and to stop sucking him. At any indication that he was about to take a more promising line, she would pat Anne's bottom to give her a cue to renew her efforts as an incentive and reward.

There was no way of knowing whether his responses were of the intellect or purely automatic but, on the whole, MIss Muttock judged them to be automatic. And as the pleasures he was allowed became more intense, so did Mary Muttock's.

Packard now had the first joint of a saliva-slick thumb firmly up her arse and was squeezing it rhythmically against the two fingers he had slipped into her vagina. In no time at all he had brushed aside all his objections to the idea that monetary value might inhere in written words, conceding that it was the discipline of the marketplace rather than literary theory that called the shots when the chips were down. 'And that,' he remarked, benignly manipulating the Muttock's rear quarters, 'is the bottom line.'

Not a word had been urged by anyone other than Packard and Dr Carton to contest the authenticity of the texts. And now Dr Carton, who seemed to inhabit an academic ivory tower of her own, expressed her somewhat restrained delight at her colleague's abandonment of his initial scruples. 'I had feared,' she confided. 'I had feared for the reputations of these fine, high-minded writers, the torch-bearers of our great tradition. Do you not share my sentiments, Professor Fargo?'

The contortions of Randle Fargo's lean features showed that he was sharing at least some of her sentiments and was physically capable of enjoying them to a much higher degree. At this moment he was gripped by passion brought on by the more literal gripping of his person under the table. Yet by exercising an iron will he was just able to get a sufficient grip on his higher faculties to make some kind of half-audible response to this appeal. 'Sure, lady,' he gasped. 'I guess it's kinda scary.'

Dr Carton beamed seraphically, her creaking joints about to twitch into overdrive as her loins thawed. 'Well,' she surmised with a certain lack of realism. 'Now we can go ahead and buy all this shameful material for Banesville and Dr Haggler can keep it under lock and key and the world need never know that poor frustrated Miss Austen and the others had those appalling moments of weakness. We can even burn it . . .' With those words she went completely uncritical, radiating mania at the imminence of meltdown triggered by an unseen finger on her button. Doomsday overtook her and she said no more.

In the chair, Dee Dee Burdle had her own distractions to contend with. As far as she could judge the sense of the meeting, the discoveries had now been accepted as genuine, so she tinkled a little bell as a signal for the second act of the ballet to commence. There was a pause, a rumbling and a bumping against the knees, calves and feet of the scholars as their unseen attendants withdrew. For the attendants themselves this was a hot and hazardous business. Mary Muttock found herself being propelled forward by a nose which must have belonged to Anne Amory nuzzling between her buttocks and forcing her to shove her own face against the sweaty fur of Joker's bum, the tights now right down round his knees to impede his progress.

At last the retreat was completed. Once more the joyful, voluptuous strains of Delibes were heard as Miss Muttock activated the tape player. The edge of the curtain was lifted back and the four dancers made their reappearance, slipping out and round to the front of the tables. Joker and Gina struck a stationary pose in which the girl's arms were extended in a gesture of yearning while her lover knelt before her wringing his hands in adoration. But the audience were more interested at this point in the two handmaidens, who stood one on each side of the motionless couple. Undulating to the music, Anne and Melanie peeled the black leotards from their bodies and stood naked save for their pretty legwarmers. Slowly they turned to display themselves from every angle; there were gasps as the extent of the indignity that had been visited upon Melanie's backside now became fully apparent. Yet fascinating as this spectacle was, there was no lack of admiration for the unblemished person of young Anne, whose tiny triangle of blonde fur challenged her partner's gingery-blonde bush in its aesthetic appeal.

Anne laid her hands on Gina's shoulders and Melanie laid hers on Joker's. All four dancers were now in motion. Melanie lifted the wreath of flowers from Gina's head to release the flimsy yellow veil. She replaced the wreath and performed a little dance of triumph, swirling the gauze above her head and letting it trail behind her as she flitted around the floor. The compass of her movements narrowed until she was circling round the hirsute Joker, who stood with raised arms while Anne knelt in front of him in the act of dragging down his tights before his prick could grow too erect for the elastic of the waist to be pulled down over it. He kicked the garment aside and pranced about like a stallion.

And now began the main part of this performance. The routine the dancers had gone through on their earlier appearance was repeated, at least in its broad outlines, by the now naked quartet. While Gina stretched languorously, stroking her limbs and contemplating her pretty freckles, Melanie and Anne skimmed butterfly hands all over her body. Joker stood by, intent on adopting the poses of a body builder, flexing and tensing his bronzed muscles.

In a bold variation on the original theme, the two handmaidens now left Gina to her own slow writhings and pounced on the narcissistic youth. Melanie stood behind him and pressed the cool length of the front of her body against the back of his. Her slightly convex belly was urged into the yielding flesh of his bum and her hard nipples bored into the skin at the base of his shoulder blades. She reached round in front of him with both hands to hold his prick while cupping his testicles. Soon a change in the configuration of his tool was very obvious. It had hung down, large but lazy, swinging in time with the music. But as Melanie stroked and squeezed, it filled out like a sausage-shaped balloon being inflated. Anne dropped to her knees in front of him. After fixing the hefty club with her violet eyes she thrust herself forward, took her small but shapely breasts in her hands and rubbed the long nipples alternately on the purple knob. When she drew back, everyone could see that they were wet with the sticky fluid that was smeared over the cockhead. Both attendants now stepped away from Joker, who appealed to them with silent gestures of his hands and his bouncing dick. For a moment they had eyes only for each other as Anne surrendered her wet gleaming nipples to Melanie's tongue. Then Melanie slapped the girl's bottom, spun her round and forced her to take the first few inches of the massive cock into her mouth.

Now that Joker was thoroughly aroused they abandoned him to his rhythmic self-contemplation and returned to attend to Gina. The auburn-haired girl had been caressing her tits with one hand and the insides of her thighs with the other; her servitors now took over these duties, as well as that of defending her from a succession of leaping attacks launched against her by the understandably impatient Joker. As in the earlier version

205

of the dance a change in the music signalled a change in tactics. Melanie embraced Gina breast to breast, kissing her ardently with open mouth. Anne broke away from Joker's clutches to change places with Melanie and they kept up this exchange about half a dozen times, so that the constant and subtle variations of skin texture, body temperature and pliancy of the handmaidens' convexities brought the lasciviousness of the separated couple up to boiling point.

And now, at last, the satisfaction of Joker's great need was in sight. His two tormentors positioned themselves to each side of him and slightly behind, gripped his arms and used their knees to force his loins lewdly forward. Gina's slim form arched back so that her chestnut-crested cuntmound was thrust into prominence. She inched her way forward. Melanie and Anne made Joker bend his knees to bring his stem down to the level of her lovelips, which she held wide open. As soon as the glowing plum was rammed against her flesh, Joker's legs straightened with the force of metal springs and the handmaidens fell back on the floor. Gina, a pretty picture indeed, crowned with her flowery wreath, was lifted right off her feet as the lusty cock drove up into her.

Joker might have been an unpolished yob, but Miss Muttock was relieved to see that at least he was chivalrous enough to assist this sudden elevation by taking the cheeks of Gina's bottom in his clumsy hands — otherwise the spear would surely have pierced right up through her vitals.

Anne and Melanie picked themselves up and, for a brief moment, the dance continued. The conjoined lovers circled round in the most intimate of waltzes, framed by the caressing hands of their lovely assistants. As the music reached a most convenient crescendo, all four performers froze in a touching tableau. Before the eyes of the audience, Joker and Gina betrayed, by a series of pulsating quivers which their utmost exertion of will was unable to control, that intercourse was taking place.

Although half stunned by this spectacle, the watching scholars were just able to applaud appreciatively. But the show was not yet over. Somewhat drained after his exertions, Joker staggered across to the end of one of the projecting tables with Gina still impaled on his rod and clinging round his neck and hips. He dumped her on the table and unplugged. Melanie and Anne stepped forward and slewed her body round so that her knees were level with the edge of the table and her legs dangled down on either side of Randle Fargo's. The first impulse of that lean academic was to reach for the gaping slit that was spilling jism on his jottings. But Melanie had now moved to stand between him and Lindy Simmering while Anne stood on his right. Both girls faced him so that he was presented with the choice of three cunts. This, however, proved to be no choice. No choice was needed — the girls on either side each took one of his hands and placed it palm upwards under her crotch. Joker, who had come up behind him, pushed him forward so that his mouth came down on Gina's pulpy mound as she lay there. The auburn hairs of her bush responded by standing up on end.

Even Miss Muttock was thrilled by the new turn of events — such a degree of audience participation had not been planned for this stage of the entertainment. Unwilling to withdraw her eye from its peephole in the curtain, she reached around until she found the hand of someone standing beside her and pressed it against her sex.

Meanwhile, Joker moved round to the inside of the table and stood facing Fargo, who was doing mean things with his tongue. The tables were quite narrow; Gina's head was almost hanging over the edge. When Joker laid his horny hands on her breasts she opened her eyes to see his sexual equipment dangling just above her mouth. The prick was still limp, though already beginning to lengthen, and reeking from its recent exercise. She opened her lips and drew it in.

But afternoon had given way to early evening and all the performers were conscious, at any rate in flashes of lucidity, that a tight schedule had to be adhered to. Suddenly the girls on either side of him snatched Dr Fargo's fingers out of their vaginas and dragged him back into an upright position. With Joker's help they slid Gina a couple of feet sideways to her right. Her vulva was now presented to the eager attentions of Lindy Simmering, and the two assistants placed themselves at Lindy's sides. And so the game progressed, allowing just a few minutes to each member of the commission as the entertainers worked their way along the table. After Professor Simmering it was the turn of the Captain. Then Gina was manoeuvred through ninety degrees and slid along the top of table to the delight of Gloria and Dee Dee. Again she was slewed round for the last leg of her journey. The porky Meldrop was too fat to get his head right down between Gina's thighs and had to be content with the sight and aroma of her twitching cunt while handling those of Anne and Melanie.

Dr Carton had been a rather distanced witness of these happenings. But the minute the tasty dish was set before her she forgot any scruples and stooped to the succulent feast. Her colleagues round the table, who had enjoyed observing each other's pleasure almost as much as their own, looked away in embarrassment. Even Mary Muttock, watching from behind the curtain, lost interest in this encounter and abandoned herself to the fingers which had turned out to belong to Derrick. She came explosively, just as Phyllis Carton's allotted time was up, and returned her somewhat sore eye to the peephole.

Wayne Packard set aside his pipe, attacked his meal with high relish and stuck in his tongue with a will, determined to bring Gina to unambiguous, climactic orgasm. This, however, was not to be. Joker's cock had been so stiffly erect ever since his girlfriend had embarked on her journey down this third table that there was no longer any question of forcing it down between her lips, however far he leaned forward. While she was being gamahuched by Meldrop, Carton and Packard he had simply stood at her head, fondling her pink-tipped breasts while his heavy ballsack dangled in her mouth. But by this time he was no longer able to contain his pent-up charge. Reaching across the table he grabbed the girl's thighs and drew them back towards him. Wayne Packard's mouth was left high and fairly dry.

Joker lifted until it was only through her head and shoulders that Gina maintained her contact with the table. Holding her in this upended position, he licked deeply into the folds of her cunt. Then he flipped her right over. Her feet were on the floor, her breasts were pressed against the surface of the table, squashed out to the sides, and her eyes gazed with some perplexity into those of Professor Packard, who had been reduced to diverting himself by toying with the freely proffered pussies of Melanie and Anne. Joker, his hands on her buttocks, shoved forward, skewered her and commenced a rapid succession of ramping heaves.

'Joker Jennings!' she cried. 'How often — how often have I told you to stick to my mouth and not stick it in the other places, you smutty yobbo?'

'Yeah, but we just . . .'

'That was for the dance, you oaf. No one said — aaah! — no one said you could do this.'

'This is OK, though, innit? Ain't 'urtin' you?'

'Well, at least — oooh! — at least it's not my cunt.'

'Shuddup, you stuck-up bitch. I'm goin' to come.'

'Ouch! It's so — so fucking *hot*. Aaah — you make me so *ashamed*.'

Gina winced as he shot into her. Miss Muttock lifted the end of the curtain and clapped her hands; the four performers came running to join her offstage, pausing only to acknowledge the stunned applause of the commissioners, who were now addressed by their Chair.

'I am, um, I'm sure we all appreciated that diversion,' gulped Dee Dee Burdle. 'Moving down our agenda we next come to the photographic materials. Any reservations regarding the authenticity or quality of these items?'

Satisfied grunts signified that any residual resistance had by now been swept aside. Dr Carton was even moved to comment favourably on the obscene material. 'Just lovely,' she said. 'So fresh they take me back to the snapshots my uncle used to take of my sisters and me when we were little girls.'

Professor Burdle continued. 'Very well. The pictorial as well as the printed and written documents are accepted as genuine. And now we come to the final part of the entertainment so, er, thoughtfully presented by our hostess. This brief item has been added as a further surprise. Miss Muttock tells me that we are about to celebrate a happy coincidence. Today, as you are aware, is June seven. What you will not be aware of is that it happens to be the first anniversary of the marriage of two of our young body servants. Mr and Mrs O'Flammery have kindly offered to act out, in abbreviated dance form, their, um,

209

nuptials and to, er, share some of the fun with you. Guys and girls, I give you — wait for it — Susan and Darcy O'Flammery.'

Out from behind the curtain tripped the radiant pair to receive the applause of the quickly reviving spectators. Wayne Packard, who hailed from Boston, had a penchant for most things Irish and was ignorant that neither of the dancers had set foot in Kilburn, let alone the Emerald Isle; his enthusiasm was particularly emphatic. Of those present or viewing from behind the curtain, only the Captain, Miss Muttock and Melanie knew at first hand that Susie and Darcy's costumes were what they had actually worn that night a year ago in the Palace of Sweethearts — the MacDonald, now quite beyond caring as Derrick screwed the arse off her, had been told this but the others assumed that the getup was some whim of the choreographer. The smooth-skinned Darcy stood stark naked, save for a white ribbon tied low around his hips. From this ribbon, at the front and back, hung two little white handkerchiefs. A red rosebud adorned the black velvet choker at his throat. His bride simpered beside him, dressed identically apart from a couple of additional touches. Instead of being bare, her feet were neat in white sandals and ankle socks. A non-functional blue and white bridal garter decorated her left thigh. Instead of displaying a nude torso, she wore a flimsy suntop, sleeveless and unbuttoned down the front, but not quite revealing the little breasts to each side of the opening. It reached to just above the level of her navel. But what most strikingly distinguished her from her chestnut-haired groom was the gauzy veil falling down her back from a headdress of artificial white blossoms fastened to her golden curls. The edges of this veil, shorter than the all-enveloping yellow one worn earlier by Gina, lay over her bare shoulders, and down the front it hung wide open, showing off the skimpy costume. The rosebud at her throat was echoed in two little red bows on the ends of the pigtails that fell forward over her shoulders.

For the last time, Mary Muttock left her peephole for a moment to set the music going again — this time Mendelssohn's wedding march. The couple gazed at one another coyly, placed their hands on each other's shoulders and leaned forward for a shy kiss, a gesture which caused their front handkerchiefs to hang forward slightly, favouring the onlookers with a brief glimpse of the bride's blonde mound and her groom's limp equipment in its little nest of soft brown fur.

They straightened up. A series of sallies, genuflexions and pirouettes in which the boy kept his distance from the girl allowed further tantalising glimpses. As the distance between them increased, their gestures became more blatant until they were quite openly displaying their sexual attractions to each other. Handkerchiefs both fore and aft were lifted and Susie held the front of her suntop open to entice Darcy with her two plump little pink-tipped breastlets. The puffy areolae, slightly larger than what had been expected by most of the audience, proclaimed her a grown woman. Stimulated by these proceedings, Darcy's cock was lengthening and stiffening slightly, though not enough to raise his handkerchief beyond an angle of forty-five degrees.

And now they were standing at the ends of the projecting tables. Darcy leapt up in front of Packard while Randle Fargo rose and gallantly assisted Susie to climb up on the parallel table. The music had come to an end. The couple processed up these side tables with a show of solemnity and modesty belied by the ease with which the seated scholars could look up and, beginning with calves and knees, enjoy the expanses of lightly flushed flesh running up their seminudity. Being so close, the bolder researchers among them were able to lean forward and peer up under the scant drapery, and the youngsters barely flinched when the odd marauding hand spidered its way over the downy surface of a leg or rested momentarily in the exposed hollow of a flank.

They had reached the corners and turned inwards to advance and meet in the middle of the top table, right in front of Dee Dee and Gloria but also well positioned for the entertainment of Mary Muttock and the others behind the curtain. Before coming together they turned slowly round to give everyone a good view of their supposedly virginal purity. By this time Darcy's handkerchief was draped from a horizontal erection and his pink balls hung fully in view. The bride opened the front of her little top. Darcy gazed at the provocative display — his cock stretched up, slender and rosy-tipped, allowing its white covering to fall right back. Lacking this means of self-discovery, Susie took the corners of her own handkerchief daintily between her fingers and lifted it to her belly. The spectators gasped delightedly at their first unobstructed sighting of her triangular patch of fine yellow curls, framing but not concealing the neat pink gash that ran down to lose itself between the creamy thightops. This sight, however, was not vouchsafed for long — the couple embraced, mouth to mouth, breast to breast, belly to belly and crotch to crotch. Whether as a result of training or simply out of pity for the spectators so soon deprived of that pretty sight, the youngsters then let their hands wander round each other's backs to uncover their bottoms. Clinging in their tight embrace they slowly turned where they stood to give everyone equal pleasure. Susie then pushed Darcy gently away from her.

His prick stood up vertically against his tummy, shining with the bride's juices. She whispered in his ear and he lay down on his back, directly in front of the privileged Dee Dee and Gloria. The others now left their seats and gathered round on the inner side of the top table, reluctant to miss any detail of the ensuing action.

Gathering her gauzy veil to one side and slipping her suntop slightly down off her shoulders, Susie knelt astraddle her groom. For a while she gazed lovingly into his eyes. Slowly and deliberately she reached behind her and tucked her back handkerchief up into the ribbon that held it. Then she did the same to the front one.

With impatient fingers she now pulled open the moist folds of her girlflesh. Her husband, seeing what she was at, raised a hand to toy with one of her little breasts while with his other hand he forced his slick rod into an upright stance. He rubbed the tip up and down the wet trench and pressed it against the entrance to the vagina. Susie slid down to sheathe it completely. Her busy fingers played with their intermingling pubic hair, fascinated by the contrast in colour. She leaned forward and he raised his head to kiss her nipples. His head went back to the table and she lowered hers further to kiss him passionately on the mouth. This gave the little crowd of bystanders an opportunity to admire the white bottom conveniently splayed above Darcy's loins. The groove looked so inviting that Cameron Meldrop was unable to refrain from running a plump finger down from the base of her spine, tapping at the puckered pinkness of her back entrance and briefly paddling in the sticky leakage where her engorged cuntlips clung to the root of the boy's cock.

Stung into action by these liberties, Susie reared herself upright and began to pump her haunches up and down as if spurring a mettlesome mount to the winning post. Her little tits, the nipples and areolae now fiercely purple, jigged in time with her fucking. On each outstroke the white truncheon that flashed into view appeared thicker. On each instroke Darcy's little bush became more sodden with the pungent fluids pressed into it by the descending cunt, until the hairs, dark in their wetness, were plastered flat against his white skin.

The whole expanse of Susie's bare front flared up in an ecstatic flush. Her bucking up and down became ever more frantic and she hit the first of a succession of orgasmic peaks. She leaned right back and her knees came up from the table as she collapsed on her husband's legs. The instrument of her pleasure slipped out of its convulsing sheath. Although he had discharged in the depths of her quim so violently that in the throes of bliss he had bitten his lower lip, the white come was still welling out of the gaping cocktip and running thickly down the stem.

And now came the real treat, a treat Miss Muttock had persuaded the couple with some reluctance to furnish for the final softening-up of the guests. Softening, to be sure, is a word that would have applied more aptly to the women of the party than to the men, who had grown harder and harder throughout the performance. The young performers got up and moved to the ends of the side tables. Susie lay on her back with her legs open and hanging down over the edge. Her handkerchief, of course, was still tucked up so as not to obstruct the view of her ravaged cunt with Darcy's semen oozing out of it. Darcy, for his part, stood with the backs of his thighs against the edge of the other table. He leaned back until his elbows rested on the tabletop and let his head hang down to touch the cloth.

In no time at all, Lindy Simmering had dropped her pale

213

mauve skirt and bared her pussy. Darcy, unable to enjoy the sight in his awkward posture, had to be brought back to full hardness by the application of her tongue and lips. She straightened up, placed her feet on either side of his and leaned against the spike until it had passed right up inside her.

Meanwhile, Randle Fargo was standing between Susie's thighs, bathing his fat dick in Darcy's sperm. As soon as Lindy and Randle had finished, their places were taken by another couple until everyone in the room had been satisfied at least once, except Dee Dee Burdle and Gloria Sweetbutts, who did not need to be convinced of the value of the Cunlip collection and therefore remained in the background, pleasuring each other. Even Dr Carton allowed her tuft of scrubby hairs to be moistened by Darcy, whose ability to maintain a measure of stiffness under adverse circumstances and to keep up an unstinting flow of fluid was undoubtedly a talent attributable to youth, health and marriage to the delectable Susie. After fucking Susie, Wayne Packard insisted on turning Darcy round and buggering him as the lad bent over the table. Behind the curtain, Miss Muttock, Miss MacDonald, Gina, Anne and Carla had to make do with Joker, Derrick and each other, but they did pretty well.

At last the commissioners, their eyes glazed over, slumped into their chairs. When Professor Burdle called them to order and asked what might be considered a realistic sum for the university to pay for the treasures under discussion, no further debate was needed.

'No question,' panted Packard. 'We pay the asking price — what was it? — three million bucks.'

FOURTEEN

MULTIPLE EXPOSURE

'Waddya d-doing to me, Doc?' stammered Gloria. 'I guess it's gotten so big you gonna split me right open.'

She reclines on the chaise longue in the Captain's Palace of Fantasies, one foot on the floor as if acknowledging the moral standards of Hollywood's golden years, the other thrown up over the back of the couch. She is naked from the navel down, but the concealed observer of this intimate scene cannot see her pussy as the space between her thighs is fully occupied by the hairy-arsed Captain. Her dissertation notes lie scattered on the floor, for this encounter began as a one-on-one counselling session. Some months have passed since the commissioners returned to Tampoon County with bulging briefcases and Professor Burdle of UCLA recommended the immediate disbursement of three million dollars from the Banesville library accessions budget. Plus, of course, her own expenses. The money has been paid out and even after recompensing all his collaborators with varying degrees of fairness the Captain is left with enough ready cash to keep his PA in fine style. It is now November. The fall semester is well under way and most of the fantasies to which this booklined fun palace is dedicated have become realities.

'C-come on, Doc,' Gloria whimpers. 'Come on, big boy. Do it to me. Come on — do it inside me. B-bathe my sex with your fuckjuice.'

A bulky male figure bursts into the room and looms over the lovers. 'On your feet, Haggler,' he thunders. 'I need to talk with you.'

'Give us a break, Dean,' pleads the panting Captain.

But Frolander grabs him by the collar and pulls him to his feet. The fuckjuice gushes from the Captain's steaming unsheathed implement and bathes Gloria's sex. But not internally, as she desired — great creamy clots are deposited on her ruffled fur and clog the outer approaches to her cunt. Stray gobbets splash her blouse, her stockings and the fine brocade of the chaise longue. Unable to hold back at this level of arousal, the young woman brings a hand down to her vulva. Pressing the thumb hard into her clitoris, she scrabbles frantically with her fingers as if determined to urge into her channel the slippery jism of which it has just been cheated. The air is heavy with the scent of lust; Dean Frolander's nostrils twitch and his batrachian eyes almost pop out of their sockets as she jerks up her loins in orgasm.

Frolander's office is severely functional. A few metal filing cabinets still contain his personal effects, but routine paperwork has long since given way to computer inputting. The steel desk is clear, apart from an array of state-of-the-art electronic gadgetry.

The boss sits back, squinting at a silver pen he rolls between his fingers. It is an implement he rarely uses except to sign letters and cheques. 'Well now,' he begins, stealing a glance at the Captain, who stands uneasily on the other side of the desk. 'How could you be so stoopid, Haggler? Like, you let them put the make on you with all kinds of sweet talk and the library winds up smelling of shit? Now, some of the goddam faculty can get away with first degree, but just remember — you don't have tenure, buddy. We play hardball round here and we play it my way. I hire and I fire. And today I guess I'm in a kinda mean, firing mood.'

Shifting his weight from foot to foot, the Captain feels the blood drain from his cheeks. So far he has never been inside an American jail and that prospect holds no allurement for him. But if his cover is well and truly blown the future looks grim. 'Maybe my judgment has been at fault,' he ventures.

'The fuck it has! Man, your fucking judgment's been so flaky we could forget the allegations of collusive fraud and kick you out on your butt as some kinda crazy airhead not safe to be let loose on campus. You screwed up, Haggler. You goofed.'

'Allegations? What allegations are these?' Perhaps a stance of indignant innocence is called for.

'I just been talking with Packard. Packard's a guy with values. Ain't you Brits supposed to have values — like, your Mrs Thing standing up to them crazy Hispanics? I guess we got our American values from you in the first place. This great tradition going back to, you know, Magna Carta and Eric the Red. Or maybe I should say the Pilgrim Fathers. Well, it don't matter where he got them — Packard's been dipped in them values right up to his ears. He don't hold with sucking the blood outa great institootions like this library. No sir. Been wrestling with his conscience these last weeks and ended up telling me everything. Just everything.'

The Captain quails. But how has Wayne Packard found out? 'How did he find out?' he asks.

Frolander contemplates. 'Guess I owe it to you to tell you this much,' he says. 'You won't be putting the word around, on account of you won't be here no more? Case of *cherchez la femme,* as they say. Seems Professor Packard got kinda romantic on your trip to England. Says he tried to resist but she seduced him. Not a worldly man, young Packard. A true idealist.'

Alarming suspicions run through the Captain's mind. During the visit to Cunlip Hall, Packard's nocturnal needs had been catered to by good old Melanie. Was it possible that some indiscretion had passed her lips, some fragment of ill-considered pillow talk? Frolander continues:

'Danged if I don't blame myself for appointing her. But we needed credibility. The Chair had to be an outsider. And this Burdle dame's real good — an international reputation, they tell me. Pity to destroy it.'

'Nothing wrong with *her* judgment.'

'Not her judgment, no. It's her morals have fucked us up, Haggler.'

'You mean she's been sleeping with Professor Packard?'

'Guess that's your typical British understatement. She's been sleeping with him and doing drugs with him and raving in her

217

sleep and telling him things would make you wanna weep. You been suckered. That Byron manuscript you purchased from her? That ain't no Byron manuscript — it's straight Burdle, by her own confession. We been taken, man. Taken. Screwed. But at least there's an upside to it.'

'What's that?'

'Think about it, Haggler. Who's your best bet when it comes to spotting forgeries?'

'Well . . .'

'A first-class forger, that's who. Set a thief to catch a thief. She wasn't a bad choice to chair the commission. She says all that Cunlip stuff's hunky-dory and I guess we can still take her word for it.'

The Captain wonders if the worst is over and he can ride this one out after all. 'Look, Dean,' he says, 'the Byron business was petty cash. And if she hadn't spilt the beans herself no one would have caught on. It wasn't just me that was taken in — I got Packard's opinion as soon as I'd agreed to buy.'

'OK, so Packard okayed it. But I guess that was *ex post facto*, right? It's your blood the library committee's gonna be after. And sure as I'm sitting here they'll have the cops on you, baby. That's right, I ain't done telling you what the Burdle broad said to Packard. Said she let you slip her a length before you did the deal? That's why the DA's sure to be looking at the possibility of fraudulent collusion. ''Shades of the prison house'', as your great poet says.'

'Isn't there any way to keep the cops out of this?'

Frolander sucks in his cheeks and squints at the pen he holds up. 'Well, it just happens there could be a way, Haggler. You been laying that Gloria Sweetbutts?'

Surprised at the question — or is it a declaration? — the Captain nods.

'A real pretty little thing, that Gloria,' Frolander enthuses. 'Could fancy her myself if I wasn't . . .'

'Oh, I'm sure we could do a deal on that sort of basis.'

'What I was saying, Haggler, was this. I can fix things with the library committee so you resign with dignity and no questions asked. We withdraw the *Don Juan* forgery quietly and don't even have to make the headlines by discrediting the Burdle woman. All you have to do is let me spy on you and Ms Sweetbutts having it away. Oh, and I'll need to take a few pictures? Plenty of come shots.'

Off the periodicals room a wide corridor is fitted out with carrels for the use of faculty and graduate students. These carrels are seven-foot-square cubicles, partitioned off from the corridor and from each other by walls as high as they are long − in other words, the cubicles are lidless cubes. Each is furnished with the bare necessities of study: a small desk with a lamp, shelves on the wall above it and a chair.

It is evening. In the darkness of carrel number five the massive figure of Dean Frolander stands on a chair, his pants down round his ankles and a camera hanging round his neck. He peers over the partition into carrel number six, where the desk lamp casts a pool of golden light on the floor. Two naked bodies swim in this pool, their heads out of sight under the desk and their feet unseen in the outlying shadows.

When the Captain first raised the matter Gloria had been reluctant. He, after all, might be leaving the university, but she was hoping to remain and complete her dissertation. Further contact with Frolander would be an inevitable embarrassment for her. But knowing what was at stake she had succumbed and promised to try to come to terms with her shyness and natural modesty. One of Frolander's kinky conditions was that both participants were to be aware that they were being spied on. On the other hand, they would not know exactly when, for they were required to go through their performance every evening for a week. The voyeuristic photographer would surprise them with his flash from time to time and they were expected to conduct themselves in such a way that whenever this happened the view they presented to his lens would be a memorable one. Another condition was that the carrel door would be unlocked so that the lovers were at the mercy of casual intruders. In fact this condition would have gone without saying, as only one of the carrels − number five − has a lock and bolt, but Frolander chose to mention it to ensure that his victims' thrills were heightened by their consciousness of the risk.

Dean Frolander has had a good week. Every evening he has

shown up in the lockable carrel at a different time, sometimes more than once. He has not always taken a photograph; often it has been more interesting just to stand on his chair in the darkness watching Haggler and Sweetbutts go through the whole routine from foreplay to afterplay. And then to let them start over if it's still early enough in the evening.

Once he takes a picture, of course, the blinding flash tends to put them off their stroke. Frolander may be a voyeur but he is not really a sadist. In this respect he is pretty much like the Captain. The Captain has a good idea of what will keep Frolander sweet, and takes care that he gets it — up to two or three photos a session, including at least one come shot, and plenty of prick-stiffening action in between.

On the first occasion the eager librarian had climbed up on his chair, collar unbuttoned and cock hanging free, a good ten minutes before the lovers turned up. He ducked his head as the main overhead light was switched on, raising it again as soon as the shaded desk lamp was substituted. He had seen Haggler wedge the chair under the handle of the door, an expedient that might have given the couple a few moments to make themselves decent if anyone came but could hardly have averted some sort of scandal. Then they both undressed, the man almost precipitately and his girlfriend with nervous birdlike movements, draping their clothes over the desk. In their haste they left their socks on. Gloria's sexiness was enhanced by the black and red striped ankle socks, but her partner's ill-matched grey ones with holes at the toes held little appeal for the hidden onlooker.

The girl was placed on her back across the small desk. Her feet dangled down from well-parted knees and her fluffy brown bush blazed directly under the lamp, a tufted island uplifted from the surrounding pool of gleaming white flesh. The salient geographical feature of this island was a narrow rift of coral which was disclosed when Gloria thoughtfully if self-consciously crushed the hairs under her fingers, sweeping them sideways and outwards for the benefit of her unseen admirer.

This gesture also suited the convenience of her acknowledged lover. Taking care not to obstruct his boss's view, Haggler knelt above her on the desk, his knees nudging her armpits, and bent forward. His tongue reached out to its full extent and the tip

220

began to flick at the upper end of the ravine. His hands went round under her bottom; she lifted her legs and planted her feet on the edge of the desk, letting her rounded thighs fall wide open so that her knees almost touched the surface. The tonguetip flicked faster. The man's fingers curled up round her buttocks and upper thighs until they tickled the stretched sinews of her groins.

Suddenly the tongue was withdrawn as its owner straightened up to stand on the desk. He pulled the bottom up with him. Gloria's face flushed as the blood rushed to her head, which together with her shoulders and elbows remained in contact with the desktop. But her back was raised vertically so that her bum stuck up in the air while her legs hung unsupported at right angles to her body. Haggler had to move the lamp a couple of feet to the side to avoid singeing the double hedge of curls that lined the soft banks on either side of the pouting, upturned trench of love.

Frolander had nearly fallen off his chair at the sight. Evidently Haggler had planned his next move with great care for the watcher's benefit. He stood astride his upended sweetheart between her waving legs and bent his body forward so that his stiff prick came down from a vertical to a horizontal elevation. Then he used one hand to force it down even further while with the forefinger and thumb of the other one he prised apart the plump cuntlips.

Both Frolander and Ms Sweetbutts gasped audibly and simultaneously as her lover's rod was plunged straight down in one fell swoop into the juicy tube. Because of the position of the lamp, what Frolander now boggled at was an illuminated patch of flesh, roughly circular. Gloria's pulpy cunt formed its centre. It also contained her buttocks, partly covered by a pair of dark-haired male hands, the whole of the groove between the cheeks round to the base of her spine, and the backs of her upper thighs, as well as the lower reaches of a shaggy male abdomen with its great black thicket of wiry scrub. In fact, what the lamp so attractively highlighted for contemplation, dismissing all irrelevant or distracting detail to outer darkness, was the very arena of lust. Frolander had bitten his lower lip and squeezed his bollocks as the lewd act was performed before his eyes.

221

Every time the hands forced the buttocks down, the ramping prick was drawn out into view. The full detail of the network of veins contrasting with the whiteness of the cockskin could be clearly made out in the brightness of the lamplight. This was so in spite of a thick coating of lovejuice sucked up from the cunt on each stroke along with the clinging petals of tender girlflesh that refused to relinquish the glans. Time and again their separation from the violating organ seemed inevitable but always, at the very limit of its withdrawal, the swollen stem drove down again, sweeping the petals back out of sight as it was swallowed up in its sheath.

At last the knob was pulled right out, already discharging. The man's fingers kept it pointing downwards so that every slug of sperm either slapped into the mushy folds of flesh in which it had been wallowing or laced the smooth skin surrounding those folds. A warm puddle of the silvery fluid formed in the hollow between those upturned thighs and bottom cheeks. It began to seep backwards into the pouting arsehole and forwards to soak the girl's bush. But Frolander had missed his chance. With the camera still hanging round his neck he had shot his own load all over the partition wall.

Another time he had arrived in his carrel, mounted the chair and found them already at it on the desk. The circle of light was almost entirely occupied by the unappetising sight of a set of hirsute buttocks and balls; Gloria's splayed thighs could just be seen disappearing into the darkness on either side as they bounced over her. And then her lover got off her, moving right out of the circle, which now spotlighted the girl's pubic region. Frolander had not even had time to unzip his pants. This time he had no intention of being caught off his guard. He steadied his camera on the top of the partition and took aim just as the shower of semen shot from the shadows and sprayed all over the smooth white skin, the chestnut curls and the gaping leaves of the cunt.

On yet another occasion Frolander had been watching them lying on their sides half concealed under the desk, where they were writhing in a sixty-nine. He nearly fell backwards when he heard an impatient tugging at the handle of his own carrel door. The rattling stopped. He heard the door of the adjacent

222

carrel open and saw the lovebirds blink up in horror. Almost immediately, the horror gave way to relieved smiles. Two clothed forms busied themselves at the circumference of the illuminated circle; the light caught their happy faces for an instant and Frolander recognised them as Warren S. Buckmaster Junior and that redhead Coralmay Connochie, the freshers he had met at the cocktail party last semester.

Gloria and Haggler had resumed their mutual licking and sucking while the newly arrived couple fussed around them. The ecstatic but more or less static mandala of the sixty-nine was now enlivened by the hands, lips and tongues which flickered in and out of the pool of light at its periphery.

After a while this activity ceased for a moment. Then, while Gloria and her man continued their mutual pleasuring with increasing violence, Warren and Coralmay changed their tactics. Instead of letting the flat of her tongue lap all over the illuminated nudity without regard for the sex of the person being licked, Coralmay concentrated on Haggler's bum. Frolander saw (or was pretty sure he saw) the pointed tip make fleeting contact with the root of the prick, tickling Gloria's chin and lips as it did so, before rasping back over the hairy balls and forcing an entry into the Britisher's back passage. At the same time, Warren's unleashed and saliva-coated ramrod homed in on Gloria's sweet butt. Once again Frolander's impression was that the first place touched by the intruder was the point of connection between the lovers. It seemed that the knob was momentarily stuffed into the girl's vagina alongside Haggler's penetrating tongue before sliding wetly back to violate the anal aperture. Unfortunately photography was out of the question, as it was important not to alert these young newcomers to the fact that the tableau was being observed. But Frolander had enjoyed a truly satisfying wank, spilling his seed just at the instant when the four on the other side of the partition came in a tumult that rolled them out of the lamplight.

Dean Frolander relishes the recollection of these exciting moments as he stands on the chair with his pants round his ankles and his camera round his neck. He raises the camera, steadies it on the partition and adjusts the focus; then he moves the zoom lens in and out until the circle of light fills his viewfinder. He will need the flash, of course, to take the picture but he finds pleasure in seeing the sportive couple so neatly framed in the confines of their golden pool.

Perhaps the cocksure Brit has forgotten the explicit instructions Frolander gave him, or perhaps he is just warming the girl up in preparation for the big moment. On all the previous occasions the action has been consciously pointed in the librarian's direction and executed in such a way as to make an enticing display for him. But tonight he has not caught sight of more of Ms Sweetbutts than her legs wrapped round the hips slamming into her.

Nevertheless, this view, though conventional, is one that plenty of guys would pay good money to see. The legs are long and slim and the attitude one of enjoyment. The shots he took on previous evenings were all rather hotter stuff, but if he fails to get the present scene he might regret it in years to come when his ardour is beginning to cool and his cardiovascular system can no longer cope with the extremes of lust.

While such reflections pass vaguely through his consciousness, the pressure of Frolander's fingertip on the firing button increases involuntarily until the shutter clicks and the flash floods the whole carrel with its harsh glare. The split-second of exposure is followed by a longer moment of dazzled blindness and in that moment rough hands seize him by the ears. The desk lamp is lifted and pointed straight at him. As his eyes slowly recover he registers that Coralmay Connochie is holding the lamp while Warren Buckmaster starts to shake him. Only the fear of being found naked by library staff obliged the youth to exercise some restraint. But if his and Coralmay's predicament is an embarrassing one, Frolander's is worse. His career is in peril, especially if the Women's Library Group or the clean-up-campus faction get to hear about his conduct. He tries to think quickly. 'Thought I'd caught some sneaky thief,' he explains. 'Real sorry to disturb you guys.'

'Ain't much to steal in these carrels, man,' replies Warren. 'Guess you know that. And everyone knows they call them fuckholes. Hanging around the fuckholes with a camera — well, don't that just speak for itself, Coralmay?'

Coralmay has pulled on a sweater, switched on the main light

224

and got up on a chair to bring herself up to Frolander's level. As he fumbles for something to say he shifts awkwardly from foot to foot and his unfastened trousers drop to his ankles. Even the shock of discovery has been insufficient to deflate the visible evidence of his guilt.

'Say,' he splutters. 'Let's just call it quits, right? I wasn't here with my camera and you weren't screwing her ass off in the library precincts.'

Warren seems relieved but Coralmay has a better idea. 'You carry much weight round here, Doc Frolander?' she asks.

'When it comes to library matters my word's pretty well law.'

'Have any, er, influence with Professor Packard?'

'Guess he owes me a few favours.'

'Well, Warren and me, we been having some problems with his 101 course? Like, we not been getting the grades we think we deserve? My mom's real mad — she wants me to have nothing but straight *A*s.'

'Mine too,' adds Warren. 'Fix it so Packard always gives us *A*s and I'll fuck her down there on the desk for you. And then we'll do it with Dr Haggler and Ms Sweetbutts. Oh, and we'd like some prints, sir.'

The first-class cabin offers far roomier accommodation for airborne lovers than the Captain experienced the last time he flew to England. And the cabin crew are discreetly non-judgmental. Bare from the waist down, Gloria stretches across the two springy seats between window and aisle. Equally free from hampering garments, the Captain lies under a light blanket and corkscrews his stiffness into her seepage.

'Ladies and gentleman, this is your captain.' A piped message informs them of their altitude above Greenland, the English weather and their expected time of arrival at Heathrow. It wishes them a pleasant journey.

Gloria gazes up with a look of devotion. 'You know, Doc,' she murmurs, 'from now on I guess *you're* gonna be my captain.'

Acknowledging that this is the end of their academic nexus — her dissertation will never be finished — the Captain agrees. He fucks harder. Fleeting images of the pleasures towards which he is winging his way, images of Melanie's gingery bush and the darker auburn of the fluff at Gina's sex, are distractions which have the effect of heightening his present excitement. His fucking becomes even harder and so does his cock; he feels the charge of sperm gathering in his ducts. 'Never thought that much of California,' he confides in the ear of the shy but compliant New Englander. 'Too sodding materialistic.'

'That's what I like about you, Captain,' she replies. 'You aim high. Take me with you, lover. Fly me as high as you like. Take me right up there to the jetstream.'

The Captain does not need to be asked — he is already losing control of his steep, accelerating ascent. Gloria heaves herself up in lustful deliverance high above the frozen north as hot jets of sperm stream into her open body. It feels as if the pulsing flow will never end.

Nexus

THE BEST IN EROTIC READING – BY POST

The nexus Library of Erotica – over a hundred volumes – is available from many booksellers and newsagents. If you have any difficulty obtaining the books you require, you can order them by post. Photocopy the list below, or tear the list out of the book; then tick the titles you want and fill in the form at the end of the list. Titles marked 1992 are not yet available: please do not try to order them – just look out for them in the shops!

EDWARDIAN, VICTORIAN & OLDER EROTICA

ADVENTURES OF A SCHOOLBOY	Anonymous	£3.99	
THE AUTOBIOGRAPHY OF A FLEA	Anonymous	£2.99	
BEATRICE	Anonymous	£3.99	
THE BOUDOIR	Anonymous	£3.99	
THE DIARY OF A CHAMBERMAID	Mirabeau	£2.99	
THE LIFTED CURTAIN	Mirabeau	£3.50	
EVELINE	Anonymous	£2.99	
MORE EVELINE	Anonymous	£3.99	
FESTIVAL OF VENUS	Anonymous	£4.50	
'FRANK' & I	Anonymous	£2.99	
GARDENS OF DESIRE	Roger Rougiere	£4.50	
OH, WICKED COUNTRY	Anonymous	£3.50	
LASCIVIOUS SCENES IN THE CONVENT	Anonymous	£4.50	
THE LASCIVIOUS MONK	Anonymous	£4.50	
LAURA MIDDLETON	Anonymous	£3.99	
A MAN WITH A MAID 1	Anonymous	£3.50	
A MAN WITH A MAID 2	Anonymous	£3.50	
A MAN WITH A MAID 3	Anonymous	£3.50	
MAUDIE	Anonymous	£2.99	
THE MEMOIRS OF DOLLY MORTON	Anonymous	£3.99	

A NIGHT IN A MOORISH HAREM	Anonymous	£3.99	
PARISIAN FROLICS	Anonymous	£2.99	
PLEASURE BOUND	Anonymous	£3.99	
THE PLEASURES OF LOLOTTE	Andrea de Nerciat	£3.99	
THE PRIMA DONNA	Anonymous	£2.99	
RANDIANA	Anonymous	£4.50	
REGINE	E.K.	£2.99	
THE ROMANCE OF LUST 1	Anonymous	£3.99	
THE ROMANCE OF LUST 2	Anonymous	£2.99	
ROSA FIELDING	Anonymous	£2.99	
SUBURBAN SOULS 1	Anonymous	£2.99	
SUBURBAN SOULS 2	Anonymous	£2.50	
THREE TIMES A WOMAN	Anonymous	£2.99	
THE TWO SISTERS	Anonymous	£3.99	
VIOLETTE	Anonymous	£2.99	

"THE JAZZ AGE"

ALTAR OF VENUS	Anonymous	£2.99	
THE SECRET GARDEN ROOM	Georgette de la Tour	£3.50	
BEHIND THE BEADED CURTAIN	Georgette de la Tour	£3.50	
BLANCHE	Anonymous	£3.99	
BLUE ANGEL NIGHTS	Margarete von Falkensee	£2.99	
BLUE ANGEL DAYS	Margarete von Falkensee	£3.99	
BLUE ANGEL SECRETS	Margarete von Falkensee	£2.99	
CAROUSEL	Anonymous	£3.99	
CONFESSIONS OF AN ENGLISH MAID	Anonymous	£3.99	
FLOSSIE	Anonymous	£2.50	
SABINE	Anonymous	£3.99	
PLAISIR D'AMOUR	Anne-Marie Villefranche	£2.99	
FOLIES D'AMOUR	Anne-Marie Villefranche	£2.99	
JOIE D'AMOUR	Anne-Marie Villefranche	£3.99	
MYSTERE D'AMOUR	Anne-Marie Villefranche	£3.99	
SECRETS D'AMOUR	Anne-Marie Villefranche	£3.50	
SOUVENIR D'AMOUR	Anne-Marie Villefranche	£3.99	
SPIES IN SILK	Piers Falconer	£4.50	

CONTEMPORARY EROTICA

AMAZONS	Erin Caine	£3.99	
COCKTAILS	Stanley Carten	£3.99	
CITY OF ONE-NIGHT STANDS	Stanley Carten	£4.50	
CONTOURS OF DARKNESS	Marco Vassi	£3.50	
THE GENTLE DEGENERATES	Marco Vassi	£3.99	

MIND BLOWER	Marco Vassi	£3.50	
THE SALINE SOLUTION	Marco Vassi	£2.99	
DARK FANTASIES	Nigel Anthony	£3.99	
THE DAYS AND NIGHTS OF MIGUMI	P.M.	£4.50	
THE LATIN LOVER	P.M.	£3.99	
THE DEVIL'S ADVOCATE	Anonymous	£3.99	
DIPLOMATIC SECRETS	Antoine Lelouche	£3.50	
DIPLOMATIC PLEASURES	Antoine Lelouche	£3.50	
DIPLOMATIC DIVERSIONS	Antoine Lelouche	£3.99	
ENGINE OF DESIRE	Alexis Arven	£3.99	
DIRTY WORK	Alexis Arven	£3.99	
DREAMS OF FAIR WOMEN	Celeste Arden	£2.99	
THE FANTASY HUNTERS	Celeste Arden	£3.99	
A GALLERY OF NUDES	Anthony Grey	£4.50	
THE GIRL FROM PAGE 3	Mike Angelo	£3.99	
HOT HOLLYWOOD NIGHTS	Nigel Anthony	£4.50	
THE INSTITUTE	Maria del Rey	£3.99	
PARADISE BAY	Maria del Rey	£4.50	1992
LAURE-ANNE	Laure-Anne	£4.50	
LAURE-ANNE ENCORE	Laure-Anne	£4.50	
LAURE-ANNE TOUJOURS	Laure-Anne	£4.50	
Ms DEEDES AT HOME	Carole Andrews	£4.50	
MY SEX MY SOUL	Amelia Greene	£2.99	
ONE WEEK IN THE PRIVATE HOUSE	Esme Ombreux	£4.50	
PALACE OF SWEETHEARTS	Delver Maddingley	£4.50	
THE REALITY GAME	Andrea Arven	£4.50	1992
THE SECRET WEB	Jane-Anne Roberts	£3.50	
SECRETS LIE ON PILLOWS	James Arbroath	£4.50	
STEPHANIE	Susanna Hughes	£3.99	
STEPHANIE'S CASTLE	Susanna Hughes	£4.50	
THE DOMINO TATTOO	Cyrian Amberlake	£4.50	
THE DOMINO ENIGMA	Cyrian Amberlake	£3.99	
THE DOMINO QUEEN	Cyrian Amberlake	£3.99	

EROTIC SCIENCE FICTION

EROGINA	Christopher Denham	£4.50	
PLEASUREHOUSE 13	Agnetha Anders	£3.99	
THE LAST DAYS OF THE PLEASUREHOUSE	Agnetha Anders	£4.50	
TO PARADISE AND BACK	D. H. Master	£4.50	
WICKED	Andrea Arven	£3.99	
WILD	Andrea Arven	£4.50	

ANCIENT & FANTASY SETTINGS

CHAMPIONS OF LOVE	Anonymous	£3.99	
CHAMPIONS OF DESIRE	Anonymous	£3.99	
CHAMPIONS OF PLEASURE	Anonymous	£3.99	
THE SLAVE OF LIDIR	Aran Ashe	£3.99	
THE DUNGEONS OF LIDIR	Aran Ashe	£3.99	
THE FOREST OF BONDAGE	Aran Ashe	£3.99	
PLEASURE ISLAND	Aran Ashe	£4.50	
KNIGHTS OF PLEASURE	Erin Caine	£4.50	
ROMAN ORGY	Marcus van Heller	£4.50	

CONTEMPORARY FRENCH EROTICA (translated into English)

EXPLOITS OF A YOUNG DON JUAN	Anonymous	£2.99	
INDISCREET MEMOIRS	Alain Dorval	£2.99	
INSTRUMENT OF PLEASURE	Celeste Piano	£4.50	
JOY	Joy Laurey	£2.99	
JOY AND JOAN	Joy Laurey	£2.99	
JOY IN LOVE	Joy Laurey	£2.75	
LILIANE	Paul Verguin	£3.50	
MANDOLINE	Anonymous	£3.99	
LUST IN PARIS	Antoine S.	£2.99	
NYMPH IN PARIS	Galia S.	£2.99	
SCARLET NIGHTS	Juan Muntaner	£3.99	
SENSUAL LIAISONS	Anonymous	£3.50	
SENSUAL SECRETS	Anonymous	£3.99	
THE NEW STORY OF O	Anonymous	£3.99	
THE IMAGE	Jean de Berg	£3.99	
VIRGINIE	Nathalie Perreau	£4.50	
THE PAPER WOMAN	Francoise Rey	£4.50	

SAMPLERS & COLLECTIONS

EROTICON	ed. J-P Spencer	£4.50	
EROTICON 2	ed. J-P Spencer	£4.50	
EROTICON 3	ed. J-P Spencer	£4.50	
EROTICON 4	ed. J-P Spencer	£4.50	
THE FIESTA LETTERS	ed. Chris Lloyd	£2.99	
THE PLEASURES OF LOVING	ed. Maren Sell	£2.99	

NON-FICTION

HOW TO DRIVE YOUR MAN WILD IN BED	Graham Masterton	£4.50	
HOW TO DRIVE YOUR WOMAN WILD IN BED	Graham Masterton	£3.99	
HOW TO BE THE PERFECT LOVER	Graham Masterton	£2.99	
FEMALE SEXUAL AWARENESS	Barry & Emily McCarthy	£4.99	
LINZI DREW'S PLEASURE GUIDE	Linzi Drew	£4.99	1992
WHAT MEN WANT	Susan Crain Bakos	£3.99	
YOUR SEXUAL SECRETS	Marty Klein	£3.99	

Please send me the books I have ticked above.

Name ....

Address ....

....

........................Post code ....

Send to: **Nexus Books Cash Sales, PO Box 11, Falmouth, Cornwall, TR10 9EN**

Please enclose a cheque or postal order, made payable to **Nexus Books**, to the value of the books you have ordered plus postage and packing costs as follows:

UK and BFPO – £1.00 for the first book, 50p for the second book, and 30p for each subsequent book to a maximum of £3.00;

Overseas (including Republic of Ireland) – £2.00 for the first book, £1.00 for the second book, and 50p for each subsequent book.

If you would prefer to pay by VISA or ACCESS/MASTERCARD, please write your card number here:

— — — —   — — — —   — — — —   — — — —

Signature: _____